## "Why didn't you hire a bodyguard, Kate? Why come to me?"

Stone asked her curiously.

"I don't know."

"The reason I'm asking is that I also remember, Kate, exactly what you said before you walked away three years ago. Do you?"

Kate kept her face averted.

"You said, and I'm quoting you here, 'I wouldn't have your baby if you were the last man on earth.' That's what you said then, Kate, right after I'd asked you to marry me, to make a family with me. And yet yesterday you asked for my help. Way I see it, that makes me the last man on earth. Am I, Kate? Am I the last man on earth?"

Kate lifted her head and faced him, warrior to warrior. "Yes."

Dear Reader,

It's summer, the perfect time to sit in the shade (or the air conditioning!) and read the latest from Silhouette Intimate Moments. Start off with Marie Ferrarella's newest CHILDFINDERS, INC. title, *A Forever Kind of Hero*. You'll find yourself turning pages at a furious rate, hoping Garrett Wichita and Megan Andreini will not only find the child they're searching for, but will also figure out how right they are for each other.

We've got more miniseries in store for you this month, too. Doreen Roberts offers the last of her RODEO MEN in *The Maverick's Bride*, a fitting conclusion to a wonderful trilogy. And don't miss the next of THE SISTERS WASKOWITZ, in Kathleen Creighton's fabulous *One Summer's Knight*. Don't forget, there's still one sister to go. Judith Duncan makes a welcome return with *Murphy's Child*, a FAMILIES ARE FOREVER title that will capture your emotions and your heart. Lindsay Longford, one of the most unique voices in romance today, is back with *No Surrender*, an EXPECTANTLY YOURS title. And finally, there's Maggie Price's *Most Wanted*, a MEN IN BLUE title that once again allows her to demonstrate her understanding of romance and relationships.

Six marvelous books to brighten your summer—don't miss a single one. And then come back next month, when six more of the most exciting romance novels around will be waiting for you—only in Silhouette Intimate Moments.

Enjoy!

Yours,

Leslie J. Wainger
Executive Senior Editor

---

Please address questions and book requests to:
Silhouette Reader Service
U.S.: 3010 Walden Ave., P.O. Box 1325, Buffalo, NY 14269
Canadian: P.O. Box 609, Fort Erie, Ont. L2A 5X3

# NO SURRENDER

## LINDSAY LONGFORD

Published by Silhouette Books

**America's Publisher of Contemporary Romance**

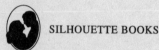 SILHOUETTE BOOKS

ISBN 0-373-07947-8

NO SURRENDER

Copyright © 1999 by Jimmie Morel

## LINDSAY LONGFORD,

like most writers, is a reader. She even reads toothpaste labels in desperation! A former high school English teacher with an M.A. in literature, she began writing romances because she wanted to create stories that touched readers' emotions by transporting them to a world where good things happened to good people and happily-ever-after is possible with a little work.

Her first book, *Jake's Child,* was nominated for Best New Series Author, Best Silhouette Romance, and received a Special Achievement Award for Best First Series Book from *Romantic Times Magazine.* It was also a finalist for the Romance Writers of America's RITA Award for Best First Book. Her Silhouette Romance *Annie and the Wise Men* won the RITA for Best Traditional Romance of 1993.

For Lucia, Tara, Leslie, Karen, Isabel, Melissa

In a business where, of necessity, the bottom line will always be the bottom line, you cross the *t*'s and dot the *i*'s with grace and rare kindness. It is an honor and a privilege to work with you.

## Acknowledgments

Russ Blumhagen, Office Manager of Rosin's Eyecare, Naperville, Illinois,

John Polak, a dear friend and a brilliant man who knows everything about insurance,

Dawn Weddle, dietician and nurse, Edward Hospital Birthing Center, Naperville, Illinois

Thanks for helping me in criminal endeavors!

# Chapter 1

"Of all the gin mills in all the world, et cetera."

"Not your best Bogart imitation, Jed." Chin up, she kept walking toward him, no hesitation, no second thoughts. She'd do what she'd come to do.

The man in the shadows clunked the beer bottle against the scarred, rickety table. Leaning back in a chair that owed its stability to a miracle of glue and hope, he yawned. "To what do I owe the pleasure, Katherine? And why do I suspect pleasure isn't what you have in mind?"

Kate studied the languid posture of the long-limbed man staring at her with a faint hostility in his gray eyes.

Even in the pitchy gloom of The Last Resort she knew his cold, hard eyes were gray. Once upon a time, in another life, she'd slept with Jedidiah Jackson Stone. Frequently. And with great pleasure, she remembered, swallowing. She damned well ought to know the color of his eyes.

"May I sit down, Jed?" She lifted her chin higher, a faint hostility of her own shimmering through her.

He ignored her question. "You look ticked off, Kate."

"Do I?" she asked through clenched teeth.

"Yeah, you do," he said, one booted foot tapping against the rung of a grimy chair. His boots were worn, dusty.

"Must be the lighting." She smiled, and her cheeks ached with the effort.

"Think so?" Glancing away from her, he studied the cheap, stained paneling where an alligator skull hung next to a rusty metal coon trap, and cobwebs stretched to the ceiling and the huge, dusty wooden wheels with burned-out light-bulbs. "Could be." His posture altered minutely, warning her. "Reckon you've never stepped foot in a joint like this, have you, Kate? A little rough and redneck for you, I'd guess."

"I didn't come for the atmosphere."

"No?" Harsh and judgmental, his gaze drifted over her, back to the walls. "Too bad. We got atmosphere up the old wazoo." Halting the movement of his boot, he lifted one dark eyebrow. "But this dive's not exactly your cup of tea, is it?"

"It has a certain charm." She didn't like the trace of chilly amusement in his eyes as she answered. "Florida beer joint. Florida decor."

"Oh, excellent, Katherine. Polite to the core, aren't you?" His foot resumed its restless tapping.

Resolutely Kate squashed her irritation. She knew exactly what Jed was doing. He was trying his damnedest to ruffle her. Well, she was on his turf. She couldn't afford to antagonize him any more than she already had by walking back into his life after three years. She'd come with one enormous problem. She sure didn't need to create more problems. If she let Jed's needling get to her, she wouldn't stand a chance with him.

Days ago she'd examined her options, which, all things considered, were slim and none, settled on her strategy and made her decision to seek him out, and enter the minefields of their past.

Taking a deep breath of grease-laden air, she disregarded

his provocation. "Since we seem to be starting a conversation after all, may I sit down, Jed?"

"Well, see, Katherine, it all depends." He yawned again, but his foot kept tap, tap, tapping. "Depends on what you're of a mind to talk about. But, sugar-pie, I don't think you could say anything I'd be interested in hearing."

Kate shrugged as if she didn't care one way or the other what he decided and half turned, ready to leave.

Jed's gravel-tinged voice stopped her.

"Interesting, Kate, that little play you just put on. It's almost convincing." His smile was genuinely amused.

Fury singed the roots of her hair. If she didn't need his help so damned much, she'd pivot on the points of her Italian heels and head for the door.

"Now you really look annoyed." His smile deepened as she didn't answer. "But since you're here, have a seat. The more I think about it, I've decided that anything that could drag you out to my neck of the woods intrigues me." He slid the edge of his boot under the chair rung and tugged the chair beneath the table even as he offered her a seat. "What'd you have in mind? Because you always have something in mind, don't you?" His smile had vanished into the angles of his face, and his eyes were colder than ever.

Kate tugged at the chair, but his toe held it tight to the table. He was going to be much more difficult than she'd dreamed. And what she'd dreamed had been nightmare enough.

It was just her damned luck that he was her only hope.

At the table next to Jed's, a man lay cheek down on the wet surface of his table, crooning softly to himself. "May I?" she asked the crooner, whisking the extra chair away and over to Jed's table.

"Determined as ever, I see." Jed slouched farther down in his chair. "You're an intimidating woman, Katherine, when the mood takes you."

"Somehow I doubt that you're intimidated, Jed." She bumped the chair over a broken tile.

"Oh, believe me, I am. Scared right down to the tips of my tippy toes, in fact. You have that effect on a man, Kate." Never looking away from her, he lifted the brown bottle to his mouth and drank. With each swallow, the corded muscles of his tanned throat moved strongly. He slapped the bottle back on the table and slid down to his tailbone.

"Pay attention, Jed," she said severely, grabbing a wad of rough paper napkins and scrubbing at the sticky seat.

"Oh, believe me, I do," he drawled, looking as if he were about to fall asleep any second, but his eyes were alert and attentive. "You're an interesting woman, Katherine. Whenever you're around, I always pay attention."

"Good." She regarded the seat dubiously. Maybe she should stand. Standing might give her an edge. She glanced at Jed. No, nothing had ever given her an edge over him, no matter what he said. Jed being Jed, he'd see right through any attempt to pull a power play. After all, he'd written the rules on game playing. Even at her best, she'd never considered herself in his league.

So, no games. She needed him in a helpful frame of mind. She dabbed at the seat again, reluctant to risk her Armani skirt on the chair.

"What the hell," he finally said sighing. "Come on, Kate. Sit down. The chair's safe. You're not going to catch anything. No guarantees, though." The hostility flared brighter. "And you're a woman who craves guarantees, aren't you?"

"I like security," she said stubbornly.

"So you do."

"And stability."

"Fine. You've made your point." He nudged the chair toward her. "Sit. If you mess up that nifty suit, I think you can swing the cleaning bill. And if you can't, I'll cover it." He curled his long fingers around the neck of the bottle and tipped it up once again, his narrowed eyes mocking her. "It's a real spiffy outfit, though, I have to admit."

In a slow, maddening scrutiny, he let his gaze move over

her, and her breath quickened as he lingered on the long, knotted pearl necklace that swung gently under her breasts.

"Thank you." She gripped her fingers together as his gaze lingered on the pearls, and the necklace trembled with her indrawn breath.

"You'll forgive me, I know, considering our history, but I can't help wondering—oh, just a bit, mind you—why you got all gussied up to pay me a visit, Katherine." Tilting back on the unreliable legs of his chair, he rocked thoughtfully, never taking his gaze from her. "Buttoned-up blouse. So I won't get the wrong idea, I'd reckon. But it's the *damnedest* thing. Because I look at that top button on your silk blouse and all those pretty pearls, and, sugar-plum, I get all kinds of ideas."

Not replying, she tightened her mouth. Heat rose fast and hot from her neck to her cheeks as one corner of his mouth lifted. Her knees trembled against each other. She should never have come looking for Jed Stone. Not in this lifetime.

He checked the skirt length. "A bit long. But professional-looking. By the way, your legs are still terrific."

As he let his gaze drift down her legs in a long, slow perusal, treacherous heat flushed down her whole body. Damn him, *damn* him.

Abruptly she sat down. If she stuck to the seat, she stuck. So be it. She wasn't giving Jedidiah Stone a second chance to make her blush.

Letting the chair rock back onto its four supports and settle, Jed folded his hands across the mouth of the bottle. Resting his chin on his hands, he continued his aggravating perusal. "And a swell hairdo to finish up the overall effect. That hairdo's just about the closest thing I've seen in a month of Sundays to a schoolmarm 'do, Kate. You never used to skin your hair back like that. Makes you look mighty fierce, I can tell you that." Never lightening the gray of his eyes, his smile mocked her. "Of course, all that buttoned-up, skinned-back look does is make a man think about popping open those teeny-tiny buttons and fluffing up your hair. You know, check out the terrain for himself.'' His grin was pure provocation.

''Fascinating,'' she said, and crossed her legs, satisfaction of her own filling her as his gaze flickered once to the flash of thigh showing in the slit of her severe skirt. She smoothed her skirt down over her knees, shooting him a look from under her eyelashes as she did.

Two could play this game. And he'd set the rules.

A dull flush touched his cheekbones.

''So cut to the chase. Why'd you risk a walk on the other side of the tracks tonight, Katherine?'' Gleaming at her from the depths of his remote gray eyes, the hostility was no longer faint. The lazy teasing had vanished in the cynical twist of his mouth. The lines radiating from the corners of his eyes held no amusement or sympathy. ''Bottom line. What do you want?''

''I want your help,'' she said baldly.

Watching her, he went very still.

Behind him, in the kitchen galley, a tray of dishes hit the floor, and the short-order cook let loose with a stream of curses. Kate jumped. ''Oh!''

Tucking her fingers under the flap of her purse to hide their trembling from Jed, she raised her chin and didn't blink. She wouldn't show him weakness. Not now, not ever again.

And then, as she continued to meet his gaze, he smiled, a slow, lazy movement of his mouth, and she almost shoved her chair away and ran. ''Let me see if I understand. You want *my* help, Kate?''

She nodded, once. Her neck was stiff with tension and uneasiness as he continued to smile. Jed was most dangerous when he smiled.

''After all this time?''

She tried to nod. Her muscles had frozen. ''Yes.''

''Three years.''

She nodded. ''Three years. Yes.''

''You never wanted anything from me before, Katherine, did you?''

She couldn't answer. Her mouth was spit-dry. She hadn't expected that he could still hurt her.

"Not even my baby." He leaned forward, and the ice in his eyes was as cold as death.

"No." Down deep in her abdomen, shivers began, moving over her in slow waves.

"But now you want my help."

"Yes."

"Let me get this clear. Exactly why should I help you?" Abruptly he leaned back, freeing her, and the slow rolling shivers in her belly lengthened, slowed.

"I'll pay you."

A sideways drift of cigarette smoke wafted between them, and the hiss and spatter of frying came from the galley kitchen. "You'll pay me."

She managed to nod. Clamped under the purse flap, her fingers fluttered and moved with a life of their own.

"You think you can...buy me."

"No." She shook her head, and felt a pin slip from the carefully arranged twist of her hair. Shoulders not moving, feet glued in place, she angled her chin in the direction of the room. "But since you're hanging out in a place like this, I think you can use money right now."

"Is that so?" Silky soft and menacingly polite, his voice came to her under the throbbing beat of the piped-in music. One long finger made idle circles on the wet table. "I'm touched. So comforting to think you care about my welfare. And after all this time."

Her breath caught in her throat. "You never turned money down before. Not that I know of. You've always been a man who followed the scent of a dollar, Jed. A man who has his price."

"Rudeness won't get you what you want," he chided, his eyes narrowing. "A suggestion, Kate. When you go looking for a favor, you don't want to alienate your potential bene-factor." But he leaned back once again and, that small space enough, she could breathe again as he asked, "By the way, how did you find me?"

"It wasn't hard." She lifted her hands and purse to the table and took a deep, steadying breath. "I know your habits."

"Do you?" His lean face was all polite attention. "I'm flattered."

"Don't be."

"Tsk, tsk, sugar-plum. There goes that attitude again. So you went looking—" He stopped as she blinked. "Ah. *You* didn't. You hired someone." His eyes were slits in the sharp planes of his face. "The little gum-smacking brunette? The female version of the gumshoe, the chick dick? That private eye who came in here about two months ago?"

Reluctantly, Kate nodded.

"Well, well, well." He held the empty bottle up to the light and then looked around, raising his index finger. "Buy me a drink, Katherine?"

She dipped her head fractionally. He wasn't going to help her. He was going to push and badger her until he provoked her, until he—

"Here." The white-hatted cook slammed a bottle in front of her and one in front of Jed.

"The lady's paying, Sparks. Right?" Jed smiled, a shark-like baring of his teeth.

The cook shot Jed a glance and muttered, "I don't give a damn who pays, long as somebody does."

Fumbling in her purse blindly, Kate pulled out a bill and dropped it into the palm stretched in front of her. The situation was out of control. Jed was only going to string her along, playing games, making her pay for what she'd done, said, in the past. And he was her only hope. "Keep the change, Sparks," she said, automatically smiling even as panic licked along her spine, paralyzing her.

She glanced up at the figure heading back to the kitchen and then spoke to Jed. "Can we talk business?" She hoped he wouldn't hear the same desperation in her voice she did.

She hoped he hadn't noticed her panic when the dishes had clattered to the floor. She hoped... But she was out of options. It was time to, as Jed had said, lay her cards on the table or fold and walk away. Bile rose in her throat.

If she walked away, where would she go? Who could she turn to?

Nowhere. No one.

The police weren't going to help her. That had been made clear.

It was Jed or—

She clicked the snap of her purse shut. Open. Shut.

"Nervous?"

She gripped her purse between white-knuckled fingers. "I need your help," she repeated numbly.

"You want my help. After all this time. Okay, I got that the first time around. But tell me, Kate, why should *I* help *you?*"

"You're the only one who can."

"And you think you can afford my price?" he said softly.

The reins of control slipped from her hands with her purse as it tumbled to the floor, spilling lipstick and tissue and her pills. She jerked to her feet. "Your price was always too high, Jed." Stooping, she grabbed her purse and the rolling lipstick case with one hand, shoving everything into her purse. She turned to go in a rush of words and movement. "I was stupid to come here. I knew better. I can't imagine what in the world I was thinking—"

His grip on her wrist stopped her.

With a whip of her head in his direction, she faced him, pins flying and pattering onto the floor.

"Let go of my hand. I'm leaving."

"The hell you are," he said pleasantly. "Not until you've satisfied my curiosity. Tell me why you need my help, Katherine. Satisfy me." Under his implacable, ironic voice, other words echoed, nighttime words from the past.

She couldn't breathe. Her stomach roiled and bounced, and the room closed in around her.

His grip firm, he jiggled her arm. "Tell me. Now."

"Someone's trying to kill me." The breath emptied out of her, her knees buckled and she sagged into the chair, his grip firm around her wrist.

"Managed to piss off someone again, have you?" He hadn't moved, but he seemed all around her, too close, too…too *everything.* "You have a knack for doing that." He flipped her hand idly back and forth, her hand so limp it flopped like a wounded bird as he said thoughtfully, "Surprise, surprise. You've managed to interest me, after all, Katie. I wouldn't have bet a sweet million you could. Not anymore, anyway." He shoved the beer bottle toward her. "Take a drink."

"No."

"You look like cottage cheese gone bad."

"You sure know how to sweet-talk a girl, don't you?" Lifting the beer bottle with her free hand, she rubbed it across her forehead. Her throat was tight, and nausea kept her swallowing, but she didn't drink.

Kate wished he'd turn her loose, wished she'd never stepped foot into The Last Resort. Wished she could stagger out the door and stop his questions. Nothing had changed between her and Jed. Running to him had been a stupid decision.

"Why didn't you ask the private detective for help?"

Lifting her chin, she met his gaze. "I did. I hired Patsy."

"Continue." His index finger slid over her pulse, and she shuddered in a dreadful mix of heat and nausea.

"Because someone broke in to Patsy's house and was waiting for her when she came home. Two months ago. She's dead." Kate felt the blood drain from her head. She pulled against Jed's fingers.

He didn't release her, but his fingers curled around hers. "Shame. I liked her."

"I liked her, too." Kate swallowed as the malty smell of beer came rolling back on her. Perspiration beaded her forehead. "She was my friend."

Not releasing her, Jed abruptly stood up, dragging her with him. "Come on, Kate. You need air."

Her hip bumped against the edge of the table, and her question came from no conscious place. "Did you sleep with her, Jed?"

"None of your business, Katherine, if I did or didn't." Jed hustled her toward the door. "Back in a minute, Sparks."

"Sure, sure." A skillet banged and rattled on the grill. "Whatever."

Outside, humid air slapped her in the face, smothered her.

"You okay?" He waited a minute, then asked, "Who found her?"

"Me." She gulped air as if she were drowning. "I identified her."

"Yeah?"

She nodded once, convulsively, her throat spasming.

"Tough. Even for a tough cookie like you, Kate."

She shut her eyes against the memory of a body sprawled across the kitchen table, milk and blood puddled on the floor. Shut her own eyes against the memory of Patsy's eyes wide open and startled. "People said we even looked alike." She flattened her palm over her abdomen, pressed against the waves of nausea.

"I remember noticing her hair. Pretty, I thought." The skim of Jed's fingers along Kate's cheek as he brushed a strand of hair off her face conjured another memory as he said, "You cut your hair. You had the most beautiful long hair, Katie."

Behind her closed lids, his voice came to her, rough, reluctant. "Sometimes I still dream about wrapping it around your throat, spreading it over your breasts." His palm slipped over the back of her head, down past her shoulders. "Long and satin-sleek. I loved your hair, Katie."

She remembered, too. He'd slip his fingers through her hair, separating it strand by strand, fanning it across the sheet, across his sleek chest, teasing her skin with the spiky ends.

"I really, really loved that silky rope against your bare

back.'' He paused. ''That's why you cut it.'' It wasn't a question. ''Because I liked it.''

''Yes.'' Cutting her hair had been a decision to cut herself free from memories, from Jed. In some undefinable way, she'd believed cutting her hair would cut her loose from him, would free her to go on with her life.

''Well, I said you were a tough cookie.'' He stared out over the half-empty parking lot fenced by live oaks and tall pines. ''Take no prisoners, do you?''

Mutely she dropped her head. She'd cried until her eyes were swollen when she cut her hair. She hadn't shed a tear for Patsy. Hadn't been able to. Eyes burning, scalding, she would have welcomed the relief of tears, but they'd stayed locked away.

But since her nature wouldn't let her cry surrender in the face of Jed's probing, she focused on fighting a battle she was afraid she'd lost the second she'd opened the door to The Last Resort, and so she spoke aloud her deepest regret. ''I think Patsy was killed by mistake. I think someone mistook her for me.''

Even as Kate spoke, the ground beneath her feet was rising and falling in waves. And all she could see, think of, were Patsy's surprised eyes, changeable hazel eyes so like Kate's own that it was as if she'd looked at her own self as she'd stared down at her friend's body.

''Are you going to be sick, Kate?''

''No,'' she whispered, clamping her hand over her mouth and remembering Patsy, remembering the sound of flies buzzing and thumping against the window screen, remembering the smell...

Jed clasped the back of her neck, not ungently, and urged her head down toward her knees. ''Sit down, Katie. Before you pass out.''

Seeing her sag, Jed caught her before her eyes closed. If he'd thought she looked bad before, that hadn't been the half of it. Under a soft streak of artificial color, her skin was green-white, and the shadows under her eyes, shadows he had missed in the gloom of The Last Resort, were deep purple bruises.

She'd lost weight, too, he noticed as he carried her to a wooden cypress chair away from casual eavesdroppers leaving the bar.

A thin line of sweat beaded her hairline and with a brush of his finger across her clammy skin, he flicked the drops away and waited, his pulse going lickety-split. "You okay?"

"Sure," she muttered, her head between her knees and her color worse than ever. Her shoulders were tightly hunched forward. "No more questions, Jed. Please. For a minute."

"All right." Taken aback, Jed let his palm rest against the back of her neck. "I'll give you a minute. And then I want some answers, Kate."

Damn her. He'd never expected to see her again. She shouldn't have hunted him down. Why hadn't she gone to the police with her questions instead of coming to him?

Jed left his hand on Kate's neck. Her air of fragility threw him off balance, blunted the edge of his anger.

Patsy Keane hadn't given him a clue who she was working for. She'd chatted, asked a few unimportant questions, and thanked him. Most people wouldn't have pegged her for a private eye. She'd been shrewd, good, but he'd picked up on the too-casual aspect of her questions, questions that weren't in the nature of a flirtation.

He'd decided she was checking up on Sparks or one of the other guys at The Last Resort for some reason. He'd answered her questions from that angle, making sure she knew the guys weren't in any trouble.

He'd been right. And he'd been wrong.

Jed frowned. He didn't like being wrong. Being wrong could kill a man. Or a woman.

Apparently Patsy Keane had had the job of finding him for Kate. No, that didn't make sense. Kate wouldn't have hired an investigator to go looking for him. She'd had another reason for sending her friend out on a tracking mission. The investigator had been looking for something else. It looked as if she'd discovered something that had killed her. Or was her death not even connected to Kate? Gut instinct told him it was, coincidences being suspect, he'd always figured.

And how badly did he want to know what the woman had found?

Enough to let Katherine March back into his life, even on his terms?

Kate believed she was the intended target, not Patsy. Kate believed Patsy's death was a by-product of whatever Kate had sent her to investigate.

Under his hand Kate stirred, and her dazed hazel eyes met his. "I must have skipped a meal. Low blood sugar," she said in a whispery voice unlike any he'd ever heard from her.

"I don't think blood sugar's the problem."

"I've never fainted in my life. But thanks for the—" she shrugged "—compassion, Jed. This was an error in judgment. I'm leaving." Placing her narrow hands on the chair's arms, she stood up, wobbled and sank back into the seat, her mouth pinched and bloodless. "In a second."

The damned woman was going to be the death of him.

Furious with her, with himself, with the fate that had led her to him again, Jed strode to the door of The Last Resort and stuck his head in. "Hey, Sparks," he yelled over the music and voices. "Orange juice and crackers out here. *Stat.*"

"Yeah, yeah. When I have a minute."

"Now." Jed was ready to tear something apart with his bare hands, his teeth. He could start with Sparks.

James McGarrity, aka Sparks on his rap sheet, looked up from the hamburger-laden grill and dropped his spatula. "Got it. Orange juice."

Jed gave the man credit. Sparks could move when motivated.

Seconds later, Sparks swung through the screen door and made his way to Jed.

"Here." Sparks shoved the glass into Jed's hands. It

dripped with condensation. "Sorry," he growled. "I didn't know it was for *her*."

"For *her* you'd move fast?" Jed about-faced toward Kate.

"Don't be a jerk, boss. She's different." For Sparks, women were broads, babes, or bimbos. It said something for Kate that Sparks had separated her out.

Scratching his back against the wood corner of the door, Sparks waited while Jed lifted the glass to Kate's lips. "We don't get her type around here."

"Yeah, there's an understatement, all right." Jed stuck his finger under Kate's chin and raised her face. "You look like someone poleaxed you, sugar-plum. Drink."

"What will you do, drown me if I don't?" Drinking, she sputtered against the rim. Drops of water splattered onto her suit, dark against the mushroom-colored silk.

"Probably." Grimly he tilted the glass and held it until it was empty. "Kate, you could drive a man to drink."

"Too late. You're there already." She gestured weakly with one hand toward the restaurant/bar. "Can't blame your failings on me, Jed."

"I never did." Examining her face critically, he turned it toward the slanting rays of the late-afternoon sun. "You're looking better. Yellow-green isn't your best color, Kate."

"I'll try to remember." She blotted her mouth with the tips of her fingers. Her hands shook with fine tremors, and she gripped them together as she caught his glance. "In the future."

Jed stepped back, relieved in spite of his bitterness to see her come back with sass and vinegar.

He handed Sparks the empty glass, and Sparks ducked his head, mumbling under his breath only loud enough for Jed, "She's a keeper, this one." Sparks lifted the hem of his stained apron and wiped his forehead. "Classy, she is. Not rough edged like you and me." Returning to the bar, he let the door swing loudly shut behind him.

With the door completely closed, Jed braced one arm on either side of Kate, trapping her in the chair. "All right, Katherine. You shouldn't have come here. It was a mistake. But you did. You're sorry you made that decision. So am I. But you're here. And damned if I'm going to let you leave until you tell me what the hell's going on.'' He gave the chair a shake.

Her hands doubled into fists. "You can't keep me here." She glared at him but didn't move.

"Think I can't? Think I won't?'' he whispered, yielding to long-buried hurt and bewilderment and rage. "You don't want to test me on this, Katherine. Not if you're smart. And you've always been smart as a whip, haven't you?'' He scooped away a strand of hair drooping into her eyes. His palm burned and he rubbed it against his gray slacks. He didn't want the touch of her lingering.

And then, unexpectedly, so fast he wasn't prepared, she straightened up and shoved him backward, her hands flat against his chest. "Back off, Jed. And don't bully me. You were never good at it anyway.'' She reached down for her purse, swayed and held her hand palm up against him. "Don't touch me. I can handle this. You were right. I made a mistake coming to you. I won't ever make that mistake again.''

Her high heels clicked against the porch boards, stuttered as he said, "Who's trying to kill you, Katie?''

Though the line of her shoulders slumped, she kept right on marching forward, straight out of his life one more time.

And an old resentment, an old hurt, coiled in him and raised its head, slid through his bloodstream.

He stood on the porch, watching as she beeped open the door of a slick little sports car. Red and shiny. All that power under the hood, just like Kate.

Dangerous, this slide of anger moving through him, but watching her walk out of his life again, he had no will to capture the anger and stuff it safely away.

Swearing a blue streak, fury knotting his insides, he stepped off the porch. As she three-pointed and came toward him in the narrow lane bordered by oleander trees, he let the anger rip loose and stepped in front of her car.

He wondered if she'd stop first, or if he'd step out of the way.

Adrenaline and energy zipped through him, and something else he didn't have time to analyze, not with Kate heading toward him. But for the first time in three years he felt alive again, not left in some limbo of grayness.

With the mix of anger and this other, unidentifiable emotion tangling inside him, he decided it would be interesting to see who blinked first. Kate? Or him?

Through the lightly tinted windshield he glimpsed Kate's pale, determined face.

He'd really, really annoyed her. On purpose. And she'd known he was rattling her chain, too. As he stood there, she raced the engine—in warning, annoyance, he couldn't decide, but he imagined the engine snarl had a lot in common at the moment with Kate's state of mind.

Kate in a temper was always interesting.

Kate would stop. She wouldn't hit him. She'd give in. Of course she would.

He grinned.

But with Katherine March, he'd never been sure. She'd always had the ability to surprise him.

# Chapter 2

Moments after Kate's car vanished from sight, the whiff of grease and hamburgers sneaked into Jed's awareness.

"So, boss, what's going on?" Sparks coughed, pulled a cigarette from a crumpled packet.

"Damned if I know." Jed stared into the distance.

"Huh. That so?" Whistling off-key, Sparks shot him a keen look.

"Yeah. You heard me." Watching the dust swirls from Kate's departure subside, Jed shrugged. At the last moment she'd stopped, the front bumper of that hot little car not quite nudging his knees. Why in God's name had he stepped in front of her car? What was he thinking?

That, of course, was the problem. He hadn't been thinking. Some primitive part of his brain had kicked in and he'd simply reacted to the moment. Well, hell, his brain had nothing to do with it. She'd strolled into his place, cool and smooth as bourbon on the rocks, and knocked him back in his seat.

From that point on, things had gone to hell in a handbasket. He'd let her get under his skin.

Then, as she was leaving, her temper flaring, he'd reacted, wanting to prove—what?

Did he think he was proving something to her? To himself?

Irritated, he kicked the sand, watched dust swirl in puffs of gray. He hadn't proved a damned thing, that's what. All he'd done was show one more time that Kate March could make him act like a damned idiot.

What he'd needed in that energy-charged moment was to make her look at him, react to *him*. Ego? But something else, too, had stirred in him as she'd regarded him with her temper-tinged hazel eyes. "Damn." Viciously, he kicked a clump of sandspurs.

Apparently considering the conversational door open again, Sparks seized the moment. "What'd the lady want?" Reflectively, he rolled the cigarette between his fingers. "I'm bettin' she didn't come here for my cuisine." Coughing again, Sparks stuck the unlit cigarette behind his left ear. "Did she?"

"Nope." Jed pondered that last moment after Kate had stopped, recalled the way her forehead had rested against the steering wheel. With a grin, he'd tapped the hood of her spiffy car, she'd lifted her head, and that close to her, he'd caught the fear filling her huge eyes. Not seeing him, she'd stared into his eyes, despair settling over her face like the fine dust of the path.

He'd never seen Kate afraid of anything.

He'd stepped aside.

She'd gunned her car past him, leaving him with that disturbing memory of her stricken face and this ache in his gut that he'd missed some crucial piece of information.

"You know her, right?" Sparks's comment was casual, easy, letting Jed know he could answer or not, but Jed heard the stubbornness and knew better. A pit bull, Sparks wasn't about to abandon the question of Kate March, no matter how easy and friendly old Sparks acted.

Glaring at him, Jed admitted, "I know her."

"Pretty well, I'm thinking."

"You think too much, old man. No. I never really knew her." Like the swirls of dust from Kate's departure, silence filled the space between them. Thoughts twisting inside him, Jed watched the breeze lift the brown-tinged leaves on the bushes.

"Huh." Sparks took his cigarette from behind his ear, thumb-flicked a match and lit up. "I'm bettin' you were in love with her. And it looks to me like you still got feelings for the lady."

Jed shifted, faced the man who'd worked for him for almost two years.

"You're wrong. She's nothing to me." Jed meant what he said, too. Too much damage had been done. Their weapon of choice had been words, but he and Kate had left the battlefield of their affair with enough scars to last each of them a lifetime. Everything considered, he'd been lucky. The wound hadn't been mortal after all. "She's just a woman in a fancy suit looking for a favor. That's all," he repeated, and felt the emptiness shift and tighten inside him.

"Don't try to con a con." Sparks watched the glowing end of his cigarette. "You and her got a history. Anybody could see that much."

"Curiosity—"

"I done heard that story already. But you watched her like she was cream and you a damned thirsty tomcat hoping to get a taste."

Wishing he'd never let the old man start talking, Jed crossed his arms. "You looking to get fired, Sparks?"

Not immediately answering, Sparks shook off the glowing ashes from his cigarette, watched as they scattered to the ground. He frowned as a speck landed on a dried leaf, flaring brightly. With the toe of his work shoe he stubbed out the ember and kicked sand over the leaf. "Can't fire me. You let me buy into this joint. You forget?"

"Nope. Didn't forget. Made a mistake. You caught me in a weak moment. Tell you what, I'll buy you out." When

Sparks's head rose abruptly, Jed almost smiled. He'd short-circuited the old man's nosiness. "Hell, what do I need a broken-down ex-con for anyway? I'll get Ben to fill in at the grill."

Sparks watched him for a second, grinned. It was, after all, a familiar game they played. "Nah. Life's getting too interesting around here. And neither you nor Ben can cook hamburgers or fish worth a damn. Young Ben's doing the books and handling all that computer stuff you keep shoving at him. Besides, the customers like me." Giving him a sly look, Sparks added, "Fact is, lots of 'em come just to see old Sparks do his thing. I'm part of the atmosphere. The *ambience,* boss."

"That what you are, you old coot? *Ambience?* Damn. Now you tell me." Relieved to have Sparks's attention away from Kate, Jed stifled his chuckle. "That changes everything. The Last Resort needs every bit of ambience it can find."

"I know what you're doing, Jed." Dropping his cigarette to the sandy path, Sparks ground it out, picked up the butt and shredded it, putting the remains in his pocket. "If you're not going to tell me about her, you're not. I've got hamburgers cooking and half a dozen hungry customers." Wiping his hands on his apron, Sparks scowled at him. "But I thought we was friends."

Jed sighed. An impulse he didn't understand drew the admission from him. "You're half-right. I was in love with her. Once. Not anymore. When push came to shove, we were strangers. Now, hell, I don't even like her." He meant that, too. In spite of the way that treacherous part of his anatomy had leapt to immediate attention, Jed didn't like Kate March.

Dislike was way too vanilla for the intensity of his feelings, for the darkness and unwanted hunger she aroused in him. If he let himself, he could almost hate her for reminding him again of that hunger. "I don't care if I ever see her again," he said, and wondered why the words sounded forced.

"No?" Sparks glanced over his shoulder, his expression

carefully blank. "Whatever you say, boss. I'm only the cook. Not my business why she was here. Or what she wanted."

"Damn right it isn't." Jed didn't want the old man walking into his brain, fingering through his feelings, but it was Sparks's expression that made Jed head toward him, catching up with him in one stride. Jed clamped a hand on the old man's shoulder and halted his trudging steps. "Look, it's no big deal. Here's the truth. I thought I loved her. I thought she loved me. I was wrong. And she left me. That's all there is. An old, boring story."

Sparks stuck a kitchen match between his teeth, chewed, worked the match around and said, "Something more between you and her. Or she wouldn't have showed up here looking like death warmed over, and you wouldn't be scowling at me like you had a belly full of bad oysters, would you, now?"

Jed poked Sparks in the arm. "You've been watching too many old movies."

"Not all the time." Sparks gave him that sly grin again. "But I'm merely wondering why a lady like her showed up not so long after that other nice babe, the inquisitive brunette packing heat, did."

Surprised for the third time in one day, Jed let his hand fall to his side. "Ah. You saw her pistol."

"Yeah. Hard to miss it." He took the match out, cracked it in two, dropped it into his pocket. "Even for an old coot."

"Most people would have missed it." Amused again, Jed shook his head. "Why didn't you say something?"

"Not my place to." Sparks patted his pocket irritably. "Coincidences make me nervous, that's all. The brunette, she a cop? She walked like one."

"No," Jed said slowly, thinking about that afternoon and Patsy Keane's questions. "A private detective."

"That so?" Sparks's expression sharpened, grew wary. "Now, that's right peculiar."

"I thought she'd come to dig up information about you and Ben, maybe Tuba Tony, but I was wrong." He'd thought

At first the Keane woman was Kate, and all the old anger had rushed in before he'd seen the woman clearly. "She was checking me out, I think. Asking questions about Ms. March and me, trying to find out when I'd last been in touch with her. It didn't seem important, and, frankly, I didn't give it another thought after she left."

He had, though. He'd spent a sleepless night wandering outside, remembering the days after Kate had walked away from him, remembering her final words, words that had seared their way into his soul, astonishing him with their pain.

"Not like you, Jed. You must have wondered what the babe was up to."

"Yeah, maybe I wondered a little. But not for long. Anyway, now that I think about it, she was trying to find out if I posed some kind of threat to Kate."

"Huh," Sparks grunted, and the caution left his face. He scratched his chin. "A threat to that pretty lady? Because?"

Jed let his gaze drift to the tall pines and oaks shadowing the parking lot. In the growing twilight their darkness seemed secretive, threatening. "Because Ms. March, the lady from my past, thinks somebody's trying to kill her."

"Your Ms. March, is she stupid?"

"No," Jed said moodily, letting pictures play in his head, pictures of what Kate must have seen when she'd discovered the Keane woman's body. "Katherine March isn't stupid. Not by a long shot."

"Then I reckon somebody is trying to kill her. Be a waste if they did. Shame a classy lady like her got nobody to assist her in her hour of need." The screen door slammed emphatically behind Sparks, and his hand pressed the screen mesh as he turned toward Jed. "A real shame, especially after she came asking somebody I won't name for a favor. That somebody being a big ol' stubborn galoot."

"You're pushing, McGarrity."

"Huh." Sparks disappeared into the gloom of the bar.

A mournful whoof echoed from the darkness under the porch.

"Hell, Booger," Jed said to the dog slinking toward him
tail swiping the dirt. "Everybody except you is leaving m
in the dust today. What's the matter? I need to change m
aftershave?" He scratched the dog's head. Coated with cob
webs and sand, Booger's pelt was rough under his hand, no
like the smooth sleekness of Kate's hair when he'd touche
it.

Her hair had slipped so easily against his palm, like warm
silk. Jed picked a burr from Booger's droopy ear. Once upo
a time in another life, he'd wrapped his hands in the thic
rope of her hair and— Fingers tangled in Booger's fur, Je
took a deep breath. The ozone-tinged air stung his lungs a
he inhaled. Not smart to take a detour down memory lane.

Collapsing onto Jed's worn boots, Booger snarfed, pol
ished the leather with his tongue and then, satisfied, rolle
on his back, wiggling and scratching his spine in the sand
dirt.

"Least I can count on you." Squatting, Jed cuppe
Booger's chin and rubbed. "Good dog. A man can count o
his dog. Even a no-account mutt like you." Jed rubbed th
dog's ears again, let his fingers linger on the sweet spot th
dog loved. "What'd you think of the lady, Booger?"

Booger's tongue lolled on Jed's boot.

"Yeah, she has that effect on me, too. Still." Patting th
dog's head, Jed glanced again at the almost dark parking lo
remembering again the vulnerability and desperation i
Kate's face.

Like some reproachful ghost, her image lingered in th
deepening dusk. "I don't need Katherine March back in m
life, do I, Booger? She doesn't mean anything to me, and I'
be nuts to walk that road again, right?"

Booger rolled his head on Jed's boot.

He lifted the dog's other ear, searched for ticks. "A ma
only needs to get sucker-punched once in a lifetime to lear
his lesson. I sure as hell learned mine." His mouth tightene
grimly as his fingers curled into the fur behind Booger's neck
"Just because a woman's got sad eyes and looks like a goo

reeze would topple her on her rear end, a man doesn't have
o be a fool twice in his life, does he? Not if he's got a speck
of the sense the good Lord gave him."

Listing to the side, the dog gathered his huge paws underneath him. "Urff." Rising, he loped off into the darkness,
his shadow merging with the bushes and trees.

"Shoot, Booger. *Et tu?*" Wiping his drool-anointed hand
on his slacks, Jed looked up at the clouds gathering in the
west.

In the distance heat lightning flashed silently.

Her expression had been hopeless in that final moment.
Almost like she'd given up. Funny. She'd never let him see
any weakness. Any vulnerability. Not his Kate. He studied
the deepening darkness, the shadows closing in. But, she'd
never been his, not really, no matter what he'd thought.

For a while he'd thought he loved her. Afterward, for a
time, he'd hated her, rawness and pain a cold nastiness inside.

Then she'd walked into The Last Resort, and anger and
his other, confusing, emotion had leapt into life again.

He wished he could stick a label on it. Desire? Yeah, he'd
recognized that right off and been caught off guard. Lust, hot
and sudden and so fierce he couldn't have stood up if he'd
had to. Oh, yes, she could still make him want her, want her
with an urgency that left him dry mouthed and furious with
her.

With himself.

Jed shoved his hands into his pockets. It was this other
emotion he didn't have a name for, this *something* that had
made the hairs on the back of his neck stand up in warning
as she'd strolled toward him. Desire was easy. Uncompli-
ated.

Nothing had ever been easy with Kate.

Not even the heat.

A heat that still licked along his nerve endings.

Head tossed back, he watched the scudding clouds, felt the
first sprinkle of rain.

Well, Kate March was a puzzle he'd never solve. Too

much water under the proverbial bridge. Too much—every
thing.

And he no longer wanted to solve the puzzle.

Did he?

Rain stung his face, rolled down his neck. The hiss an
crack of lightning snapped through the air. So what if she'
asked for his help? Her problems weren't his. *She* had walke
away from him.

Now, three years later, eyes carefully polite, manners spi
polished and shining, she'd come back to him, asked for hi
help.

But in spite of her gussied-up, in-control outfit, hopeless
ness had stared back at him from the depths of her soft haze
eyes. All that sadness and vulnerability. And fear.

Kate, afraid?

His fingers curled into a fist. He didn't like that idea. No
sassy, mouthy Kate, who'd never taken any guff from him

Her friend had been killed. Brutally.

And Kate was terrified. She hadn't been able to mask tha
flick of panic in her eyes.

"Damn it all to hell." Feeling trapped, like a bull herde
into the ring, Jed shook his head, swore viciously and heade
back into The Last Resort. Like the bull, he recognized th
smell of danger. Of death.

Hands shaking, Kate slammed the bleached oak file drawe
shut. "Calla, do you have any clue where I stuck the printo
of our Guatemalan suppliers?" She fanned through a stac
of papers on the credenza next to the cabinet. If her nos
weren't stuck on her face, she'd lose it, too. Everything wa
disappearing, falling apart around her, and she couldn't fin
the blasted printout and—

She stopped, pressed cool fingertips to her flushed face
breathed in and out slowly. "Calla?"

After she'd left Jed on the island last night, she'd drive
around the mainland for hours, down to Sarasota, up to Pa
metto, afraid to go home, afraid not to, seeing a threat i

every pair of headlights behind her. Finally, nerves shot, she'd driven home, left every light in the house on and checked the locks and security system three times.

Everything sent her pulse jumping. The creak of the stairs. The brush of a tree branch, the shifting shadows on her bedroom wall. She hadn't slept, and in that haze of exhaustion, memories had darted in and out of her mind, tormenting her, destroying sleep. Jed. Patsy. And, finally, Frank, his face accusing her until she'd crawled out of bed and trudged to the office.

She hadn't told Jed about Frank.

She couldn't.

Anyway, the subject of Frank was no longer an issue. Jed wasn't going to help her. She couldn't blame him, could she? Going to him had been a long shot. She'd lost.

Now she was truly on her own. She would deal with whatever was lurking in the darkness.

Bracing both hands against the file cabinet and leaning her forehead against it, Kate forcibly stopped the direction of her thoughts, brought herself back to the moment. The printout. She needed the hard copy of their suppliers to check against the computer disk. "Calla! Help. I would have sworn I had the list in my hands—" Inhaling, she brushed her hair out of her face.

"Here, honey. Sorry it took me so long." Pushing Kate's office door open with her hip, Calla, her reliable, efficient partner, dropped a sheaf of computer foldouts into her hands. "You left it on my desk yesterday afternoon when you left." Short and compact, dressed in flaming red trousers and a knee-length vest embroidered with golden birds and scrolls, Calla made Kate think of a fireplug with wheels. And unlimited energy.

"Right." Kate sank into her chair. "So I did. Right before I left for my—appointment, we were talking about expanding our South American sources." Her stomach bounced, evened out. "Thanks."

"Are you okay?" Calla perched on the arm of the hibiscus-flowered pink-and-green sofa and crossed her arms under her full breasts. "Because you look like something my cat dragged home." Her cherubic face creased, her intense blue eyes sharpening. "You haven't looked well in weeks. Not since Frank was killed. I'm worried about you, you know."

"I know." Kate found herself curiously vulnerable to the sympathy in Calla's face. Maybe she should tell Calla— No. Not yet. She shrugged. "Touch of this stomach flu. That's all. Some kind of bug." As Frank's genial features flashed in her mind, Kate closed her eyes, opened them. "But thanks. For the worry. For the help. We've both been putting in long hours setting up these new accounts. We're both strung out and tired. In fact, I'm amazed you haven't picked up a virus. Must be all those vitamins you take by the handful every day."

Suddenly her stomach roiled. She smiled weakly as she shoved back her wooden chair, nausea churning viciously. Rollers squeaked on the bare floor as she bolted for the door of her office and the rest room down the hall, her hand flat over her abdomen. "Excuse me."

"Sure." Calla thrust a wad of tissues and the trash can into her hand. "Take this. Just in case."

"Thanks," Kate gasped, and ran as her stomach whip-sawed.

Head down, lips clenched, she was at the outside door of the suite, reaching for the glass doorknob, her stomach bouncing and whipping like a roller coaster. The door crashed back toward her, she dropped the trash can and tissues, and slammed into Jedidiah Stone's chest.

"Oh, God," she moaned, and tried to push past him.

"Not anywhere close." His warm palms cupped her elbows. "Steady, Kate. Where you goin' in such a rush?" His drawl drifted into her ear, butter rich, soothing.

With his arms around her, she wanted to burrow into him, hide from the night terrors and imaginings, wanted to sink into the floor so that she wouldn't have to look at him. None of those actions was possible. Not with Jed. Not ever. And especially not now.

Calling on the strength that had carried her through the past months, she lifted her head from the deceptive comfort of his hard chest and faced him, swallowed the nausea that had sent her racing for the door and the rest room. "Hello again, Jed." She edged backward as he stepped closer. "What a shock. I didn't expect to see you."

Lightly gripping her elbows, he glanced at the old-fashioned cuckoo clock on the wall. "It's only eleven. Headed for an early lunch, Kate?"

The idea of food made her stomach roller coaster again, and she thought for a moment that she would disgrace herself. "No."

Stiletto heels clicked against the plank floor. "Hi, I'm Calla Bowen, Kate's partner." Calla stuck her hand in Jed's direction.

Keeping Kate close to him, Jed took Calla's outstretched hand. The cuff of his shirt pulled back slightly, revealing a flat silver watch face. "I'm Jedidiah Stone, Kate's—" He draped his other arm around Kate's shoulder and Kate shut her eyes momentarily, desperate for control as her nausea unaccountably waned. "Well, what am I, Kate?" A message to her in the way he held her close to him.

*Hired gun,* she almost said. *Ex-lover,* she could have said and watched Calla's mouth drop open. *The biggest mistake of my life* would have been the truest answer. She didn't know how to answer him.

She wasn't sure she understood that nonverbal signal he was sending to her as he tucked her under his arm, so she settled for simplicity, finally responding, "Jed's a colleague from my old job." Not positive why she'd followed the impulse to lie to her friend, comprehending only that it sprang from the sudden pressure of Jed's arm across her shoulders, she stepped away from the weight of his arm and left the shelter of his lean body.

"Kate and I worked closely together. For about eight

months.'' Not a trace of innuendo in Jed's smooth voice, but his hip brushed against hers, and knowing what he was doing, Kate wanted to slap him, wanted to scream, wanted to lean against him and let his warmth seep into the coldness that had kept her in thrall since she'd found Patsy.

And Frank.

Annoyed with herself for the reflexive response to Jed's presence, irritated that she'd reacted without thinking to the slight pressure of his hand encouraging her to lie, she was now trapped by that lie. Meeting Calla's eyes straight on, she added awkwardly, making up a history as she talked, ''We met when I worked for SA Textiles, Calla. About four years ago. Before you and I met.''

''Really?'' The tilt of Calla's head toward Jed would have been flirtatious in another woman. From Calla, the tilt was contemplative as she looked from Kate to Jed. ''Kate's never mentioned you.''

''Oh, I reckon Kate forgot about me after all this time, right, Kate?''

''Not in the least.'' She pasted a smile on her face. ''How could I ever forget you, Jed?''

''Aw, thank you, darlin'.'' His mouth curved, but his eyes stayed the same remote, chilly gray. ''Anyway, we'd lost...touch.'' Jed's smile was all sunlit charm as he cocked his head sideways and returned Calla's look. ''You might say we ran into each other again by accident.'' His slight pause before he said *ran* was barely perceptible, a reminder of the moment when he'd grinned like the devil himself as she'd braked hard and her car had slewed greasily sideways in the dusty sand in front of him. ''Just one of those coincidences.''

''How...interesting.'' Calla glanced quickly at Kate, back to Jed.

''Yes, it was. Very.'' And his smile widened, encompassed Calla in its brilliance. ''Like old times.''

Kate wondered if Calla caught the cold glint in his eyes, eyes left untouched by his smile. But Kate saw. She understood. Jed was on the hunt.

She wondered, too, if that were a comfort or a threat.

Softening under the sun of Jed's smile, Calla tugged at a straight swath of streaky blond hair. "You must have been pleased to see Kate again."

"Pleased? I'm not quite sure that's exactly the word." Jed reached out and tapped Kate's shoulder, lightly, gently, nothing more than the brush of a butterfly's wing before he dropped his hand.

She shivered.

Without taking a step, he seemed to angle himself toward her, filling her view, but she didn't move, wouldn't give him the satisfaction of letting him think he'd intimidated her. He slid his hands into the pockets of his charcoal-gray worsted slacks. The fabric tightened across his thighs in a way that once would have made her pulse thunder. "What do you think, Kate? Were you *pleased* to see me?"

And as he turned his smile onto her, Kate felt like Aladdin. She'd uncorked the bottle and let loose a power she'd never controlled or understood.

"Oh, *pleased* doesn't begin to cover my reaction," she said, smiling back at him through tight lips, promising herself that hell itself could freeze over before she'd let him see again that he could make her shiver at his touch.

"That's what I thought," he said softly, and turned once more to Calla. "Kate and I had made plans, but you're more than welcome to join us. If you like?"

Puzzlement pleated tiny lines in Calla's forehead. "You didn't mention a lunch date—" She stopped. "I'll take a rain check, but, Kate, are you…?" Calla's thin eyebrows drew together as her glance dropped to the overturned waste can.

Her stomach tightening once more, Kate ignored Calla's pointed glance and prayed that Jed wouldn't attach any significance to Calla's concern. He would notice, of course. He noticed everything. He always had, but if she were lucky, he might think…anything. Let him think anything except guess at the truth. Kate grimaced, lied again. "I forgot we'd talked about going out to eat, Jed. Sorry, but I don't think I can—"

"Of course you can." Clasping her elbow once more, he stooped, straightened the waste can and turned Kate back toward her office. His smile was so warm it made her teeth ache. "Grab your purse and we'll be on our way. You can't imagine how much I've been looking forward to this."

This time Kate was sure she heard a threat behind the velvet words.

"I'm right in the middle of something," she managed to say, and tugged against his hold. "I didn't realize we'd made definite plans."

"No? My misunderstanding, then. But since I'm here…" The narrow palm of his other hand flattened against her back as he studied her. His dark gray shirt and tone-on-tone gray tie deepened the smoke of his eyes, and their intensity almost unnerved her as he added, "Let's catch up. What do you say?"

Kate didn't say anything. Whatever had made Jed decide to seek her out, she didn't know, but she would pay for it before the day was over, one way or the other. When she'd decided to approach Jed, she'd opened a Pandora's box. She'd let loose the demons of their shared past. If she were lucky, hope still remained.

If Jed had decided to help her, she would need to be very, very lucky.

"You look like you could use a good meal." Jed's warm hand at the back of her waist propelled her toward her office, and she reached behind her to push his hand away, to separate herself from him in that small way.

As she did, he caught her hand with one of his, clasping it firmly. The cool cotton of his shirt brushed against her wrist. "Got a favorite restaurant? For a long, leisurely lunch?"

Spoken in his whiskey-dark drawl, the word *lunch* seemed a euphemism for behind-closed-doors activities, and Calla's head jerked toward her. Flushing, Kate dragged her hand free, the slip-slide of that cool cotton on her skin an awareness she didn't need, didn't want.

Jed paused. "No?" He urged her forward toward her office door. "Oh well, not a problem. I'm sure I can come up with a couple of ideas."

"I'm sure you can." Whether those ideas had anything to do with food, though, was another matter entirely. She stomped toward her desk where she'd stowed her purse.

"Such faith, Kate. How touching." Amused, his voice was that of an old friend, a close friend, and everything in his body posture as he leaned toward her reinforced that picture.

Kate understood Jed was acting out a scenario for Calla. She just wished he weren't so damned good at setting the scene and creating his character. Being the focus of Jedidiah Stone's attention was seduction beyond belief. A woman could be lured into believing anything she wanted to. Bending so close that his clean, soapy smell enveloped her, he seemed to surround her, and remembering everything, she still felt her pulse flutter.

Of her own volition, she'd opened the door to Jed. She'd sought him out. Now, whatever would be, would be.

She needed him. She needed his skills.

And he'd decided for his own reasons to help her.

"I'll get my purse," she said resolutely, and yanked open her drawer. Lifting out her purse, Kate slammed the drawer shut with a soul-satisfying *thunk.*

Calla's wide-eyed stare caught hers as the picture of Frank on her desk wobbled, fell face forward, the rattle of the silver frame appallingly loud in the sudden silence.

# Chapter 3

From the corner of her eye, Kate saw Jed's thin fingers close around the picture, lift it, and place it carefully upright on the burled finish of her desk. Too casually he surveyed her office, his gaze passing over the bolts of fabric piled on the worktable, the stacks of papers on the credenza, the basket of yarns and small squares of rough fabric next to her desk. When he turned to her, his eyes were carefully expressionless. "Got everything, Katherine?" Only the slight formality, a formality anyone else would have missed, revealed that he'd reacted to the picture.

"Yes." She gripped her purse tightly, lifted her chin and walked toward the door, Jed close behind her, so close she was aware of the heat from his body even in the cool office. Glancing over her shoulder to Calla, Kate said, "We'll be at Coco's on the Pier. I have the cell phone if you need me." Coco's would be fast, probably noisy, and in all the confusion, she and Jed would find a kind of public privacy to discuss their business.

Jed rested his hand lightly on her shoulder. "I know Coco

She runs a swell little spot.'' He patted Kate's shoulder, and she knew the approving touch was one more part of the scenario he was playing.

"There's a relief.'' She sighed dramatically, fluttered her hand in front of her face, did her best Southern belle imitation. "You know I live for your approval, Jed.'' The second the words were out of her mouth, Kate wanted to kick herself. Damn him. He'd pulled a string, and she'd reacted again, not thinking. At least she'd spun her reaction so that he wouldn't know he'd provoked her.

But she saw the glint in his eyes.

He knew.

Business. No matter how he tried to nettle her, she *had* to keep what was between them impersonal, a business arrangement only.

He drew her close and she was irritated and comforted at the same time. "You know everything you do meets with my approval.'' He opened the door, smiled at Calla. "Kate's very special to me. I can't imagine how I lost contact with her.''

"You'll have a chance to renew your friendship, then.'' Calla's expression was uncertain. Though she hadn't said anything in front of Jed, Calla, of course, would be thinking of Frank. She would think Kate had a new interest in life. "How terrific you ran into each other.''

The creaking of the door as it slowly opened had Jed swiveling from Calla to the door. His stance altered so fast Kate wasn't even aware he'd moved until she realized he was suddenly between her and the backlit form still standing in the hall.

"Hey, Ma.''

"Hal, what on earth are you doing here?'' Calla's quick steps closed the space between them. "I thought you were in classes today.''

"Came to see my favorite mom instead.'' He grinned, teeth sparkling in his tanned face and lighting his bright blue eyes with mischief. Glancing at Jed, Hal shrugged. "My one and only ma, but still my favorite." Shrugging again, Hal said, "Anyway, Ma, the professor booked on us, so I escaped from the palm-lined confines of Sunshine U. to come visit." He referred to the highly expensive, laid-back university twenty minutes down the Tamiami Trail.

"You knew I'd be working, Hal. I don't have time to visit." Calla frowned, but she stepped back, giving Hal room to enter.

"I'll keep you company. You don't have to entertain me." As Hal stepped in, his sharply pressed khakis brushed against Kate's leg.

At her back, Jed was a silent presence, his shoulders still angled toward her, a surprising tension in their slant.

"Maybe I'll go pick up carryout for us. My treat. How's that sound, Ma?"

"Swell, kid." Calla stood on tiptoe and pecked Hal on the cheek. "And I could sure use an extra pair of hands. No, no, Kate," she said as Kate turned in concern. "Everything's under control."

Hal reached out to Kate, drawing her into a bear hug as he wrapped his arms around her. "Haven't seen you in a couple of weeks, but you doing okay, Auntie Kate?" Deep for a young man, his voice was troubled. "I know…"

Caught between Jed's rangy strength and Calla's gangly nineteen-year-old son, Kate abruptly felt claustrophobic, the too-sweet citrus smell of Hal's cologne stirring her almost-forgotten nausea.

"Fine, Hal. Busy, like your mom. We're running late. Sorry to be so rude. Catch you later, sweetie," she managed to say through clenched teeth as Jed held the door open, and Kate ducked under his arm and through the door into the cool quietness of the hall. Not even checking to see whether Jed followed her, once out of Hal's and Jed's sight she double-timed past the doors of the other suites on the floor until she reached the rest room.

Perspiration beaded her clammy forehead as she shoved through the door. She heard Calla's voice in the background introducing Hal and Jed. The door whooshed behind her, leaving her finally, blessedly, alone with her misery as she leaned against the sink, her stomach heaving in spasms.

Afterward, splashing cold water on her wrists and face, Kate heard the door open. Expecting Calla, she was too miserable even to look up from the bowl of the sink. "Sorry for barreling out of the office the way I did. This damned flu has really knocked me. Explain it to Hal, will you?"

"Not a good idea, Kate, to run into rooms with concealed hiding places, especially not when your life's been threatened." Reflected in the gold-framed mirror in front of her, Jed opened each stall door, letting it slam metallically behind him. "Anyone could hide in here. Biding his, or her—" another door slammed like the punch of her heart against her rib cage "—time. Waiting for you to come in."

She couldn't speak. Pictures clicked too fast in her head, pictures of Frank, of Patsy. Black-and-white pictures where blood was dark against a white floor.

In the mirror, Jed's eyes finally met hers. "You're a sitting duck, cookie. But you know that. I figured you were real desperate, Kate. Or you wouldn't have tried to hire me, would you?" His voice was softer, colder than the well water gushing into the sink. Watching her through slitted eyelids, he leaned against the blue-tiled wall. "No comeback? No clever reply? Cat finally got that acid little tongue of yours?" He handed her one of the heavy linen hand towels. "Dry your face, Kate. We're going to have lunch, and you're going to finish that conversation you walked away from yesterday. We have a lot of…catching up to do."

"I didn't think," she said dully. "I never even thought about someone hiding in here. My God." Her laugh rose shrilly even to her own ears. "This is the *women's* bathroom!"

"Think that would stop someone who's already murdered your friend? Killers find it easy to bypass the social niceties, Kate."

"I know, I know." Her fingers trembled slightly as she

wadded up the towel and dropped it into the wicker basket under the sink. "I didn't *think*. Damn. I was so *stupid*."

"Careless. Not stupid." Jed's arm brushed hers. "Come on, let's blow this joint."

As she slid her purse strap over her shoulder, she stopped, struck by a sudden realization. A chill slithered over her skin. "If someone had been hiding in one of the stalls, you would have been too late. You were talking to Calla and Hal."

"I was seconds behind you, Kate, and I never took my eyes off this door. No one could have left this room without my seeing him. I'd checked to see if there were window exits in here before I came to your office. Three people walked by the bathroom while you were in here. They made enough noise that no one with half a brain would have attacked you while they were in the hall."

"And a killer with no sense of self-preservation?" Once Jed had planted the idea, it was growing with terrifying power. She couldn't think of the closed stall doors now without picturing someone watching her as she'd dry-heaved over the sink, waiting for her in secrecy. Waiting to kill her. Her voice rose shrilly. "Maybe he wouldn't have cared about the people in the hall. Maybe he would have killed me and hidden until everyone in the building left!"

"That wasn't going to happen, Kate." Calm, implacable, his voice promised safety, a security she was beginning to see might be only an illusion.

She slicked lipstick across dry lips and dropped the shiny tube back into her purse. It clattered against the high-tech plastic of her palm-sized cell phone. She was afraid her teeth were about to echo that sound any second and she clenched them, saying flatly, "Someone could have killed me so quietly that you wouldn't have heard a sound, Jed. That's the truth, and you know it. You couldn't have done a thing to save me." She shuddered, long, rolling, unstoppable vibrations. "I made a mistake going to you for help."

She wasn't aware he'd moved until his narrow fingers cupped her face, and he had her backed against the sink, moving her backward into the corner with the push of his legs against hers. He wrapped his hand around her nape and pressed her chin up so that she was forced to meet his accusing gaze.

"You never trusted me, did you, Kate?" His face was grim, a dark flush slashing his cheekbones. Sibilant, dark, his words hissed into her ear. "Nothing's changed, has it? You were willing to let me into your bed." The palm of his other hand curved over her belly, lower, touched her briefly, familiarly. "Into your body."

The thunder of her pulse was loud in her ears. Her chest shuddered with each breath she tried to take. She couldn't move. Worse, oh, so much worse, she didn't want to move away from the heat of his skimming touch.

"But never into your heart." His face filled her vision as he trailed his fingers upward, spread them across her left breast. "No, you never allowed me there, did you, Katie?" Soft, seductive, memories spinning out of control with his words, with his touch. Old hungers spiraled through her, kept her still as he continued. "You kept me out of that cold heart of yours, didn't you?"

His mouth was so close that her lips buzzed as his breath whispered against them, and his thighs bumped aggressively against hers, insistently, turning her bones into warm honey.

His thumb slipped along her cheek, feathered a course to the corner of her mouth, and all the while, his eyes darkened, deepened, the cold gray turning to molten silver.

And her arms moved without conscious decision, closed around the width of his shoulders. Her hand tightened against his shoulder, and on tiptoe she lifted herself toward him blindly.

His belt buckle pressed against her stomach. She took a deep breath, somewhere an instinct for survival surfacing. "You don't scare me, Jed."

"Is that what you think I'm doing?" He tilted his head closer and his mouth brushed hers lightly. "Trying to scare you?"

"I don't know what the hell you're doing, but I've had enough." She lifted her chin, freeing it. Slapping his hand away, she tried once more to step away and couldn't, not with his legs still cradling hers, not with her own knees turned to jelly. "I told you yesterday. I won't let you bully me."

He tapped her chin, a light touch that felt like a caress. "Unfair, Katie. You've never been afraid of me. That's twice now you've accused me of bullying you. I haven't. I never bullied you. Not once. Admit it."

"All right. Fair is fair. Maybe I was wrong. Now give me space."

His mouth tightened. "Not yet." Moving closer, he bent his knees until he looked her straight in the eyes. "You welcomed everything we did three years ago. You craved my touch on you. My body on yours." He took her hand and flattened it against the zipper of his slacks, curved it against the hard ridge beneath.

She didn't blink. "Yes. I did. I wanted you, Jed. I don't anymore. Not that way." She jerked her hand away.

"No?" He still hadn't moved, and she didn't think she could catch her breath, not with the memory of him burning her, not with him warm and hard against her once more after so long. He brushed the back of his hand against her breasts, against the hard pebbles of her nipples. "You're such a liar, Katie." As he stepped away from her, his open palm slid over her breast and cupped it, his thumb resting against the tip. "But your body isn't." His thumb moved infinitesimally, and she inhaled sharply, unwillingly.

"Fear, Jed. Thinking about killers hiding in the women's stalls will have that effect on a woman. That's all. Don't flatter yourself," she said sweetly. Her skin tingled as if she'd touched a bare wire.

"While I can understand how you might tempt someone to kill you, you were safe today. Make no mistake about that. No one was going to harm you. Not on my watch." And that fast, his smile turned feral, frightening, as he finally released her, turned and slapped the door open. Holding it, he waited.

She'd always been aware Jed was a man who'd made his living solving problems in violent situations, but she'd never before seen him like this. She shuddered, glimpsing the side of him that she'd only vaguely sensed before. This man with the ruthless glitter in his eyes was also the man she'd once loved, this man who'd pleasured her gently, exquisitely, until she'd drifted in a haze of physical awareness, unable to think of anything except him. For a time.

Jed said he would drive. Her car, he told Kate calmly, was a darlin' little thing, but riding in it would turn him into a human pretzel.

She argued.

"I trust your driving, Kate. I don't want to ride in a sardine can. No matter how expensive a sardine can. But if it'll make you feel better, here." He took out the keys to his Chevy Blazer, tossed them to her, opened the passenger door and waited.

Of course she drove.

Watching her hair whip in the wind coming through the open car windows as she drove across the causeway to Anna Maria Island, Jed wondered how much longer she'd be able to stay silent. He reckoned the incident in the bathroom had disturbed her more than she wanted to admit. He'd hated the terror in her eyes as he'd pushed open each stall door. No matter what he felt about her, he wasn't going to let anyone terrorize her. Common decency, that's all, nothing more, but he was quickly developing an urge to wrap his hands around the neck of whoever had put that stark fear in her eyes and squeeze. Hard.

Coco's on the Pier was deserted.

"Y'all can have your choice of tables." The hostess gestured to tables draped with brilliant tropical fabrics. Folded into bird shapes, parrot-colored napkins—hot pink, shrieking green and chrome yellow—rested on top of white plates. "We haven't been all that busy today. Kind of surprising, since it's high season." The heavily tanned hostess lifted her arm to reach for the menus, and her plastic lei slipped off one bare, brown shoulder.

"Outside?" Kate scarcely glanced at Jed before she nodded to the hostess and moved toward the patio.

Kate's take-charge attitude had returned. For what might be ahead, she would need all her grit and intelligence. "Sure," he said.

And if someone had trailed them, the surf would act as white noise, hiding their conversation. He'd checked to see if anyone had followed them. As far as he'd been able to see, no one had. Still, better to have a plan in place, even in Coco's emptiness.

Kate sank into one of the metal chairs and faced the water. Crossing her legs, she stared out at the gulf. One sandal dangled from her toes, and the high arch of her foot gleamed in the sun. Her silvery-blue dress flickered in the sun like minnows in shallow water, rippling against her legs in the breeze and drawing his eyes to the pale curve of her calves.

Once, he'd kissed his way up from the arch of that foot, over the sleek calves of her legs and across the soft skin of her belly. Everywhere. He wished he could forget the taste of her skin, the salty sweetness of her breasts on a hot afternoon, an afternoon spent exploring one another's bodies in an adventure of the senses.

But it had all gone wrong.

Until he'd seen her again, he'd convinced himself he had forgotten the particular taste and scent of Kate March. He wished he had. Combined with salt spray and warm air, her scent drifted to him and mixed with his every breath, reminding him.

The sun was warm on his face, and the moment had a curious peacefulness to it in spite of the melancholy settling over him. Loss, that's what it was, he thought, finally giving a name to the emptiness. Loss.

The incoming tide moved heavily against the huge stack of rocks down below, and spume from the water blew over them as they flipped their menu pages. As Kate absently turned the pages, not looking at the selections, her profile was a clean sweep of straight nose and sharp chin.

The sense of loss still filling him, he tugged at the top of her menu. "Why so quiet?"

She faced him, her face pensive and calm, the earlier tension and fear gone for the moment. "Oh, I was thinking how much I love watching the water. How peaceful this is." She gestured toward the rocks, to the empty dining room behind them. "Sometimes I think I could live on an island. Away from people, noise. Away from all the confusion."

"You wouldn't like an island for long." Diverted by the picture of Kate on an island, he grinned and pulled out a sweet potato strip, offering it to her. "Bugs. Dirt. No phones."

"You may be right." Nibbling on a bit of vegetable, she waggled her hand at him, not conceding a thing, and the filmy sleeve capping her shoulder fluttered with the movement. Underneath the edge of the sleeve, her skin gleamed mysteriously, and he almost reached out to lift that gauzy hem and trace the line of her shining skin. "But the idea's very tempting these days." She sighed and dug into the mound of potato slivers the waitress had brought, biting thoughtfully into one strip. "Sometimes I'd like to disappear, vanish and not have to think about anything, anybody." She dusted the spice off the ends of her fingers. Red-brown specks fell to the table. "Oh, I wish I could wake up and everything was the way it was before. I want my old life back."

Her voice was so wistful, her face so forlorn, that he was touched. He didn't want to be, didn't want to feel anything for her, didn't want any personal connection with her. He'd decided in the early-morning hours that he would help her, but it would be a business matter only. Nothing else. "A lot's been going on, Kate. Are you ready to talk about it?"

"Yes. All right." She placed the menu down carefully. "I'm assuming you've decided to—take me up on my job offer?"

"Sure." Irritation bubbled inside him. "You got the

money, cookie, I got the time. Like you said yesterday, I can always use some extra dough, and I'm not particular.''

"That's not what I said."

"Oh? Sure sounded that way to me."

"I thought you looked as if you might be short on money. That you might be interested in a job. That's all."

"No, you said that I was a man—let me see, how did you put it?" Tipping his chair back, he crossed his arms and balanced one foot against the pedestal stand of the table. "That I was a man who followed the scent of a dollar. A man who had his price."

"I didn't mean to hurt your feelings, Jed." She reached out a small hand toward him, let it fall as he kept his arms crossed. Frowned, the feathery line of her eyebrows pulling together, as she stared down at the menu on the table. "That wasn't my intention. Truly."

"Sure, Kate, I understand. No harm, no foul. You called it as you saw it. We've both been good at saying what's on our minds, right?"

"I suppose." She continued to frown. "I shouldn't have said that, though. You had your reasons for what you did, for choosing the jobs you took. It wasn't—isn't—my business to sit in judgment. To accuse you of taking on any job for the right price."

"Especially not if you're the one making the offer." He wondered why her observation cut to the quick. It did though. He moved the flatware in front of him back and forth, thinking. "Back then. We didn't always argue, did we, Kate? Remember?"

Quiet, almost a whisper, her words came to him. "No, we didn't." She turned her head away from him, toward the water.

Overhead a seagull screeched, his wings blinding white in the sun.

Jed waited a moment before he asked, "Why didn't you hire a bodyguard, Kate? Why come to me?"

She didn't answer him right away. Unwrapping her neon-pink napkin slowly, she draped it over her lap. "I don't know."

"The reason I'm asking is that I also remember, Kate, exactly what you said before you walked away three years ago. Do you?"

She kept her face averted.

"You said, and I'm quoting here, 'I wouldn't have your baby if you were the last man on earth.' That's what you said then, Kate, right after I'd asked you to marry me, to make a family with me. And yet yesterday you asked for my help. Way I see it, that makes me the last man on earth."

He thought for a second she flinched, but, eyes downcast, hiding her thoughts, she stayed silent.

"No comment?"

She shook her head, and her hair belled out around her face in a nimbus of light brown gilded by the afternoon sun.

"Well, *am* I the last man on earth, Kate? Now?"

She faced him, warrior to warrior. "Yes."

That admission hurt, too. He wondered, though, at the blank resolution in her eyes as she'd spoken. He lifted one shoulder nonchalantly. "Okay. So I reckon the deal between us is clear. All cards on the table. Let's order and talk about the terms of this job." Speculating, he watched her carefully. If she could still hurt him, was she, somewhere under that brittle armor of hers, still vulnerable to him? It might be…interesting, he decided suddenly, to find out. Testing, he added, "And negotiate the price."

"I can pay you—"

"So you said. But I haven't decided what this job is worth to me yet. What my fee will be." He lifted the ring finger of her left hand. "Tell me about the picture on your desk first, Katherine."

Her hand jerked, but he held it tightly, curious as to what she'd say, how she'd explain what he'd already figured out.

Interrupting them, Beth, the waitress, said, "Y'all might want to try the grouper today. It's really good. Lemonpeppered and broiled? But the beer-boiled shrimp are nice and fresh, too.''

"Grouper," Jed said, not looking at the waitress. "Salad. Couple of glasses of your house white."

Kate started to speak, stopped.

"Excellent choice." Beth scribbled on a pad and sauntered off, sticking her pen in her hair as she pushed through the patio doors.

"You know, don't you?" Kate's eyes glittered, whether with temper or frustration, he couldn't tell. Probably both. "You've figured it out?"

He nodded.

"Fine, then. What else do you want me to tell you?" This time she yanked her hand free and tucked both hands under the table.

"Nothing wrong with the truth, is there?"

"Frank." She swallowed.

"Me?" He grabbed at the green sail of his napkin as it billowed up from his lap, anchored it against the breeze. "I try to be. Be nice if you were, too."

"My fiancé."

"Ah. *Frank.* The fiancé." Jed raised his glass of water to his mouth and was surprised to discover the nastiness uncoiling inside him once more. He didn't like this intense animosity toward a man he'd never met, either, the urge to take him out in a back alley and work out the nastiness. "Tell me about Frank. Why didn't you ask him for help, Katie?"

"He's dead." Her breasts rose quickly with her inhalation, trembled against the silvery-blue fabric. "Dead."

"Well." Jed stared at the surf below them, thinking.

"No, not *well* at all." Drawing his attention back to her, Kate's voice was shaky.

He handed her his napkin as she fumbled futilely for hers. "I'm sorry, Kate." And he was. Thumping a man into a pulp was one thing. Discovering he was dead was another matter. The nastiness drained out of him and he focused, knowing at a gut level he wasn't going to like the answer to his question. "What happened?"

It was the look in her eyes that told him.

"Murdered?"

"Yes." Nothing whispery about her voice now. Something cold and implacable, something he identified with. As terrified as she was for herself, Kate was beyond anger that people she'd cared about had been killed. "With Patsy."

"Why?"

"Frank was with Patsy the night she was murdered. I was supposed to meet her. She said she had the report ready for me. I could pick it up or she'd drop it off, but she wanted to explain a couple of points in person, not over the phone. I was running late."

"Not unusual."

"I know. A character flaw." Almost as if she were reciting, she continued, her voice empty. "Frank and I had planned to have dinner that evening. Afterward." She took a deep breath—to steady herself, he thought as he watched. "I told Patsy I'd meet her at her house. While I was in the parking lot, though, Frank called on my cell phone. When I told him I had to make a stop first and was running behind schedule, he offered to pick up the report for me. He had to go right past Patsy's on his way to the restaurant anyway, he said. No problem. I thought it was a good idea. It would save time, and I could always talk to Patsy later."

Her hands lay flat on the table as if she were trying to support herself. "I found both of them. They were there together." Her fingernails scratched once against the cloth, went still. "At Patsy's," she repeated.

"Where were you going to meet Frank?"

"At the restaurant. That was the whole point."

"So why did you go to Patsy's?"

"I drove past the restaurant, Frank wasn't there, and on the spur of the moment, I thought I'd surprise them both. I thought maybe they'd started talking and lost track of the time. I went to Patsy's. That's why I found them. I made good time," she said dully. "All the lights were green."

"Did Frank know what he was picking up?" Listening to the subtext of what she was telling him, Jed went still. He was curious. Her explanation was off-kilter, and he sensed that, like yesterday, she was omitting details, holding back information. "Did you tell him why you'd hired Patsy?" Jed's insides knotted as he asked the question. Kate had never let him help her. Had she, however, leaned on Frank, the man whose rawboned face had shone with such amiability back at Jed from the silver frame?

Her head resting in her hands, she hesitated. "No. He didn't know anything about what had been going on. I hadn't told him why I'd hired Patsy. Sweet Frank volunteered to help me in a tight spot, and he was killed for his kindness." Abruptly she lifted her head. Her eyes glittered fiercely. "Still want the job, Jed? Still want to help me? You might get killed, too. And then what good will any amount of money be?" She pressed her palms against her eyelids. "Back out, Jed. I'll understand. This isn't a game. Two people have already died. No matter what happened between us in the past, I don't want you dead, too."

"Nobody's going to kill me, Katie." He took one of her hands in his. Despite her fierceness, her hand was cold and small. Defenseless, he thought, though Katherine March had never in his experience been helpless. "Enough people have tried. I'm reasonably confident no one's going to succeed any time soon."

"I don't want to open a door and find you dead," she repeated, a scratchiness in her low tones.

"Aw, Katie, you care after all."

Like she hadn't heard him, she continued in a monotone. "I've caused too much pain. Too much death."

"I'm kill-proof," he said. "Relax, Kate. I made up my mind yesterday. Nothing you've told me has changed it. You've got yourself a bodyguard. I'll take very good care of your body, Kate. And we'll talk afterward about my fee."

Curling her fingers into his, eyes closed, she nodded.

That easily it was settled. He'd made his decision. Willingly, he thought. Hoped.

He wondered if the bulls in the ring went willingly. Or if some far-off scent lured them forward, kept them thundering toward the bloodstained sand.

# Chapter 4

Moments later, Jed looked up as Beth interrupted them.

"Sorry it took so long, folks."

"No problem. We're not in a hurry." Kate smiled at the waitress. "Smells good." Taking a quick sip of water, Kate smiled again, an odd strain in her smile that made him lean in and watch her even more closely.

Deftly Beth palmed the plates onto the table. "I think you won't mind the wait, though, once you taste what Martine has done to this fish." She put her fingers to her lips in a Southern version of the French ooh-la-la. "Spectacular," she drawled. "The man's a genius."

"I'm sure he is," Jed said, and watched as Kate once more quickly sipped her water.

After Beth had served their food and vanished back into the main restaurant area, Kate picked at the grouper with her fork, poking at it until the thick meat lay in flakes.

"You don't like the results of Martine's genius?"

She lifted a chunk, chewed. "It's wonderful." She stabbed another chunk. Chewed.

"No appetite? Flu will do that to you."

"Flu." Her fork hovered midair, dipped slowly back toward Martine's grouper of the day.

"Yeah. That flu you mentioned to Calla?" At The Last Resort, he'd thought stress had made her look washed out and thin. Flu could have the same effect.

"I'm fine. Really." She dug in to the fish. "Don't worry about me."

"Okay," he said easily, letting the subject drop for the moment. But there was too much effort, too much dogged determination in the lift of her fork to her mouth. He couldn't quite put his finger on what it was about her behavior that triggered a faint *alert! alert!*

Something had.

But that was Kate. She'd fall over in a heap before she'd give up or admit she couldn't handle something. If it was important, sooner or later he'd figure it out. He was still astonished she'd sought his help.

And that was what he wanted to get a handle on first.

The main dining area inside Coco's had filled, and diners were spilling outside onto the patio in a buzz of talk and laughter. Kate became quieter and more withdrawn as the patio filled. Jed felt her slipping away from him, going somewhere inside herself where he couldn't go.

He didn't want to examine why her withdrawal bothered him. But it did. Forbidden territory. His reactions to Kate March was best left alone.

He scowled at the tip of his shoe. Enough. He needed her back in the moment. He needed her thinking about the situation facing them. Facing *her*. He was only the bodyguard of the moment. Doing his job, that's all. Everything else had been burned out not long after she'd left him. He'd made sure of that.

"Kate. Pay attention. What did the police say when you told them you thought Patsy was killed by mistake? That you were the target?"

Startled, she glanced up. Her fork clattered against her

plate and flecks of grouper bounced. "They said it sure didn't look that way to them. Oh, they were nice, understanding. Concerned. But it didn't make sense to them that I might be the target. I mean, gee whiz—" Kate's mouth twisted "—Patsy was killed in her own home. Why on earth would I think she'd been mistaken for me?" Picking up her fork again, she toyed with the ruined grouper fillet, laid the fork down. "They suggested ever so courteously that Frank and Patsy might...be interested in each other and, oh, by the way, did I have an alibi?"

"Did you?" Jed watched carefully as she raised her chin and glared at him.

"You want to know if *I* had an alibi, Jed?"

"Yeah, I reckon I do."

"You think I killed Frank?" Her face flushed, chasing away the sick paleness of the flu or fear, or whatever it was that had her looking like a carton of bad milk.

"Murder's usually a crime of passion, opportunity, or economics. You were engaged. Hey, there's passion." Jed resented the pain that corkscrewed through him with the words. Funny, that he could react that way after all this time. "Come on, Kate, the police would have wondered if you'd killed him and Patsy in a fit of jealous rage. That would be their first, automatic reaction. They'd start with the most obvious motive. That's how they're trained. From their viewpoint, cookie, you had the best motive." Knowing it would irritate her out of her quietness, he grinned. "Besides, you have a temper, Katie. Who knows what you might do?"

A tray of dishes crashed behind him. The table rocked as she shifted her legs, bumped the pedestal underneath.

"Damn you, Jed. I don't have a temper." Her attention sharpened on him and her eyes sparkled, the hazel deepening to that mossy green he liked. "Except with you. And you'd tempt a saint to murder."

He reached over and carefully slid her knife to his side of the table. "Making sure, Katie," he said as she stared at him, her eyes flashing. "Watching out for potential hazards. Staying alert."

"Good idea." She smiled then, her bottom lip curving in a sweetness that made him reach out and touch its softness. "Since I've never laid claims to sainthood."

"Me either." As he touched her mouth, his throat went tight with hunger, and he couldn't look away from her mouth, his words coming out all scratchy and harsh. He'd loved her mouth, been fascinated by the richness of its curves and texture, its sweetness that gave the lie to the vinegar of her words. He cleared his throat uncomfortably. "I'm nobody's saint, Kate. You, of all people, should know that."

"Right." Her gaze skittered to the side, her eyelashes shadowing her eyes, hiding her thoughts. "You're not. I knew that from the beginning. But I never wanted a saint."

Her mouth was so soft against his thumb. He moved it one small space, delicately across her lip. "What did you want, Kate? I never understood." He hadn't. This was the question that had haunted him long after she'd left.

Avoiding his gaze, she pleated the tablecloth fabric. "You."

"You had me."

"No. Never." She looked at him then, her gaze locking with his, thoughts swirling secretively in the depths of her eyes like shapes barely glimpsed in a dark river.

Sleek and smooth, her mouth was slightly damp from her last sip of water. If he leaned forward and took her mouth with his, she would taste of the lemon that floated in the water, of the coffee she'd asked for and drunk instead of the wine he'd ordered. He sighed, distracted by the feel of her mouth, by the scent of the salt water and the lure of Kate March's eyes going so deep and green that a man could drown in them if he was reckless. Letting his thumb linger, he tugged on the fullness that lured him to taste.

"Don't, Jed. That's not a good idea." With her words, her lip slipped against his thumb and the tip of her tongue grazed his finger, damp and warm. Slick.

An accident.

But it reminded him of Kate touching him in a hundred ways, a hundred places, with her mouth, her tongue.

"You're right." Abruptly he reached for his wine, noticing distantly that the fine vibration from his hand sloshed the wine against the side of the glass. Like liquid sunshine, a drop fell on the table, glistened against the brilliant colors. "Clumsy of me, Kate."

"Yes." She brushed the drop into the bright fabric. "But no problem. This fabric washes well." Rubbing harder and harder, she went on in a rush. "It's one of our products."

"You've done well, haven't you?"

"Yes."

"And in such a short time. Three years ago you were happy managing that interior decorating firm down in Sarasota. You'd just started there, hadn't you? After leaving SA Textiles?"

"Yes."

"By the way, quick thinking. We met at SA's, huh?" He smiled. "You might have a future in espionage with that kind of fast recovery."

"It seemed best to stick as closely to the truth as I could. Calla knew I'd worked there. I had to give some explanation for our acquaintance."

"Oh, excellent, Katie. Our *acquaintance*. Nice touch."

"What else could I say? Calla didn't need a dossier on us, and I thought you didn't want me explaining who you really were."

"No, I didn't, and you did a good job. Unless she starts to ask me about fabrics. And then I'd be up the proverbial creek." He adjusted his chair so that he could see her without the sun shining into his eyes. "Anyway, quite a career switch for you. Going into business on your own. Risky."

"I needed to change my life. I had a little money saved. Borrowed more." She shrugged. "Calla and I saw an opportunity for an upscale fabric supplier on the Gulf Coast. It was the right time for us, for the market. Things fell into place. We struggled, but now it's all we can do to keep up with the demand. We're the hot name in custom fabrics. If you want the unusual for your wedding, your house, for anything, the word's out. Go to Bowen and March's Import Imprints.''

"I'm impressed. You've worked hard." He'd recognized the quality of her office furnishings, the classy lines of her shoes and suit, and he knew to the dollar how much her jazzy car cost. "Quite an accomplishment in next to no time." She'd changed everything. Her hair. Her address. Everything. "When you decide to overhaul your life, you don't play around, do you?"

"Making a change was important."

"New broom sweeps clean, huh? Out with the old, in with the new." Ego intruded again, left him peckish and on the edge of cranky. "You sure created a whole new life damned fast. So when did Frank enter the picture?"

Not answering, she smoothed her hand over the tablecloth and changed the subject. "You shouldn't touch me, Jed."

He sipped the wine, swirled it and silently cursed himself for breaking the one rule he'd made when he'd decided to let Kate hire him. No entanglements. Nothing with emotion. Frank wasn't important. Jed tipped his glass in her direction, saluting her. "I always liked touching you, Kate. And, like I said earlier, if you're honest, you'll admit you liked touching me. Old habits die hard."

"Three years ago, Jed. Both of us have new habits by now." Again the brittleness that tweaked his curiosity, but she lifted her coffee, drank, and the moment passed. "You know the old saying about repeating history."

"That those who don't learn from history are doomed to repeat it?" He'd wanted to take her mouth with his with such urgency that his body ached. At some strange, disconnected level he was amused by the way his body reacted to her. At another level, a level that went soul deep, he wanted—

What? He gripped the stem of the glass. Nothing. He wanted nothing from her.

"We've learned our lessons. And we both survived. Hearts and souls intact. We don't want to repeat history, do we, Jed?"

"Hell, no." He upended his wineglass and downed the last of the golden liquid. "Shoot, we did enough damage to last both of us a lifetime." He smiled, plunked his goblet down and went in for the kill. "So, Katie, did you have an alibi or not?"

He'd always admired Kate's ability to recover, never more than now. She didn't miss a beat, bless her.

"Yes. Because I was rushing to meet Frank, I got a speeding ticket. Can't find a better alibi than having one of Sabal Palm's finest vouch for you. And since you're so interested, it was physically impossible for me to have been at Patsy's at the time she and Frank were killed." She crumpled her napkin and stood up, dropping it on her chair seat as it rocked behind her.

"Good."

"What?" Soft brown hair drifting around her face, she whirled toward him in a billow of silver-blue dress and annoyance.

"Well, cookie, your alibi eliminates a detour for the dudes and dudettes in khaki. Makes it easier for them to look at things from, oh, let's say *your* perspective." He gestured with his head. "Have a seat, Kate. We need to talk—"

Frowning, she suddenly whipped her head to the left, looking down at the walkway along the rocks.

"What's the matter?"

"I don't know." She leaned over the wall and peered down at the surf and rocks. "Nothing."

Jed stood and stared down at the wash of foam and surf against the rocks. The narrow walkway was empty. Where it made an L and disappeared around the edge of the building, he saw a flick, as though someone had walked by.

Puzzled, Kate looked at him. "I thought I saw Calla. But that doesn't make sense. Couldn't have been Calla. She would have called me if she needed me. Or come up here looking for me. Odd.'' She gripped the edge of the rail, and the pinched white around her mouth told him she wasn't as unconcerned as she pretended.

He stepped on the bottom rail, vaulted down to the rocks and dropped to the walk. In a flat-out run, he sprinted toward the corner.

The sun beat down in a mellow haze on the crushed shells in front of Coco's. The parking lot was full. Rapidly scanning the lot, he didn't recognize any of the automobiles he'd scoped out in Kate's office parking lot, didn't see anyone rushing off.

Shading his eyes, he looked into the distance down the road that led back to the causeway. Packed now with cars, vans, trucks and motorcycles, it was a fume-spewing parking lot, a faint gasoline haze obscuring the day. Nothing caught his eye. Too damn many tourists jamming the roads.

Kate thought she'd glimpsed Calla. He gave a lot of credence to Kate's observations. Like Sparks had said, Kate wasn't a stupid woman. If she thought she'd seen something, Jed wasn't about to ignore her suspicions.

Before he could return to the patio, she came walking toward him in a flutter of dress turned ghostly silver by the bright sun. With her purse in her hand, she raised her arm to shove her hair out of her face. Cast into shadow, once again the skin of her underarm seemed the essence of femininity in some unexplainable way that stopped the breath in his chest. ''Hey, there—''

''Yes,'' she muttered. ''I left Beth a lovely tip.''

''Wasn't asking.'' He straightened his tie and slid his hands inside his slacks pockets to keep from stroking that shadowed strip of skin. ''Would have expected you to. You've never been…ungenerous, Kate.'' In fact, she'd been the most generous of lovers, giving and taking pleasure in such a way that taking her to bed had felt like being given a gift beyond price. Every time.

''Thank you.'' She stumbled, seemed surprised, as if his

compliment had caught her off guard. Glancing down the road, she asked, "Did you see anyone?"

"No." He turned to stare at the road again and off in the distance in the direction of the causeway. "Easy for someone to lose himself, herself, in the crowd. You thought you saw Calla, huh?"

She nodded.

"Why?"

"I don't know," she said slowly. "Something. A color? An impression, that's all, Jed. I'm sorry. I wish I could be specific. I guess it wasn't important. It's only that I'm so damned jumpy. I never used to be like this." She frowned. "I was wrong, I guess."

"Everything's important, Kate. You didn't overreact. Best to check stuff out. If your gut tells you something's making you uncomfortable, listen to it. It may save your life."

"Maybe. You're right, of course." She frowned again. "But it was so unexpected, and all my reactions are off these days." A whip of wind lifted her skirt, tightened it against the V of her thighs and sent a pang of hunger down his groin.

"Do something for me, Kate."

"All right," she said hesitantly, and walked toward him. Her square, pewter-colored heels crunched on the shells, flexed her calves into parentheses that his hands had once known as familiarly as his own body.

Her dress wrapped her body, rippled around her and held his gaze in spite of his effort to look away. The delicate shape of her, the dip and curve, burned his eyes. Almost in slow motion she came toward him in a glow of silver-blue and golden autumn sun, and he knew he would remember the look of Kate March in this parking lot when he was an old man and well past longing and desire.

"What do you want me to do?"

"Call Calla."

He expected her to argue.

She didn't.

Instead, she pulled the tiny phone out of her purse and

punched a couple of numbers, spoke into the palm of her hand. "Hi. I thought I'd let you know I'm running late. Right. Nothing new there, but I—" Kate looked toward him and he nodded "—I don't think I'll be back in the office before you leave. Take care." She pushed a button, snapped the phone shut and tucked it back into her purse. "Calla's at the office. I couldn't have seen her on the walkway."

Cupping Kate's elbow in his palm, Jed led Kate toward his car. "No, reckon you didn't. But you saw *something* that triggered your alarm."

"No third degree? You believe me that easily?"

He nodded. "Yeah, I do."

She tipped her head, and the sun turned her throat to a golden shimmer. "Two compliments in one day." Touching his forehead, she smiled gently. "Can't think what's wrong. You must be running a fever, Jed."

"Think so?" He couldn't stop himself. He ran the back of his hand down that long, smooth column. Her eyelashes fluttered, lifted like the material of her dress, and, in truth, he felt like a fever heated his blood, coursed through him. A sickness of the blood. "Maybe you're right."

"Gosh, and you're agreeing with me on top of everything." She made a mocking face. "Has the world come to an end and no one told me?"

"No, no, Katie." He touched the entwined silver loops dangling from the tender lobe of her ear, set them chiming. "I said *maybe* you're right."

"Oh, very good. Quite the tricky little two-step you just executed. But that's okay. An almost agreement will last me for a while." She patted his arm. "Don't let it throw you." She made a face at him. "That you came so close to saying I could be right about something. I won't rub your nose in it."

"Of course you will. Every chance you get." He smiled right back at her. "Wouldn't be any fun if you didn't, Kate. You know that." He stepped back, pointed his key at his car and beeped the remote.

Wrinkling her nose impudently, she climbed into the passenger seat. "Okay, honcho, I did all the work last time. You drive."

"Bossy as ever."

"Bossy? Not me. I'm the soul of accommodation."

"You? Ha." Hand on the driver's door, he let his gaze skim under the car, looking for a disturbance in the pine needles he'd driven over. Nothing. No one had crawled under the car while he and Kate had been in Coco's. "But I hear and obey."

"Oh, sure. And the moon's made out of green cheese. You'd already planned to drive. *I* was merely being gracious and keeping the truce going." Clipping her seat belt, she said, "Even if I had seen Calla, Jed, she would have had a good reason to be here. I know she would. Calla wouldn't hurt me. Why on earth would she?" Kate gave the seat belt an emphatic shove. "She's my friend."

"Maybe. Maybe not."

"No maybe about it." She smacked the seat between them. "Look, Jed, if you're going to work with me on this, you have to understand something. I won't have you harassing my friends. None of my friends would have killed Patsy. Or Frank."

"And what makes you so sure that your friends aren't responsible for those deaths? In my experience, people are capable of almost anything."

"Your experience isn't mine. You've never trusted anyone, have you, Jed? Always on guard, always suspicious."

"Come on. Someone killed them. I'd be loony if I didn't suspect the people around you. Of course I'm checking out their motives." Like a bit of grit in an oyster's shell, her certainty ground against him. "I'd really like to understand, cookie, what makes you trust them? And…" Repeating her earlier question mockingly, he added, "So *easily?*"

"Because I know them. They wouldn't hurt me. For any reason."

Her absolute confidence frustrated him. "Kate, *someone*

has killed two people. It wasn't an accident. Both people were connected to you. You're at the center of whatever happened. The killer could be anyone around you. Someone you trust. And whether or not Patsy was killed by someone thinking Patsy was you isn't really significant—''

"Tell that to her." Her voice spiked bitterly. "I'm sure she'd be thrilled to know your opinion. What a relief for her, to know that her death was insignificant."

"You know that's not what I meant. I told you. I liked her."

"Oh, I know you didn't mean her death wasn't important." She cupped her face, and her hair slid forward, curtaining her. "I'm sorry. What I said was uncalled for."

"Hell, Kate. If we keep up like this, all this apologizing and understanding, we might wind up being friends." He started the engine and backed, turning the car to face the road.

"There'd be a miracle, all right." She leaned her head against the seat and closed her eyes. "We—" she searched for a word "—cared for each other. Once. I'd like for us to be friends."

"I never wanted to be your friend, Kate. I can't be one now. You're asking too much."

"I see." She closed her eyes again, disappeared from him into that far place.

"I'll save your life, Kate. That's what you've hired me to do." He thought she flinched, but with his eyes on the road, he couldn't be sure. It was more a sensation of slight movement, a shifting in his peripheral vision, and then her voice came as soft as the smell of oranges on the damp air.

"All right. That's what you agreed to do. Anything else would be too much to hope for, I guess."

"Damn right, cookie." He spun the wheel to the right and out of the path of a slow-moving turtle crossing the road. "Me and you being friends isn't even in the realm of the possible."

"No, of course not. I can see that now." With both hands

she pressed her skirt flat over her knees. "I don't feel like talking anymore, Jed."

"Yeah, this kind of talk isn't productive, that's for sure. Mixing up the present and the past isn't getting us anywhere except stuck in old patterns. Let's concentrate on the job at hand, okay?" He spared a glance for her, and didn't want to see the smudges under her closed eyes, didn't want to feel that sneaky urge to comfort her.

But he did. And nothing he felt had anything to do with friendship. He shook his head, clearing it. "How about taking a ride with me, Kate?"

"Where do you want to go?"

"Think you could handle a side trip to the murder scene?"

Turning toward him, she pressed against the door, all fatigue vanished. "Why?"

"I'm curious."

"Is there a point to your curiosity, Jed, or is this some game to see if you can push me over the edge?" Sudden tension buzzed from her. "Because you can't."

"What?" Stunned by her accusation, he took his foot off the accelerator, slowed the car.

"What are you after, Jed? You want to see how I'll react to viewing the scene where Frank was killed? Is that it? Did curiosity make you decide to help me?" Her mouth curled in dismay. "Is that why you showed up at my office? Because you were curious to see how I was holding up to murder and mayhem?"

"No. Not curiosity." He wasn't sure he was telling her the truth. Maybe curiosity had played a part. Maybe he had been curious to see if he could break through her coolness toward him, make her regret—what? "I'm not sure why I decided to help you, Kate. I just did, that's all. Don't try to turn an impulsive decision into a major deal, okay? Don't overanalyze my change of heart."

"I need to, because this investigation isn't a puzzle to me. It's not a mind game where the adrenaline comes from outsmarting an unseen opponent. The rush is what you love. The game. But this is reality, not a game. You're not involved. Nothing's at stake for you, Jed, so you can distance yourself very nicely.''

Her intensity rolled over him.

''My goal's real clear, Jed. I want to know who killed Patsy and Frank. I don't care about pitting my wits against you or against some killer. I don't have the inclination to be clever. Or the energy.'' She kneaded her forehead.

''Whoa, Kate.'' Turning the steering wheel and watching for a break in the traffic, he pulled off to the side of the road and parked under a stand of pines. He left the engine idling, and the air-conditioning hummed in the silence as he sorted through the elements of what she'd poured out.

The causeway was ahead, a solid line of cars headed back to the mainland. The narrow path bordering both sides of the span was packed with fishermen dangling a line in the intercoastal waters below. Even focusing on what she'd thrown at him, he let his gaze search the crowd of fishermen, the campers parked like him beside the road. Looking for anyone out of place. Anyone who shouldn't be there at this time of day.

Satisfied, he asked the uppermost question on his mind. ''You said, pitting your wits against mine? I don't get your point.''

''Why not? I thought I made it as clear as spring water.''

''I heard the words. I don't get the message. Why in God's name would you think I was trying to push you over the edge?'' He laid his arm along the back of her seat. ''What would be the reason?''

She crossed her arms, a protective, nonverbal message he understood very clearly. ''To tie up loose ends.''

''I'm not following you.'' He felt as if she'd suddenly begun speaking in tongues. And why should she feel defensive? What was she protecting?

''I thought—'' she hesitated, stumbled over her next words ''—I thought you might have decided to use this mess as a way of getting even with me.''

"Ah. Revenge. And why on earth would I want revenge Kate?" Interesting, he decided, that she'd thought revenge could be a motive for him. "Because you walked away from me? Because when I offered marriage and children, you tossed the idea away like yesterday's garbage?"

"Yes. For all those reasons." She lifted her hand toward him, clutched the seat belt instead.

"But revenge," he said softly, touching the curve of her shoulder under the sleeve of her dress, "suggests that a person has been hurt. A person wanting revenge would have to care, wouldn't he?"

She shifted, and the gauzy material skimmed his wrist, the tiny hairs rising in its wake. "Didn't I hurt you, Jed? I think I must have. If nothing else, your pride?"

"What a very convoluted, Machiavellian plot it would be. Katherine, for me to wait three years for revenge. Like some nasty, poisonous spider weaving an intricate net. What a low opinion of me you have if you'd think for one instant that I'd spin that kind of plot if I wanted to get even with you." He let his words slow into a drawl. "For what you did. For what you said."

"No?" Doubt and weariness hazed her face.

"Cookie, if I were looking for my pound of flesh—and. granted, it's very nice flesh indeed…" he let his gaze drift lazily over her, deliberately lingering on her breasts and thighs. "If that's what I wanted from you, I wouldn't take you to the scene of your lover's murder and watch you fall to pieces in front of me."

Her hand fluttered toward him again, and he was angry with her for knowing him so little. How could she have taken him into her body and understood so little about him? Her fault? His?

"What would you do, Jed?"

"If I really wanted revenge, Katherine, if I really cared about what you'd done, I wouldn't have waited three years. I've never believed that revenge is a dish best served cold. Isn't that how the line goes? Me? Shoot, I'd have come after you and seduced you until you thought you couldn't breathe, couldn't think if I didn't take you. And then when you wanted me with every cell in your body, wanted me until you ached with the need to have me inside you, why, then I'd walk out the door.'' He looked her full in the face. ''That's what I'd do if I cared.''

She inhaled, a sharp, pained breath, as if he'd struck her.

## Chapter 5

The sound of her gasp struck Jed like a knife.

For a few minutes he listened to the passing hum of the tires on the road, concentrated on the flow of traffic and the drivers in the cars, automatically checking each one even as he admitted the unwelcome truth to himself.

Sometimes he could be a bastard. At her attack, some of the old pain had made him go cold and mean inside, made him want to see if he could hurt her a little, too. But he hadn't believed he could.

And then she'd gasped.

Until that moment, he'd never seen any evidence that he could touch her emotions.

Oh, sure, he could turn cool Katherine March inside out with pleasure, with a touch, a stroke. Her eyes would go that misty, mossy green, and she'd sigh softly, almost silently as he entered her. Her sigh nothing more than an exhaled breath as if she yielded to pleasure in spite of herself, surrendered to a need that overrode her will. And then, lost in the pleasure they created together, she would give of herself and leave him breathless with the wonder of *her,* his Katie.

Only she wasn't. And she never had been, except in his bed. There, communication had never been a problem.

But today he'd let her get to him again, just like yesterday. He shouldn't have. Shouldn't have let the past sting him into nastiness. He had, though, and he'd been a first-class jerk. Period.

He'd been thrown by the way she hid the fact that she was hanging on by her fingernails, and, touched by the way she clung to her tough-cookie armor, he'd let down his guard. His immediate dislike of her Frank, a dead man who didn't deserve antagonism, had jolted him and left an unpleasant taste in his mouth. Had made him…careless.

Sighing, he tapped her on the shoulder. ''Oh, hell, don't worry, Kate. Revenge didn't influence my decision. I'm not trying to collect a debt.''

''Understand me, Jed. Even if you wanted revenge and that was the only reason you decided to help me, I'd use you. I'll do whatever has to be done to save my life and—'' She bit her lip, went silent, her face pale. ''I'll use you, Jed. Because I have to. If you're going to back out, do it. Just don't waste my time.''

''Explain something to me first, Katherine. Just so I understand. Why'd you make that long speech about games?''

''Because you like to push my buttons, Jed,'' she said wearily. ''Admit it. You always have. I can't do that anymore. I can't play any kind of games with you.''

The exhaustion he'd seen in the smudges under her eyes weighted her words, crimped the corners of her mouth into tiny lines and made him regret the impulse to prick at her self-control. ''I wasn't playing games.''

''That's what it suddenly felt as if you were doing.'' She rubbed her eyes. ''I told you, I don't have the energy to keep my sword and shield up around you.''

Moved when he wanted to feel nothing, he slid his hand

under the fluff of her hair. "Aw, Katie, I'm not trying to push your buttons. Hell, I thought I was being considerate."

"Considerate?"

"Yeah. Sensitive. You know, asking if you could handle going back to the murder scene? Seemed like a considerate act to me. Instead of driving along and wham, bam, ma'am, there it is."

"I see." She regarded him as if he'd grown two heads. "Only you could come up with an explanation like that. You were thinking of my feelings?"

"I didn't want to upset you. While I may have my Terminator qualities, I'm working on becoming a nineties guy."

"The nineties are almost over, Jed." Her mouth curled, one corner tucking into a dimple on the left side of her face. "You're running late."

"Hey, I may be a dinosaur, but I'm not dead yet." He could see that her mood was shifting. He'd amused her.

She shook her head. "I don't know whether to laugh or cry."

"Might as well laugh, cookie. Can't dance."

He'd never seen Kate March cry, and he didn't think he could bear it if she ever broke down. Catching one smooth strand of her hair, he wound it loosely around his finger, the slippery silk sliding over his skin. "It's the only advice my old man ever gave me. So I cherish it. Kind of a one-size-fits-any-situation philosophy of life. You might try it. On a bad day."

"Oh, Jed, you make me so crazy sometimes, I could throw something at you." Her shoulders trembled, and he was sure she was laughing—shakily, but laughing all the same.

"Violence never solved anything," he said somberly.

"This from a man whose life has been spent dealing with violence? From a man who never walked down a dark, dirty alley without a song in his heart?"

"Don't get nasty. But I know what I'm talking about. I'm well acquainted with the beast. I know its limitations. And its power.'' He rubbed the silk of her hair between his thumb and forefinger, remembering.

During the months they'd been together, he'd come back to Kate each time after one of those explosions of violence in his life, grateful for the peace she gave him with each touch, each kiss. She'd saved him during those days of blood and misery, days when everything had been locked so tight inside him that words wouldn't come. ''I know all about violence, Kate. I chose that kind of life. But you're right in the middle of a situation that's already turned vicious, and it wasn't your choice. Why I decided to take you up on your offer of a job doesn't matter. I'm here. And if you don't trust me about anything else, Kate, believe me about this. Violence has never been a game to me. And it sure as hell isn't now. I didn't show up at your office for a round of games, not when your life is at stake.''

''If you say so.'' The strand of hair slid out of his grasp as she leaned forward, and his arm jostled against the back of her shoulder. ''Well, Jed, our truce lasted about fifteen minutes.''

''If that.'' He reached for the gearshift. Facing her, he said regretfully, ''We have the damnedest time communicating of any two people I've ever seen, don't we? All that passion we had, and we still cut each other to shreds. Why?''

''I don't know, Jed. It doesn't matter anymore.''

''Maybe not. But I remember the passion, Kate. It was real.''

''I never denied that, Jed. But passion doesn't last. It's like sand. You can't build your house on it. It shifts, changes.'' This time the weariness in her voice was tinged with sadness. ''All we had was that heat. That passion. It wasn't enough.''

He edged onto the causeway in the gap between a van and a truck hauling a cigarette boat. ''But it still feels like we have unfinished business.''

''We don't.''

''Funny. I'd have bet a couple of thousand dollars that we did. For instance, if nothing else, we never finished the conversation you started yesterday. Did you forget? Because I haven't.'' He reached toward the glove compartment to find the Gulf area map. ''Sooner or later, Kate, whether you want to or not, we're going to talk about the day you left. You owe me that.''

As he moved, she leaned forward to turn the air-conditioning levers away from her, and her arm, like chilled satin, slid against his.

''Let's go to Patsy's. I can handle that,'' she said grimly, and he wondered if she meant she couldn't handle talking about that final day together. Staring out the window, she cleared her throat. ''Let's satisfy your curiosity about what's there.''

''Or what's not there. Remember? The dog didn't bark.''

''Sherlock Holmes.'' She rubbed her arms and shivered.

''Yeah.'' He wondered whether it was the air-conditioning or the thought of seeing the murder scene that made her shiver. Or maybe even the idea of tying up the loose ends of a three-year-old encounter.

With Kate, it was anybody's guess. She'd hide a weakness like a coquina squirming for sanctuary under the sand. Pride, maybe. Or did she think she couldn't admit her vulnerabilities to him? He'd never known why, but even in the most intimate moments with her, he'd sensed that she kept some part of her essential self always apart, a part of her he'd never been able to touch.

Rolling the edge of her skirt over and over between her hand and the seat, she said, ''I never saw you as a Sherlock Holmes type, Jed. More the Terminator. Silent and frighteningly focused. You versus the world. Alone.''

''That's how you see me, Kate? Alone and solitary? Not needing anyone?''

''Yes.'' Regret shaded her voice. ''I'm sorry.'' She gestured, palms up.

''Well, Kate, I've always admired your ability to cut to the chase.'' He'd have to think about her comment later, when she wasn't around distracting him. Watching the traffic for the chance to move into the manual toll lane, he added, "Here's the situation. While I'm not old Sherlock, I still want to see the scene for myself and draw my own conclusions."

Kate blew a raspberry of irritation. "The police scoured the area. Interviewed Patsy's neighbors. The detectives on the case didn't find anything. And after two months you seriously expect to find something there that will give us a clue?"

"Nope. Not seriously."

"Then why?" Now she was twisting her hands in her skirt restlessly, the only external sign of her agitation.

"Stubborn, I reckon. At any rate, it's what I do. I look where everyone's already searched. That's one of the reasons very serious folks used to pay me real serious money. To find out why the dog didn't bark." He hadn't decided what his fee was going to be for doing this job for Kate. Not money. Something. And the price just might turn out to be the truth from her about that day. "I like to form my own opinions."

"It still seems a waste of time to me."

"In a nutshell, Kate, am I going to have to defend anything I do? If so, go find someone else to play bodyguard."

"What?" She gripped her skirt tightly. "You're bailing on me, Jed?"

"It's up to you. You stated your conditions. I have mine. I can't work with you second-guessing every decision I make because you're trying to figure out if I have some hidden agenda. Where's your faith in me, Katherine?"

For a moment she didn't say anything. Finally, as if she was walking through broken glass, she said very carefully, "I'm not questioning you. And you're right. You know your job. I'd be stupid to hire someone for his expertise and then try to tell him how to do his job. I was surprised, that's all. Okay? Going to Patsy's seems futile. As if we're wasting time."

"So what? Most investigative work is an exercise in futility and false starts. Besides, Kate, this is your life we're talking about. So what if we waste three or four hours in what turns out to be a fruitless exercise?''

"Fine. I wasn't thinking straight." The fidgety twisting of her hands ceased. "We'll start with a baby step, then."

"That's the ticket. First rule in investigating. You never know what's important until you see it. So you look five times, and then you go back the sixth time and look again."

"What's the second rule?" She lifted one shoulder carelessly. "So that I don't throw roadblocks in your way."

"I'll let you know when I decide."

"Ah, well, that makes it easy. I twiddle my thumbs and wait for you to tell me what to do?"

"That's about it." He grinned at her.

"You know that'll never work."

"Of course it won't. I just wanted to hear how it sounded. To see if you'd changed over the years. I mean, it was possible, since Frank seems to have been such an all-around nice guy, that maybe you'd become the fiancée version of a Stepford wife?"

"Oh, wouldn't you love that?" she scoffed. Her chin rose and he sensed rather than saw her glare.

"Actually, I'd be bored to tears inside of five minutes."

"Of course you would be," she said, echoing him. "You crave excitement, adventure. Frank liked the familiar. He liked routine, regularity—"

"Good God, Kate." He shot her a quick frown. "You make him sound like an advertisement for prune juice."

"Don't, Jed." Regret shimmered in the depths of her eyes. "He was a good man, maybe one of the kindest I've ever met. And, no, he didn't like upheaval, and he didn't try to push my buttons for fun. You and Frank are one hundred and eighty degrees apart."

"Is that what drew you to him?"

"Probably." As the road swooped toward the south, sunlight blazed through the windshield, and she lifted her hand to shade her eyes. "Don't sell him short, Jed. He was quiet, but he was a good person. That counts for a lot."

"Of course it does. But you didn't tell him you were afraid, did you? You didn't tell him why you'd hired an investigator, did you? At least, that's what you said."

"No," she whispered, covering her eyes. "I didn't tell him everything."

"And now you hold yourself responsible for his death, right? That's the reason for the tears?"

"Yes. I shouldn't have left him in the dark about what was going on. That wasn't fair." She sighed, started to say something and then went silent.

"Wouldn't have made a difference, Kate. Your Frank—" and the words were sour in his mouth "—was in the wrong place at the wrong time. That's all. If he'd had all the facts, it wouldn't have made any difference. Not in the long run. Even if he'd known what the subject of Patsy's report was, he would still have gone to pick it up, right?"

"I—maybe."

Her voice broke, but he didn't have time, not now, for her to spend in regret. He'd thought he wouldn't be able to bear the sight of Kate in tears, but he discovered he had to. They had to reach an understanding.

"So, Kate." He turned more fully toward her. "Take a moment or two to think real hard about that question I asked you."

"Which one?" With her hand still shading her eyes, she looked at him, puzzled. Under the umbrella of her hand, her eyes were damp. "You've asked so many."

"I asked why you came to me instead of hiring a body-guard. Remember?"

Pressing the palms of her hands hard against her eyes, she was silent a moment. When she dropped her hands to her lap, he could see that she'd blotted the tears from her face. "Yes."

"You said you didn't know. Well, think about that question, Kate. And trust me. Just a little. Think you can manage that?"

He waited for her to nod, waited for her to acknowledge that she'd already answered the question by coming to him.

"You're the best I know at what you do," she finally said. "I trust your talent for dealing with violence. Is that the answer you want from me?"

With an enormous dose of self-irony, he was amused to realize it wasn't.

Life could be a snake in the grass sometimes, rearing up and biting a man in the ass when he was least prepared. Throwing his head back, he laughed out loud at the sheer ridiculousness of it all.

"What is it, Jed? What's so funny?"

"Me, Kate. Life, that's what." He threw the coins in the toll basket and headed toward the mainland over the shining white bridge that stretched over brilliant blue water.

And down in the bright blue, deep in the depths, sharks swam, silent, deadly.

For miles after leaving the causeway and the island for the crowded two-lane back into town, they drove in silence. Kate knew there would be a reckoning. Jed was right. Too much unfinished business lay between them.

He had said, *And trust me. Think you can manage that?*

Avoiding his direct question, she'd responded as honestly as she could, answering that particular question in the only way she could. So she'd told him she trusted his talents, and even as she did, she heard how wimpish, how inadequate a response it was.

Because the hard truth was, she was asking him to put his own life on the line for her.

Immoral, she thought suddenly, no matter what her reasons, to deal with him this way. In all their time together, they'd been honest with each other. But wasn't she being truthful about this situation? Really? She'd played fair. She'd given him the choice of backing out.

He hadn't.

He was an experienced, powerful man. He didn't need her

to protect him. He was her hired gun. He knew the score. But she couldn't squash the pang of dismay that kept acid burning in her stomach. Jedidiah Stone didn't need her concern. In a corner of her heart, though, an old yearning returned. She'd wanted, long ago, to soften the edges of the tough world he lived in, to protect him from himself. Silly. If he knew what she was agonizing over, he'd laugh at her compulsion to shield him, to take care of him. Jed wouldn't appreciate this attack of conscience on her part. He was capable of making his own decisions.

If he had all the facts.

He didn't.

Troubled, she mulled over her dilemma. Her deception dismayed her. It went against everything she believed. She owed Jed one more warning. Didn't she?

But at what cost?

She couldn't think clearly anymore. All she knew was that she couldn't ask this of Jed. There must be some other choice, something else she could do—

Straightening in her seat, the decision made, she turned to him, ready to tell him everything, to lay the whole ugly business out for him. "Jed, you don't want to be involved in this mess." She had trouble saying the words because she was knotted in contradictions. Like a pendulum her thoughts moved between fear for her baby—the baby whose existence she'd kept secret from everyone—and concern for Jed, a man who'd never needed her to worry about him.

"Don't I, Kate? And why would that be?"

She studied his strong, capable hands on the steering wheel, hands that had given her pleasure beyond words.

Paralyzingly, her thoughts continued to swing back and forth. She needed him, she had to give him a chance to back out. She could manage by herself, she had to protect her child.

Fast, before she could think over her decision, she blurted, "The situation's too ugly. There are things you don't know. I shouldn't have asked you, shouldn't have involved you. If you're killed, it will be my fault. It's my mess. I'll handle it. I don't want you on my conscience, too.''

"I'm not Frank, Kate," he said softly, and the steel in his voice should have warned her.

"I can manage," she repeated insistently. "Just take me back to the office. I'll be okay." She'd warned him.

"Changed your mind, have you?" He didn't slow the car.

"Don't do this, Jed," she pleaded. Trying to save him from his own quixotic nature, she hated her inability to be candid, even now, hated being trapped. Despised this sense of being out of control of her life. "It's not too late to re-consider."

"Wrong. It's way too late. You made your decision yesterday. I made mine last night. See, cookie, golly darn, you went and made me curious. I wouldn't back off for a million bucks. I'll find out whatever I need to know. And I'll tell you one more time. I have no intention of being killed or of letting someone kill you. You're stuck with me, Katie.''

She pressed her hands against her face, not knowing what to do. She'd warned him twice, and he wouldn't listen. She should have told him everything, right from the beginning, and risked his turning her down.

But she hadn't.

If it were only her life at stake, she would never, even to save herself, have walked back into his life. She wasn't that cruel. She wouldn't have saved herself at his expense, not after what she'd already done to him.

But it wasn't just her life that was at risk.

She had asked him, without his knowledge, to put himself in danger for the child she was carrying, a child that would seem the ultimate betrayal to Jed.

Because it was Frank's child.

Jed would never understand. Couldn't.

Not after the words she'd left him with three years ago.

But what other choice had she had? Then or now? Then, it had been a matter of her own heart's survival. Now, though, the stakes were impossibly higher. She'd warned him and still kept her secret because the truth was, in some tiny, protective part of herself, she'd weighed the danger to her baby and the danger to Jed, and she'd chosen her child.

Unfair to Jed.

Marshaling her arguments once more, she frowned and tried to reassure herself, tried to remember the reasoning that had finally taken her to Jed against her best judgment, against every instinct she had.

Anyone connected with her was in danger, and Jed was the only man she trusted to protect her child and the people around her. Ironic, that she should trust him about this.

Now, with him at her side, she hated what she'd done. Even though she'd gone to him only in desperation after sleepless nights, her actions seemed so self-serving, so cold. She needed his special talents to save this child, a child barely established inside her, but there all the same.

A child she'd wanted. A child who needed the best she could provide.

And Jed was the best.

He knew the risks of what he was doing.

All right. If it had to be, it had to be. She'd kept the complete truth from him. And, as awful as it seemed to her, she would continue to keep her secret as long as she could. Because if he knew, he would never forgive her.

She could live with that if she had to, but when push had come to shove, even as she'd tried to warn Jed, she hadn't been able to face the possibility that he might turn and walk away. If he did, her baby would be left defenseless.

No matter which way she twisted the likely outcome of Jed's discovering her secret before they unmasked a killer's face, she hadn't been willing to take the risk that Jed would turn his back on her.

Frowning, sick at heart, she felt all the old confusion coming back.

All the issues between her and Jed were still the same. The unbearably powerful physical pull was there, too. And worst of all, cruelest, perhaps, was that while she'd trusted him with her body, she'd never trusted him with her heart.

He was right. She *had* welcomed him into her life, her body. On some primitive, incoherent level, she must have trusted him in that sense.

And she had. For those brief, blazing moments, for pleasure beyond words, she'd given her body into his most intimate keeping.

Now she needed him in order to protect her child. As long as he didn't know, he might continue to help her and save this child. She pressed her hand flat at her waist. Her baby was her priority.

She trusted Jed's ability and his expertise, trusted all the extraordinary competency he'd mastered in those exhilarating strolls he'd taken down the dark alleys of the world.

He'd said he knew the limitations and the power of violence. He did. Jedidiah Stone was a master of surviving in the darkness of an explosively violent, physical world. Oh, yes, she would put her life in his hands without a second thought. And that's why she hadn't sought out a bodyguard, why she hadn't even considered that solution.

Because no one could protect her unborn child the way Jed could.

Curling her hands protectively over her belly, she watched beach and waterfront developments yield to the sandy scrubland not far from Patsy's housing development.

Racked by her betrayal, by the impossibilities inherent in the decision she'd made, she knew she'd done what she had to.

A faded sign announced that they had arrived at Pine Woods. The main road, a strip of bleached white cement, split off into a series of cul-de-sacs before curving away toward a sun-washed section of older houses where hedges of hibiscus and overgrown oleanders backed up to a muddy creek framed with bracken and ferns.

"Take a right, here, and then a left. Follow the curve. Patsy's house is at the back of the subdivision."

"Which house?" Jed slowed as they drove down the silent street. "Quiet. Even at this time of day. No kids."

"Working families, kids in day care. A few retired folks. Patsy used to joke that sometimes she and the mail carrier were the only human creatures in the area from seven in the morning until six at night."

"Was she home during the day on a regular basis?" Jed pulled the Blazer into a sandy dirt driveway that led to a small cinder block house and parked, leaving the engine running. Strips of bleached-out yellow crime-scene tape fluttered from an oak at their right. A For Sale sign leaned crookedly in the front yard.

"Depended on the job. She set her own hours. If she were working a divorce case, she might work most of the night and be home all day. Her routine changed all the time." Kate took a deep breath. "It was dark, before."

"You okay, cookie?" Jed rolled down the windows and turned off the engine.

"Fine." With the car engine and the air-conditioning off, the quiet of Pine Woods seemed oppressive. "It's so damned *silent*." She shivered.

"Cold?"

"No. Couldn't be. Must be eighty degrees even in the shade back here." She shivered again. "Spooked a little, I think. All this quiet. I don't even hear birds."

Jed reached into the back of the Blazer and snagged a light wool jacket that matched his slacks. "Here."

She shook her head and unclipped her seat belt. Jed's jacket would have the scent of him, would disturb her concentration, her resolve. "Really, I'm fine."

"Hell, Katie. It's only a jacket. Don't be so damned stubborn." He slung the jacket over her shoulders.

A light presence on her shoulders, Jed's jacket did have a lingering scent, a clean masculine smell. She slipped her arms through the sleeves, and the soft wool caressed her bare arms. "This is silly."

He leaned over and slipped the top button through a beautifully bound buttonhole. "Sure, but you look kind of cute in my jacket, cookie. When you get too warm, drop it on the ground or tie it around your waist."

"It's a gorgeous jacket." Surreptitiously she slid her fingers over the gossamer fine wool, reluctant to leave what felt like the haven of the car. For someone hanging out in a dive like The Last Resort, Jed had lovely clothes. His scarred boots and that dingy bar didn't match the stuff that came from his closet. "I'd never leave this on the ground. It would be a sacrilege."

"I like nice clothes, but it's only a piece of cloth, Kate. The cleaners can clean it, repair it, or dump it if it's ruined. Come on. Let's get going before it gets dark. I don't know how long we'll be here, and, while I have flashlights in the back, daylight's better." Opening his door and stepping down onto the dirt, he said, "Unless you want to wait in the Blazer?"

Stung, she clambered out of the car. "Right. This is more of your consideration, Jed? I told you I could handle this. I can."

"Thought it was time we got this show on the road. Not waste any more time," he murmured slyly. "After all, you did say coming here seemed like a waste of time. Just trying to give you your money's worth, Katie, that's all."

"As if I'd sit here by myself while you wandered around mysteriously, throwing cryptic comments and provocative looks my way."

"Didn't expect you would."

Hurrying to match her shorter stride to his, she caught her heel on the root of the oak tree, stumbled, righted herself as Jed's arm slid around her waist, steadying her. Inexplicably she longed to lean against him, slide her arm around his waist, too, and forget all the horror that had happened in this quiet place.

When she should be thinking of Frank, she was aware only of Jed's scent, the press of his arm against her. She wondered vaguely if he'd reached out for her on purpose, to distract her.

She wouldn't put it past him, to use the sexual tension between them against her once more.

And in Patsy's yard, walking toward the house where her friend and her fiancé had been murdered, Kate couldn't understand why she felt grateful to be surrounded by Jed's scent, by *him*.

But she was.

And she didn't step away from him.

Not even when he stopped and looked down at her, bent his knees to bring his face level with hers and leaned so close to her that his wine-fragrant breath mingled with the clean scent of his jacket.

"You okay, cookie?"

"I don't think so, Jed. I don't think I'm okay at all."

He reached around her with his other arm and drew her close to his chest. "This is a hell of a note, isn't it?"

"Yes." She wanted to shut her eyes and not look at the house, not look at the yard. She wanted to keep her eyes open, fill her senses with Jed and forget everything else.

Jed could make her forget.

Worse, he could make her remember.

## Chapter 6

"**I** wish we hadn't come here. I hate this damned place. It's horrible." She rubbed her hand against his chest fretfully. Memories of the last time she'd been here flooded in on her, swamping her, invading her senses with remembered smells, sights. Textures. Jed's shirt, though, was smooth, slick, soothing to her touch. "It's haunted." For her, it was.

"We can leave. I'll come back by myself. Later." His arm settled in the curve of her waist, anchoring her, his touch the reality in the midst of images crowding in on her.

"No." A thin line of sweat beaded her forehead, and yet she was cold, so cold. The afternoon warmth fled in the wake of this cold filling her. She longed to bolt for the car, the impulse so strong that she was amazed to find that she hadn't moved. But the same stubbornness that had kept her going for so long now kept her rooted even as her knees threatened to give way. "If you think checking out the murder scene is important—" she swallowed "—I should be with you."

"No *should* or *have to* on this question. You don't have to prove anything to anyone, Kate. Certainly not to me."

"No?" Her shaky, derisive laugh was muffled by his chest. "Sure feels like I have to prove—something. To make amends to—someone." *Frank,* she owed Frank. She needed to let his sad ghost know that she had valued him even though she'd never been able to love him the way he'd hoped, the way she'd hoped. Was that where her guilt lay? In that failure of caring?

She couldn't tell Jed that.

She owed Frank and Patsy justice for what had been done to them. More than concern for herself, this truth weighed on her. She couldn't hide in a corner out of fear. "I'm not a coward," she stressed, ignoring the shaking inside her, wanting him to see that he wouldn't have to walk on eggs with her. "I'm not afraid. Really. I'll do what has to be done. You don't have to worry about me. If that's what you were doing." Her teeth clicked against each other.

"Hey, listen." Stepping back, Jed gripped her chin with one hand, but she couldn't meet his searching gaze. "C'mon, Kate, this isn't a test. Nobody's going to flunk you on life's little report card if you back out. I'm not going to tattle on you. Nobody but you and me would ever know if you change your mind about going inside." With that, he tipped her chin up so that she had to look at him, and the pity in his face was so unexpected that tears sprang to her eyes. "You don't have to punish yourself, Kate. Nobody's keeping track of who's toughest."

A cloud drifted across the sun, turned the bright October day murky. The heavy quiet under the trees spooked her. No birdsong, no hustle and noise of a neighborhood intruded, only this disquieting sense of evil reaching out and smearing its finger against Patsy's house.

"No? I didn't grow up the daughter of a marine colonel without learning that you're always being tested. Maybe I'm still trying to prove things. But it's the shadows, Jed. They haunt me." She wound her fingers in the smooth cotton of his shirt and held on. At that moment, he seemed the only reality in her world. Touching him kept her from flying into a thousand pieces. Kept her from screaming as she thought of what she'd found in this spot.

"And, Kate, I doubt that Patsy—or Frank—would hold it against you if you decided you didn't want to face the scene of their murders."

Needing to escape that pity gleaming from his eyes, Kate dipped her head again. She'd thought she could hide her feelings, but they were bubbling up, spilling over, and Jed was there, listening, his breathing slow and easy, his presence a shield against the horror.

Regret flitted through her that it was Jed who was keeping the darkness at bay when it should have been Frank on whom she leaned, Frank to whom she'd turned for help.

But she hadn't.

Hadn't even considered it. That was the curious fact that disturbed her even with the emotions engulfing her. That she should find comfort with Jed when it was Frank's face she saw behind her closed eyelids.

A long ripple of revulsion skipped down her spine.

"Easy, Kate." Nothing mocking in Jed's voice, nothing sexual in his embrace, only solace as he settled her closer to him.

She splayed her hands against his chest. Solace was easier to accept than pity. It had been so long since she'd leaned on anyone. "Every time I shut my eyes. I can't sleep. I can't think. But I remember. And I'm so tired I can't reason things out clearly. I imagined I saw Calla and immediately panicked, started thinking crazy things. That's not like me, Jed. I don't panic."

"Nope. Not to my knowledge you don't, cookie. At a guess, I reckon you've never given in to panic or fear in your life."

She realized she was shaking her head over and over again, and made herself stop. "I don't know. That Kate seems another person. Now I hear voices in the hall of my office building, and I jerk open the door, but no one's there." Wadding his shirt in her fists, she punched him once, hard. There was relief in letting go, in not pretending. "Nothing there except these damned shadows."

"Not unusual, Kate. Post-traumatic shock. It doesn't hit you right away. You haven't talked about the reasons you hired Patsy with anyone except the police, have you?"

"You. No one else."

"What about Calla?"

"No." She shook her head rapidly. "I didn't even tell my mom or sister. I couldn't. I didn't want to worry them. And until Patsy and Frank were killed, I kept hoping I'd imagined everything. And then afterward, I couldn't tell Mom and Sissy. The words stuck in my throat."

"Might have been better if you'd talked to someone. The body works in its own way to cope with the unthinkable. What you saw, here, was unthinkable." He gestured toward Patsy's house, punctuating his words, and then captured Kate's fists with one of his hands, gentling them against him. The slow beat of his heart shuddered against her wrists as he continued, his lulling, whiskey drawl blurring the pictures in her mind. "You pretended that your life was fine, that you were dealing with all that you'd seen, with everything that had happened. Well, Kate, even tough cookies can pretend only so long."

Yesterday he'd called her sugar-plum. Today, *cookie*. *Tough cookie*. Whatever his reason for choosing the nickname, she found to her surprise that it braced her every time he used it. Reminded her that she was strong.

She lifted her head and surveyed the overhanging bushes and trees, and in her mind's eye she watched the stealthy progress of a killer toward Patsy's house, pictured the moment of surprise on Patsy's face. "I keep seeing Patsy's face. Frank's. In those final moments." She pushed her face into his shirt. "Over and over, I see their faces. The overturned chair. Patsy's hands. She looked so helpless, Jed. So small. All her self-confidence and cockiness gone." Words crashed into each other as she clutched Jed's shirt once more and watched the movie play again in her head.

"Pictures, Katie. You're not ever going to forget what you saw. I don't expect you to believe me, but it will get easier. After we find whoever killed your friend." His voice roughened. "And Frank." He cupped her nape, massaged the tightness there. "Hang on. You may be irritating, argumentative and bossy as hell at times..."

Like cold water in the face, his astringent tone shocked her out of the memories and brought her to herself. She lifted her head and replied automatically, "I'm not argumentative."

"Of course you are. It's part of your charm." He tucked her head back into the slope of his chest. "But you're not crazy. And you're right to be scared. Shadows are real, too. *Something* casts them." Running a hand down her back, he worked his fingers over the tense muscles lining her spine. "Like that writer guy said, something wicked this way comes."

"I keep trying to figure out what I did to attract this kind of viciousness, and I can't. But the evil comes back to me. I did *something,* and then all the dominoes starting falling. And you may be next."

"Or you. If I don't do my job." His hand flattened on her waist, and he gave her a slight shake. "I told you. I made my choice. So did Frank. Patsy, too. And someone else, for reasons we don't know, chose to get what he or she wanted through violence. Deliberately. Because that's where the evil is. In the mind of that person. I understand that kind of wickedness, Kate, and I'll find the son of a bitch. We'll get through this, and your shadows will gradually slip back into the dark."

"And then the sun will come up tomorrow, tomorrow?" she chanted, miserably trying to lighten the moment.

"Sure, cookie." Secure and solid, his chest vibrated against her breasts with his chuckle. "It's going to be okay. A happy ending, rainbows, and all the Munchkins singing while Dorothy slaps her red shoes together and heads home. I guarantee it."

"I wish I could believe that, but I can't see anything except shadows. I can't feel anything except this bone-shaking cold.'' She wanted to believe in happy endings, in rainbows, but she couldn't. Not anymore. Shaking, she stood on her tiptoes and reached her arms up, around his strong neck, plastering herself against his length and strength. Leaned into his heat because she was so cold inside, cold as death. In this place of horror she needed that heat.

Even if she were being foolish. Even if, like the moth, the heat and fire would destroy her.

Illusory, this sense of safety and comfort, but even illusion was better than the cold that turned her blood to ice and left her teeth clicking and chattering.

On the kitchen floor Patsy's blood had puddled, warm, dark. Her hands, curled and empty against that darkness.

Jed clamped his hand at the back of her head and drew her face to his, abruptly, a little clumsily. His lips brushed the corner of her mouth, missed, and angled in again, awkwardly, as if he'd never kissed her before, as if they were teenagers discovering each other for the first time.

''I'm so cold, Jed,'' she whispered. ''I can't seem to get warm, no matter what I do. Make me warm again.''

He stood still. Then, suddenly, he moved in closer, drew her tight to him and closed his mouth over hers. No inexperienced boy in the way he fitted her mouth to his now, he traced her lips with his tongue, dampening them, easing the slide of lips over lips, his pelvis locking to her, his movements those of a man who knew what he wanted, who knew how to make a woman want him in return.

The movements of a man who'd learned early how to give and take pleasure, skillfully. Tenderly.

In this place, she needed his skill. To make her forget. To get her through the ordeal ahead.

She needed his tenderness more.

And would never have asked for it, wouldn't have known tenderness was what she wanted.

But tenderness was what he gave her, almost, she thought, in spite of himself.

He stroked her hair lightly, carefully, one hand brushing her hair back from her face. And all the while he caressed her hair with a touch as light as air, he kissed her. His mouth slanted across hers and sealed them together, his breath hers, her breathing his.

She'd wanted heat.

She'd expected fire.

And he gave her comfort. His touch softened the edges of her doubt and self-recrimination.

In this place of violence, unaccountably and miraculously, Jed Stone gave her peace.

For a long moment he held her that way, rocking her against him in that strangely comforting motion. And for the first time in months, she felt safe.

"It's a place, Kate. Nothing more. Trees and dirt. A house. It can't hurt you. After a while the memories will dim, like oil on a driveway, washing away with the rain. You'll be all right, Katie. Trust me on this, at least." He slid his hands down her back again, over her fanny, and cupped her to him intimately.

And then she couldn't speak, not with Jed's teeth nipping at her bottom lip, not with Jed's mouth taking hers hard and fast.

Blazing through her, heat licked at the ice in her veins and turned her blood to steam. Behind her closed eyes a red mist of heat glowed, and it was toward that fire that she reached.

This heat was what she'd hoped for before she discovered comfort was what she'd needed.

She thrust her hands into the roughness of his heavy hair and tugged, tightening the press of his mouth against her even as his clever tongue teased and traced the edge of her ear. Even as he shifted, widening his stance and making room for her in the cradle of his thighs where a different heat pulsed and scorched, she let her mouth speak a silent language of need and want against the cords of his neck. She trailed her mouth down, down to the stiff edge of his laundered collar, down to the crevice at the knot of his tie. As she turned blindly, seeking his mouth, the silken knot slid sleekly over her cheek, and her belly tightened in a spiral of anticipation.

Tugging frantically at the knot in his tie, her fingers slipped into the gap of his collar, and his skin blazed against her fingertips, scorched her down to her toes. He was so hot, so alive, and his heart no longer beat slowly against her. Like the thunder of hooves against dry earth, his heart betrayed him, and she knew he wasn't playing games with her, teasing her. Somehow he, too, had dropped his guard, and his body spoke insistently to hers.

This language she understood. Familiar, its cadences, its rhythms, the parsing of her body with his.

No games. No lies between them in this moment. No pretense.

He'd told her that she'd welcomed his touch. He'd been right. Her body hadn't lied. But his couldn't, either, and she was pleased that her touch had this kind of power over Jed Stone, who was always in control.

Except in this.

Here, she'd known she had power and strength equal to his. But only in these moments, only in this act had she ever felt his equal.

Walking backward, he braced himself on the Blazer and lifted her right out of her shoes. She heard the soft plop of them against the sandy dirt. The hunger racing through her made no sense, disturbed her in the darkest corner of her being. But for the first time in weeks, she was warm. Everywhere Jed's mouth swooped, everywhere his hands shaped was warm, his energy filling her and leaving no room for the terrible pictures.

With a thud his jacket fell to the ground behind her. She didn't remember sliding her arms out of its sleeves. His palms, rough and urgent, skated up and down her bare arms, pushed at the material of her sleeves until his palms cupped her shoulders and his thumbs rested on the points of her collarbone.

And the only sound in her ears was the hammering race

of his heart, of hers. Her cheeks burned and her toes curled in her nylons as his thumbs followed the midline of her breasts and brushed against them, curved underneath them and teased their soft points hard against him.

"Jed." The quiet moan came from her, the hiss of breath from him.

"Yeah, Katie. *Me.*"

If she could have, she would have crawled inside him, burrowed into his heat. Her head fell back and his mouth, damp and hot, seized the lobe of one ear and tugged at the loop of her earring, a tug that snapped through her and made her ache. Made her lift her leg restlessly against him, her knee bumping his hand as he reached behind her to lift her. She needed him to ease the ache, needed the swelling heat of him against her, in her.

She would have let him take her standing up, on the ground, on the front seat of his car. It didn't matter. Only this pulsing ache inside her mattered, only the tremble of his arms as he gathered her closer mattered. Only *this*.

She was alive in every cell of her body, warm with the beat of life against her, in her.

In her.

She opened her eyes.

Overhead a sweetly sad, plaintive call shivered through the afternoon. With a flurry of wings, a cloud of mourning doves passed on their way to water, their olive-brown bodies flashing in a burst of movement and sunshine.

Life grew inside her.

She didn't have the right to take this kind of comfort from Jed. Unconscionable to forget, even for an instant.

But she had.

The forgetting unnerved her. It had been so *easy*. Later, away from him, she would have to figure out why she'd let herself go with the tide of emotions. Sensations.

She couldn't do that now. Not with him so close to her that her breath came in skips and hitches. Not with the tumult of need prickling her skin with electricity.

She would think about these moments later.

But for her sake and for Jed's she would have to decide on a way to prevent a repetition of what had just happened.

Kate rested her hands on Jed's shoulders. He took one quick, deep breath and went still. But the pounding of his heart shuddered through her.

She didn't know what to say. What she'd done went beyond an apology. Worse, with her blood drumming warm and thick inside her, she would be lying if she told him she was sorry. She wanted to be. She should be.

She wasn't.

And if she were truthful, if the situation were different between them, she'd tell him so. She had made her choice three years ago, though, and she couldn't go back and take a different fork in the road. She'd chosen her path and it had led her to this place, this moment, and, impossibly, back to Jed.

Earlier, when she'd told Jed passion didn't survive, she'd been wrong. Passion, desire—it seemed they survived after all.

But she still believed in the innermost core of her being that passion wasn't enough. Like a riptide, it would carry you beyond the shelter of the shore, to the deeps where monsters stirred. A riptide could sweep you under so fast that you were in over your head before you realized what was happening. She'd always been out of her depth with Jed. Stupid to think that had changed.

Worst of all, though, was that she'd been unfair to Jed. She'd been unbelievably selfish to allow herself to lean on him.

She was deeply troubled that she might do so again.

"Well, Kate." He straightened, eased her down to the ground. Smoothing her hair back from her face, he smiled ruefully at her, the expression in his eyes hidden by the sun that suddenly broke through the gathering clouds. "I reckon we both proved something to ourselves."

Nodding, unable to speak, she stepped back.

Turning, she looked for her shoes. She stooped and picked them up, collected her thoughts. Brushing the sand and grit from her feet, she slipped into her shoes, balancing herself with one hand on Jed's Blazer while she tried to figure out what she should do next. Jed's beautiful jacket lay on the ground not far from them and she lifted it, shook it free of debris. "Let me take this to the cleaners?"

Hooking a finger under the back collar, he took it from her. "It's fine, Kate. Do you want to put it back on?"

"No. Thank you, though."

"Ah, Kate of the exquisite manners has returned." With an easy, looping motion, he pitched the jacket through the open window of the Blazer. As he moved, sunshine gilded one side of his face and threw the other into shadow. His back to her, he asked, "Are we going to talk about this?"

"Do we need to?" She wished she could see his eyes.

Facing her now, arms crossed over his chest, he leaned against the Blazer. "Not if you don't want to. Not much I want to say. We can chalk it up to hormones and tension and go on from here."

"Okay." She nodded in agreement. Maybe a rush of hormones was the reason. She didn't think so for a second, but if she and Jed could skate over this thin ice with that excuse, she was willing. "All right." She nodded again decisively. Maybe he'd been as shaken as she was by what had transpired.

Like her, maybe he was trying to achieve distance. The intensity of the moment had caught them both unprepared, like a tornado whipping out of the west and roaring down on them.

Abruptly, he shoved himself away from the car and walked past her, keeping a careful distance. "I'm going to go look around outside first, get an idea of what our killer might have seen. Then I'll want to go inside. Any chance you have the house key?"

"No. I sure didn't expect to see you at my office, so there's no way I could have foreseen we'd wind up here today."

She caught up with him as he stopped at the low, thick hedge framing the sidewalk that led from the driveway. "Do you want me to call Patsy's lawyer and have her bring over the key?" Kate thumbed open a flap on her purse and reached inside a narrow pocket for her phone.

Jed's glance down at her was casually amused. "Sure, if you want to wait around for a couple of hours. By then it'll be dark. Your call. Literally."

"You're going to break in?" Appalled and fascinated, she glanced quickly around toward the shade-shrouded windows of Patsy's neighbors.

He studied the house, the high bushes at the back and the overgrown grass. "I don't plan on breaking anything."

"I don't know, Jed. What will we do if someone calls the police?" She pushed the phone back into its compartment, carefully closed the flap and snapped her purse shut. They were going to break in to and enter a crime scene. "Someone might see us."

His grin was reckless and brilliant. "I reckon you know a good criminal lawyer, don't you, Kate? Someone you could call in an emergency? Not scared, are you?" He raked a hand through his hair and then waggled his fingers in front of her. "Ever picked a lock, cookie?"

"Oh, sure. Every other week. I like to keep my hand in." She waggled her fingers right back at him. More and more, the challenge appealed to her, a diversion from the ghastliness of what awaited them inside. A prudent diversion. Yielding to the need to touch him, to have him touch her, wasn't at all prudent. Danger there of an entirely different kind.

In a peculiar way, Jed's version of cops and robbers allowed her to distance herself from what she would see again, remember again, once they entered Patsy's house. Cops, like doctors, had to find ways to distance themselves from the daily awfulness of their world.

Like a cop, she would examine Patsy's house as if it were a puzzle.

And if they were caught, she'd think of some explanation. Or Jed would.

"So, we going in, or are we waiting for the legal eagle?"

"We're going in," she said, and felt her heart thump hard against her rib cage with the rush of adrenaline that surged through her. Her pulse had given that same, sickening lurch when Jed had kissed her. "What do we do first?"

"Let's wander around for a while. See what we see. Get the lay of the land, so to speak, and then we'll go inside. Okay, boss?"

"What do I look for?" Anxiously she searched the ground, intent on not missing anything that was there. Or that wasn't there and should be.

"You'll know it when you see it." Jed's face was intent, focused, as he looked along the hedges leading to the house.

"You might." She was afraid to take her eyes off the ground. "I need some direction here, Mighty Hunter."

"Loosen up your eyes, Katie."

"What?" She blinked.

"Let your gaze drift from side to side. Keep your vision relaxed. Not so tense. Things jump into view if you don't stare so hard." Stepping behind her, he placed his hands on either side of her forehead, directing her gaze toward the left where the backyard sloped back to the creek. "Now stand still. Watch for a minute."

His hands were warm and steady, impersonal, on the sides of her face as he held it in the direction he wanted her to look. She fixed her gaze back toward the creek, staring hard but not seeing anything.

"No, no. Relax, Katie."

"You're having way too much fun at my expense," she said, but she closed her eyes and then opened them quickly, waiting for something to pop into view.

At her back, Jed was a solid, warm presence. As she watched, she began to see the way the sun silvered the leaves of the oleander bushes as they moved slightly in the breeze. She saw that the corner of the cinder-block house was hidden by bushes. Hidden, too, from the driveway or from the street was the patio door.

"See him?"

"Who?" She jerked.

"Easy, cookie. The crow."

Suddenly, delighted, she saw the purplish-black shape perched on the edge of Patsy's air conditioner at the side of the house near the patio. "I see him. But what's the point, Jed? Are you taking me on a bird walk?"

"Nope, but crows are curious critters. They pick up stuff. Anything bright and shiny attracts them. And they're smart. Did you know," he said, urging her forward with his hand against her back, "that when crows are looking to make a foray into a farmer's cornfield, they keep track of how many farmers go into and come out of the field or into nearby sheds? These birds actually perform a kind of elementary addition and subtraction so that they know when it's time to make their raid."

"Nice little story, Jed." She rolled her eyes.

"Fact." He guided her around a mound of fire ants. "See, Kate? That's what I mean. You have no faith in me at all."

"Not when you tell tall tales, I sure don't."

"I read it in a Chicago newspaper, and I always believe what I read."

"Sure." She blew a raspberry.

He tapped her back. "Anyway, I'm curious as to why that crow's spending so much time in that one spot. Something's holding his attention, because he hasn't left that corner since we drove in. Let's amble over there and take a look."

"Crows can really count?"

"If you believe what you read in the papers. And, Lord knows, I do." His flicker of a smile teased her.

That sneaky twitch of his lips made her wonder if he really had seen an article about counting crows. Jed did love bits and pieces of information. Trivia. Quotations.

She'd decided he had a photographic memory. Or had trained himself to recall details and unrelated facts.

He used to amuse her over glasses of wine with his abilit
to dredge up some obscure fact about any topic she intro
duced. When she'd accused him of having a photographi
memory, he'd teased her, saying, "Sure, believe that if tha
makes you feel better."

Another game, one of many they'd played.

A lifetime ago.

She bent to a pile of wet leaves under the hedge and poke
at it with her finger. A skittering sound against the leave
was the only evidence of the snake's presence as its body
S-curved away in the direction of the creek. Stooping, sh
watched its quicksilver motion until it was out of sight.

"Country girl Kate. There's an eye-opener. You'll get you
dress dirty."

"Hey, a woman's got to do what a woman's got to do.'
Gingerly she pushed at the leaves again, determined to se
this through even as she bunched her skirt up.

From this vantage point, almost eye level with the ground
she saw bits of paper, cellophane. A beer can. The debris ha
collected against the base of the hedges, the roots of the trees
A tuft of fur was caught on the low branches of one of th
sections of hedge.

Jed plucked it loose. "Coon. Not a neighbor's cat."

"I like cats."

"I know. It seemed out of character for you." Jed watche
the crow as it hopped from the air conditioner to the ground
"What happened to your kitten? The one you rescued fron
the garbage dump. Clyde, I think his name was?"

"Clyde." She sighed. "I couldn't help him. He was to
sick."

"I'm sorry, Kate."

"Me, too."

Jed turned to her, frowned, stuck his hands in his slack
pocket. "You were so ticked off when you hauled him ou
of the bin that I thought you might deck the first person wh
crossed your path."

"I couldn't believe somebody had been that cruel. I thought I could save him. I couldn't."

A tiny fluff of gray with a torn ear and a cough, Clyde had stolen her heart the second he poked his smoke-gray nose out of a paper bag in a dumper outside a restaurant she and Jed had gone to. Only days later, alone in her apartment in that first week after she'd left Jed, she'd cried for Clyde, for the waste of his small, brief life.

"He was a cute little thief. I liked him."

"I wish I'd known that." She wiped her sandy hands down her skirt.

"Would it have changed anything?"

"I just wish I'd known. That's all."

"Yeah, well, history. Like you said." He stood there a moment looking into the distance, or maybe the past, she didn't know.

She wondered if he, too, back then had felt some of the confusion that she had. Perhaps not. Maybe all the sense of loss and regret had been on her part only. She'd never know.

And it no longer mattered.

# Chapter 7

Staying silent, they carefully avoided further discussion choosing instinctively to skirt emotional pitfalls that would complicate the job at hand.

Kate wandered from spot to spot, not expecting to find anything. Occasionally she spared a glance for the crow that had flown away with a squawk as they'd neared his spot near the air conditioner and returned in a few minutes with a cackling, territorial rush of wings and noise to resume his lookout

Minutes passed, the only sounds the cackle of the crow and an overhead airplane droning low in its approach to the nearby airport. Kate fought the growing depression triggered by the overhanging branches and scruffy growth.

In such a short time, luxuriant had become claustrophobic neglected. In another month or two, the yard would be wild with weeds and vines, unrecognizable, Patsy's efforts erased

People were nothing more than footprints in the sand erased by the incoming tide.

She shook her head, refusing to succumb to that bleak

view. Memories endured. The spirit lasted. *Things* didn't. Things weren't important.

Because somewhere, in the air, the dust, in *her,* Kate knew Patsy and Frank would live forever. She had to believe that.

And she intended to make sure that their deaths weren't one more set of statistics, one more unsolved crime.

"Jed, I'm not helping much. I really don't know what I'm doing. Give me something specific to do. Please."

"No patience, Kate?"

"Not much. I hear this clock ticking in my head, and it infuriates me that someone believes he's gotten away with *this.*" She fairly spat out the words as she waved her hand, indicating everything. The yard. The deaths. The waste.

Jed looked at her and then at the sky with its fitful mix of bright blue and scudding clouds. "Okay. Time to finish up out here. I want to check the perimeter of the house and the points of entrance. It may be rough walking down toward the creek. Stay with me, Kate, even if you ruin your shoes?"

"Certainly. You just can't help trying to annoy me, can you, Jed?"

"Nope. It's so easy."

"Ha. Not likely. Anyway, easy bores you."

"Sure. But I make an exception in your case, cookie. Because you're so cute." He glanced at the sky again.

"Of course I am. And I'm not easy." Like him, she looked up at the sky. She didn't want to be here if a storm blew in. She definitely didn't want to be here at twilight when the shadows would deepen and grow darker under the hedges and in the corner of the lot, menacing in their silhouettes.

Kate followed Jed as he began a slow, methodical search of the overgrown yard, searched with him as he lifted straggling branches of oleander and shoved aside the drooping feathers of the willows at the edge of the creek.

"The break-in was through the patio door." Jed pivoted, his back to the creek, and studied the house.

"Yes." Verifying what he seemed already to know, she

took a deep breath and looked up from the soggy creek edge, toward the shaded gloom of the rear entrance.

"Where would you stand, Kate, if you were watching the people inside?" Jed had stooped near a submerged root that humped up from the brackish water. "What would you look for? Up there?" He pointed to the patio door.

"I don't know." Surprised, she surveyed the thick underbrush and thought about his question.

A trellis walkway covered with morning glory vines screened the patio from the creek. She could see the air conditioner and the bushes around it. During the day, like now, the patio had a certain privacy. At night, though?

Letting the possibilities sift through her awareness, she tried to see the scene through someone else's eyes, someone who'd had malice in his heart. Or hers. She had to keep reminding herself that Jed had told her anyone, male or female, could be a killer.

His gaze fastened on her. "Getting into the mind-set of a killer? Looking at the location with an eye to mischief? A mind to murder?"

"Maybe I'd want to make sure no one was in the kitchen. I think I'd need a chance to make sure the coast was clear—isn't that the term?"

"You're getting the lingo down pat, cookie." Still stooping, he raked the ground near him with a stick, tossed it into the creek with a dissatisfied mutter.

"What is it?" She walked toward him. Her heel caught in a tangle of roots and mud and she staggered for a moment before she caught her balance. The last thing she wanted was to pitch face forward into the muck. Or into Jed's arms again. Very carefully she scraped her shoe against a patch of dried weeds. "Did you find anything?"

"Thought I found a stash of buried cigarette butts. Nothing, though."

"The perp," she said, striving to keep her tone impersonal, "might have stood here?"

"More cop lingo?"

She nodded. "Television."

"Ah, educational in spite of all the criticism." From his squatting position, he shot her a shrewd look. "Anyway, Kate, you're doing swell. You're pretty good at this. Keep going. Keep looking. How would you feel? What would be going through your head?" His eyes, intent and interested now, no teasing in their cool gray, met hers.

Looking away from that disturbing intensity, Kate pictured the scene. "I'd be nervous. Maybe even panicky."

"Or you might be a pro. Simply examining the terrain for easy access. What then?"

"Either way, I'd want to be cautious. The killer didn't rush in. He took his time. So, let me think." She hesitated, frowned. "Okay. It was night. The lights might be on in the kitchen. Even with the bushes and the trellis, I'll bet I could see into the kitchen. If Patsy had turned on the patio lights, though, I'd be reluctant to come real close. I'd be seen. Wouldn't I?"

"Works for me." He patted her knee companionably as if she were a very bright six-year-old.

"Don't patronize me."

"Never."

"Because I may not be a TV detective, buster, but I know I wouldn't want anyone to see me out here. And I'd want to be able to see inside." She frowned, held her hand out, palm up, to stop him as he started to speak. "But I'd have to be close to the house. So that I could pop in before I was seen. So I could get out fast if anyone heard me. The creek area is secluded, but it's too far away."

Jed grinned up at her. "Excellent."

"You agree with me?"

"Sure do, cookie. But I still wanted to check down here. Doesn't pay to skip any steps. But, yeah, I'm thinking along the same lines you are. Want to play some more?"

Pleased, she nodded and pointed to a pittosporum hedge not far from where they were. "There." The hedge offered cover, good sight lines, proximity to the patio door and privacy. "A person could stand there without being seen from the house or the street. He or she could easily observe whatever was going on in the house. And the noise of the air-conditioning unit would cover any sounds. The patio door was bumped off its runner but still upright." Kate's breathing speeded up. She forced herself to slow down, to think of what she was saying as a logistics problem, a design problem. Not to put faces on what she was imagining.

"That's how I think it happened, too." Jed stood up. "Wonder how our bad guy got here, though. Boat or car?"

"I'd guess a boat. He could cut the motor before he got close, row in. No noise."

"Could have. That's what I would have done. Silent. Fast. I could go up any of the offshoots of the creek and hide out if I had to."

"I was only a few minutes later than I'd told Frank I would be. Only minutes." Kate was pleased she wasn't stumbling over the words. "But quite a bit later than Patsy had expected me, when we'd talked earlier."

Shifting, Jed stared toward the front, at the street, watching. Alert. "I need to talk with the guys who worked the case. I'd sure like to know if they had any reports of prowlers that night. If any license plates from parked cars were run. A long shot, but a possible lead if someone reported an unfamiliar car." He rubbed the mud from his hands down the length of his slacks. The muscles of his rear bunched and knotted, smoothed out as he straightened.

Jed's body had always pleased her, and even now she found she liked watching his easy movements, the play of his muscles under his beautiful clothes.

He scowled in the direction of the hedge. "I can almost *see* the bastard. Sitting there, waiting. But for what? Who? Was Patsy already home? Was he waiting for her to come home? If you were the target, was he waiting for you to arrive? And if so, how did he know you would be here? That's the twist in the puzzle."

Shrugging, Kate bit her lip and turned toward the house.

Too hard to keep her mind focused on the *puzzle*. Damn him. It wasn't a puzzle to her. She couldn't fathom how Jed could remove all emotion from what had happened here.

Leaving him behind, she walked quickly to the hedge, pushed through its branches, scanning the ground the way he'd told her to. When he rejoined her, he didn't speak, merely scrutinized the ground and then moved on.

Forty minutes later, they finished walking the perimeter. Jed had found nothing. He'd pointed out a section of underbrush near the pittosporum hedge that looked to be new growth and explained that it might have replaced a bit of broken-off shrubbery as the killer had stood there. They searched that area particularly thoroughly. Nothing.

Kate could feel disappointment and frustration draining her energy. "What next?" She brushed a cobwebbed strand of hair off her face and slapped her hands in front of her, knocking off bits of leaf debris and mud. Dried mud caked her knees, clung to her skirt and clotted her shoes. She'd never been this grubby in her life. She felt as if spiders were crawling through her hair. She wanted to go home, shower and climb into her bed.

For another sleepless night.

"Tired?" Jed reached forward very carefully and lifted a strand of sticky spiderweb from her hair.

She squared her shoulders, slapped at a bug that had crawled up her arm after her last wiggle through the hedge. "Not in the least."

"Yeah?" His grin taunted her with her lie. "That's what I figured." He stepped onto the grass and walked to the front door. "Ready to begin your life of crime?"

"At the front door?" She couldn't believe his chutzpah. "We'll be seen for sure." But she followed his casual stroll to the front of the house, past the For Sale sign and up to the cracked concrete square that formed the stoop in front of Patsy's door. "We should go to the patio entrance. The same way—"

"Nah, too obvious. Everybody breaks in that way. Way too suspicious-looking to sneak around like that."

She hoped he was teasing her. "This is dangerous, Jed. Isn't it?"

His eyes glittered. "Who knows? Not scared, are you, cookie?"

She shook her head. "I should be." But she felt an answering sparkle tingle through her and chase away the fatigue as she spared another quick glance toward the empty street and blank windows. Instinctively she stepped closer, letting her body shield his actions. "You idiot. You love this."

"Sure." He studied the lock in the doorknob and then took out a slim, rectangular packet of thin metal rods of different sizes, selecting two as he said, "So do we look like a couple of hot prospects to buy the house or not?"

"What?" She whipped her head in his direction as he jiggled an L-shaped rod in the lock.

"House hunting, sweetie."

"I see. We're lookie-loos."

"Yep." Inserting a thin second rod, he inhaled, pressed and gave one more flick and fiddle. "People see what they expect to see. Of course, I could have made this a whole lot easier and called the real estate agent and asked for the key like you suggested." His smile was brilliant as he looked up at her from under the bend of his arm.

Even with her heart thumping sickeningly, she couldn't help returning his smile. She fought the pull of the smile on her face, but Jed's exhilaration was contagious. The fool. Making a game out of a criminal activity. "Why didn't you?"

"This way is less complicated."

"Oh, sure. Unless someone calls the police."

"Not going to happen. Good. That was faster than I expected. Patsy should have had better security." He swung open the door. "C'mon, Kate. Let's see what we see."

Stale, warm air rushed out to her, air that still seemed to bear that sweet, coppery scent of blood.

The inside of Patsy's house was dim. Musty underneath that metallic scent. Ignoring the clenching of her stomach, Kate took a deep breath and a long step inside. The front door opened from the concrete stoop immediately into a compact living room and the hall leading to the small kitchen that faced the creek.

Black powder mixed with dust filmed the horizontal surfaces of side tables, lay in smears on the carpet.

"Okay?" Jed touched her elbow briefly.

"Sure. What do you want me to look for? What are you looking for?" She clipped the words out, concentrating on the smudges of black on the walls, places where fingerprint powder had been dusted, prints lifted. Her own prints would be there. She'd clutched the edge of the kitchen door. Held on to it until she'd broken her fingernails into the quick.

"Let's walk through, slowly. See what pops out."

"Let's hope nothing pops out," she said grimly. "Or you may have to scrape me off the ceiling." She walked steadily over to the glass-topped coffee table in front of the slick vinyl green sofa. "*Gun Digest* and *Vanity Fair*." She tried to laugh.

Running his fingers along the edge of one of the pictures hanging on the wall, Jed stuck his head out. "Patsy was an eclectic reader, huh?"

"Yes. A woman of many interests." Kate picked up the July copy of *Reader's Digest*. Flipping through it, she saw that Patsy had bent the corner on one of the humor sections, marking her spot. Maybe she'd been reading it when Frank arrived and had marked her page, thinking she'd return to it later.

Abruptly Kate placed the magazine carefully on the table, lining it up precisely where the black powder showed its original position. She could see faint fingerprint ridges, blurred but visible. Patsy's? Frank's? Or the trace of someone who had made a mistake that would trap him?

"All right, Jed. Where to next? The kitchen?" That was

the room she'd steeled herself to face, and she wanted to get it over with.

"Not yet." Straightening the last of the pictures he'd examined, Jed ambled toward her, his gaze on the cream carpet. He pointed out the vacuum marks that streaked the carpet. "The evidence techs swept for hair and fiber. Wonder what they found?"

Stooping, he ran his hand up underneath the coffee table, searching the crevices where the wood legs met the wide frame border into which the glass was set. Tightening, his slacks molded his thighs and buttocks as he reached to the opposite corner. A tiny smile tightened his face.

"What did you find?" She stooped beside him, peered underneath, ran her own hand along the edges of the table. Their fingers bumped, his callused skin rasping hers. Hastily she smacked her hands flat on the tabletop.

"Nothing."

"Oh." Still stooping, she rested her face in her hands, disappointed. "What did you think would be under there?"

"I didn't expect anything. Curious, that's all. Thought it would be interesting to see if someone had stuck some kind of bug under there. No phone, but she seemed to spend time here." He pointed to the burn marks on the side table where an empty ashtray rested. Next to the ashtray a thin white circle was the size a glass would be. The evidence techs would have removed the butts and ashes and taken them to the lab. "Patsy smoked? Frank?"

Kate nodded. "She tried to quit every day. Frank didn't smoke."

"Well, I thought someone might have bugged this room either before or after she was killed. Didn't really think I'd find one, though. Just checking."

"Why would someone bug Patsy's house after the murders?" Kate tilted her head toward him, an immense and unexpected sadness sweeping over her as she thought of Patsy's struggle against her cigarette addiction and her last moment as she'd put down the magazine she must have been reading.

"One reason would be if someone came prowling around Patsy's house after something and didn't find it, he or she might think it was a cute idea to stick a bug somewhere and see. if anyone else came looking."

"The house might be bugged right now?" Kate stood up, crossed her arms around her waist. "That's creepy. Someone could be listening to us right this minute?"

"Possibly." Jed rose to his feet and surveyed the room. "One phone's in the kitchen? Another in the bedroom? Any others?"

Not about to utter a word even though Jed didn't seem concerned, Kate shook her head violently, pointed down the hall and followed him to the kitchen.

Like the living room, the kitchen was dim, the air heavy and tinged with the smell of blood.

Minimal cleaning had removed the blood from the floor and the wall, but the kitchen was caked with dust and hard-to-remove print powder. The Realtor had made only a half-hearted attempt at best to prepare the house for a sale.

Kate motioned to the sliding glass doors leading to the patio. An older-model beige phone hung on the wall next to the door. When she'd last seen the phone, its receiver had been on the floor. Since then, someone had hung it up. Greasy black powder smeared the beige.

Jed took the phone off the wall base and separated the parts, unscrewing the round receiver and speaker components. "Nope. Empty. We'll check the bedroom phone, but the living room and this phone would be the most obvious places to stick a listening gizmo, so my guess is that her house wasn't bugged."

"Good." Relief skittered uneasily through her.

"Well, cookie, don't relax yet. The bugs could have been removed. The fact that I haven't found any doesn't mean diddly. Could have been that there never were any. Or that there are bugs here that haven't been found."

"That's awfully complicated, Jed. It's like a chess game where you can't watch the other person's moves."

"You got it, Kate. That's exactly how it is." Energy hummed from Jed in spite of his ever-narrowing stroll around the perimeter of the kitchen. He cut each circle so that he wound up at the kitchen table. Balancing himself with his hands on the table, he leaned toward her.

Here it comes, she thought, bracing herself. Here it comes, ready or not.

"Tell me about what you saw, Kate. That night." Jed hit her right between the eyes with his question. He'd given her all the time he could. Now she would have to talk about that night.

When she looked up at him, one hand resting lightly on a kitchen chair, her face was pale but calm. She didn't sit down. Jed figured that wasn't possible for her, but he was encouraged. She would get through this. She would drag herself through her memories one more time. For him.

For her Frank?

Definitely for Patsy.

And for herself, too, because Kate was walking upright under a ton of guilt that wouldn't let her give up until she'd found the answers she was looking for. That was what had driven her to find him, to ask for help.

For a while during the afternoon he'd worried that she wouldn't be up to this exercise in masochism. He understood that now, months later, reliving that night when she'd walked into a fresh murder scene would be worse.

That night Kate would have pulled herself together for the police. Later, after all the official business had been dispatched, she would have shoved away the terror. The sensory assault of that kind of a scene. She would have gone on, faking, pretending that she had coped.

He'd learned that much about her in the time they were together. And he wondered a little as he watched her gather herself together now what else she had pretended when she'd been with him during that long ago time. Unwanted, the thought waltzed into his head. What had she faked?

During her interviews with the police and the newspaper reporters, she would have hidden behind a stiff upper lip and acted like everything was hunky-dory if it killed her.

And it could have.

That's why she was strung out like a twanging wire about to snap.

Might yet get her killed. Unless she trusted him with whatever she knew, with whatever she was hiding. He knew to the nth degree exactly how much danger she was in. He didn't believe she understood the nature of what threatened her.

"Okay, cookie, throw it at me. Start at the beginning again and take it step by step. I want to hear it all one more time. Where was Frank's car? Wouldn't that have been a tip-off that he was here? Alerted the killer that Patsy wasn't alone?"

The soft fabric of her dress fluttered as she took a breath and blinked. "He used my car that day. He had a lot of appointments. I didn't. His car was in the garage for repairs. He dropped me off at work before anyone arrived. Later in the afternoon the garage sent a driver over with his car, and I drove it to Patsy's. I didn't stop at the restaurant because I didn't see *my* car there, the car Frank was driving. *My* car was here. If anyone were looking, he would have assumed I was inside, with Patsy. I *should* have been inside, not Frank." Her eyes glazed over.

"Enough, Kate," he said roughly. "We don't have time for any more self-flagellation. Get to the point."

Her mouth thinned in annoyance, a better emotion for what she had to do right now. "You know," she said her voice as elegant as a duchess's, "it's a wonder to me you've survived as long as you have, Jedidiah."

"Me, too." He leaned right into her space, caught her gaze with his and held it. "All right. You got here in Frank's car. Yours was in the driveway?"

"Yes." A pale pink skipped along her cheeks. "I rang the

doorbell. Knocked on the door. No one answered. And then I heard a sound. Maybe a cry.'' She rubbed her stomach, and he wondered if she might throw up. ''From the rear of the house.''

''What did you do? Scream? Call out?''

She shook her head rapidly. ''I didn't scream. I called Patsy's name. Then Frank's. It was unsettling. The lights were on, my car was there, but Patsy didn't come to the door. And then that sound.'' Her voice trailed off into a whisper.

''How long did you stand on the stoop?'' He couldn't afford to give her sympathy. Not until he'd squeezed the last possible fact from her. He hoped that she would remember some detail she'd neglected to pass on to the police. ''C'mon, Katie. Five minutes, fifteen? What?''

''Seconds.''

''Really?'' He let doubt ride his face. ''You must have stayed there a minute or two. Most people would have.'' And that was the truth. People seldom reacted immediately to a crisis. That was why women got mugged in dark parking lots. They hesitated too long. Waited. Trying to be polite, they fell into traps. And not only women. It was a jungle out there, and most folks were walking victims. ''You probably stayed there a good five minutes. You must have forgotten.''

''I didn't forget, Jed. I'm positive. Half a minute. No more. You see, it was that sound. It raised the hair on my neck.'' She rubbed her arms hard.

''Did you push open the front door?''

''No, it was bolted. I ran to the patio door. I had scratches on my face and arms from the bushes.''

He understood why she kept rubbing her arms. Like Lady Macbeth, Kate was lost in memory where bushes slapped and cut at her. He reached out and stilled her hands, bringing her back to the moment. Less frightening for her here in the present. ''Then what?''

''The sliding door was wide open, crooked in the frame.''

He held her hands with his, keeping them from that eerie

movement that set his teeth on edge. She'd been closer than she knew to the killer in that moment. "What did you hear?"

"What?" Kate looked up at him with dry, bruised eyes and pulled her hands free.

"You mentioned the sound. What was it?"

Gripping the back of the chair, she slumped over it. "A sigh, only it was loud, so loud that I heard it even from the front of the house, even over the air conditioner. As if someone had said 'ah' on a long, drawn-out sigh. But loud, Jed. I still hear that sound in my dreams."

Knowing he couldn't allow her to retreat, Jed jiggled the table with his hands. "C'mon, cookie. You must have heard footsteps. Something else."

"The police said the same thing. But I didn't. Nothing."

She spoke so softly that he had to reach out and lift her chin to hear her. Her chin was cold and soft as a gardenia petal. Her gaze, rueful and tormented, met his. For a long moment he studied her, willing her to come back to the moment. Once he was sure she was focused on him, on his questions, he released her chin.

"Are you sure you didn't hear a car? A motor?" He wanted her to have heard *something,* because he had a terrible fear that the murderer had been very close to her in those seconds. Why the killer hadn't struck her down on the patio, if the target was Kate, Jed didn't know. A cold slide of fear made him impatient. "Come on, Kate. What did you hear? Bushes rustling? The scrape of a boat against the creek bank?"

"I found Patsy then, you see. Here. Next to the table. Frank was there." She dipped her chin toward the floor near the phone. Her eyes stared at him, but Jed wasn't sure she saw him. "Both of them. And then there was all this silence in my head." Exquisitely polite, like she was talking to a stranger, she finished, "So, I'm very sorry, Jed, but I don't believe I would have heard anything. Not with that silence."

"All right, Katie. So you didn't hear anything. No big deal. It's okay." He gave in to the need to cup the tender, fragile shape of her head with his palm. A second. One minute. And Kate, stubborn, opinionated, argumentative Kate would have been on the floor with the others. Gently he tugged at the lobe of her ear, worked his finger into the silver loop of her earring, set it swinging. "You were lucky."

She just stared at him, a bleakness beyond words in her eyes.

And then with a calmness that turned him cold, she said, "You think I'm lucky?"

He tightened his hold on the curve of her shoulder and neck. "God damn it, Kate, you *were* lucky. That's how life is. Sometimes you're on that bridge that falls. Sometimes you just miss the plane that crashes. And sometimes you're the son of a gun standing next to your friend when he steps on the land mine and you don't."

He shook her shoulder. Her head wobbled. "And you know the real awfulness, Kate? *You* don't have a damned bit of control over *any* of it. But, yeah, cookie, I think you were lucky that night. Because life's a real swell gift, and you got a second chance. *They*—" he forced her to look at the dark spots on the floor "—didn't. Your life means something, Kate. And, yeah, it's absolutely lousy luck that Patsy and Frank were killed. But *we're* alive and *we're* going to fix the creep that ran out that sliding door. You and me, Katie. We're going to nail his hide to the wall."

He gave her another slight shake. Her shoulder was thin, slight under his touch. Death had brushed its wings against her, paused, and then, inexplicably, moved on when it might have folded her within its dark embrace. He gripped her tightly, the bones under his fingers so fragile he could have snapped them with a flick of his hands. "We're going to find him and make him pay for what he did. Because that night we were lucky, and they weren't. You're alive. They aren't. You didn't make that choice. He rubbed the points of her shoulders, hard. "Get it?"

She blinked. "I get it, Jed. They died. I'm alive."

# Chapter 8

Jed was furious.

Oh, not with Kate. Well, maybe a little, he decided as he studied her pale, drawn face.

He hadn't been angry before. Disturbed, annoyed with her, intrigued by the situation, but not angry. Not until he'd inhaled the stale air of this house and sniffed the scent of a killer lingering like a bad aftertaste. Not until he'd seen for himself how close Kate had been to death.

In that moment all detachment had fled.

Out of necessity he'd learned to disengage himself from the horror of what he so often had to look on. Over the years that ability to detach his emotions, to remove himself from the devastation in front of him, had made it possible for him to function. He'd been able to look on scenes of such gut-wrenching ugliness that he wondered for a while if he'd stepped over some civilized line into the world of madness, of evil itself. To look on the work of insanity, coldly, calculatedly.

And feel *nothing*.

Wasn't that entering into that world of depravity? Wasn't it becoming the thing he despised?

But he'd looked.

He used what he saw to solve the puzzle of that evil.

Because he'd always been able to distance himself.

Until today.

Fear, rising up out of some dark place inside him, translated into this hot, unexpected anger.

Kate could have been killed, and he might never have known.

And she didn't seem to understand how lucky, how damned lucky in an insane world she'd been.

"I get it, Jed," she repeated, almost as if she were reading his mind, and her voice was so calm that he wanted to punch a hole in the wall.

"Do you?" He lifted his hands away from her shoulders, straight up into the air, unable to bear touching her without hauling her smack up against him and taking her right in this kitchen, releasing his anger and fear in the most powerful act of life he knew. Instead, he took three steps backward toward the patio door. "If you *get* how lucky you were, what took you so long to ask for help?"

"I had my reasons." Her chin rose, firm in that stubbornness that told him the subject was closed.

For now. "You could have been killed, too," he said, pushing at her with words, wanting her to accept the reality that she'd been spared.

"I know." She turned away from him abruptly, walked to the sink, her back straight. "But I was careful."

"Like in the bathroom at your office building?"

Her hair swung around with her movement. The soft curve of her bottom lip thinned in anger. "That's mean, Jed. Uncalled for."

Leaning against the wall, he forced himself to tamp down the ferocity that raged inside him as he pictured Kate crumpled to the floor beside her friend. Beside her fiancé, her blood mingling with theirs. "I don't think so. You're in over your head, Katie darlin'," he drawled, "and you don't realize how deep the water is."

"Believe me, I do." Her heels snapped against the floor as she approached him and poked his chest with her hand. "And that's exactly why I hired you. To teach me to swim. To show me how to be smarter. That way I won't make mistakes. So stuff it, Stone, and get on with the job. Keep me alive. Don't lecture me. I've had enough of those to last me a lifetime. And my daddy could lecture you into the ground on any given day." Giving him one final slap to the chest, she whirled away.

Hiding the rip of anger and fear, he lazily applauded. "Nice speech, cookie. And I'm real impressed that you tried to be careful. But you haven't been careful enough, Kate." Pushing off from the wall, he circled her arm with his hand, stopping her.

"Don't grab me every time you want to make a point." She pried at his fingers and jerked away. "I don't want to listen to any more speeches."

"And that's what scares the hell out of me." Ignoring her, he swiveled her toward him. "Because there's a fiendishly nasty mind out there, and it's focused on you, Kate. I said no one is going to get a chance at you while I'm around, and no one will unless it's over my dead body."

She covered her ears. "Stop. I don't want to hear any more."

"Too bad." Pulling her hands down, he stooped so that he could look her in the face, let her see how furious he was, how uneasy he was about the way things had played out. "I said that, and it's true. But, Kate, I know my limitations. Listen to me. *Anybody* can get to anybody. If someone wants to kill you bad enough, he will, no matter who's on guard. Because if the obsession is strong enough, a murderer will find a way. You were within arm's reach of a murderer the night you raced back to this room. And that scares the living daylights out of me. As for grabbing you, cookie, sometimes that's the only way to stop you in your tracks.'' He thought he could hear the hiss of steam coming from his ears.

Reaching up, she brushed her fingers over his face, as if she were learning his features. Tracing his cheekbones, her touch featherlight and shivery against his skin, she stared wonderingly at him. ''You're scared?''

''Hell, yeah, I'm scared. And it makes me feel out of control. I don't like feeling out of control, Kate. I'm not comfortable.''

''Yes,'' she said gently, ''I can see you aren't. You like to be in…control. Usually.''

''Yeah.'' Covering her hand with his, he smoothed their joined hands over his face and turned his lips into her narrow palm. Her skin was cool against his mouth. Pressing a kiss against the slope of her thumb, he closed her hand into a fist, held it. ''I'm scared. Isn't that a story for the ages?''

''Thank you, Jed,'' she whispered. Her eyes dilated, the pupils going dark and mysterious, drawing him into their depths. ''For caring, a little. For caring still, in spite of everything. It makes all this less—less *lonely*. I didn't realize until right now how alone I felt.''

Her fist closed in his, he leaned closer, drawn in spite of himself.

He didn't want to feel the slick softness of her mouth under his, didn't want this piercing sense of loss as her lips met his and moved against him. Didn't want to think of her cold and lifeless on the bloodstained floor where he stood. Most of all, he didn't want to want her, the desire so painful that his muscles tensed and cramped with it.

But he did.

His heart ached with the need to hold her.

All of it senseless, pointless. Unexplainable.

Dangerous.

But there, beating inside him, this *need* for Katie.

As if she'd never left him, never gone away.

''You weren't scared yesterday.'' Her head rested on his chest.

"I wasn't." He knew he had to step away. And he would. In a minute.

"You acted as if you couldn't care less."

He sighed. "Well, I was pissed off."

"Because I showed up? Because—"

"Aw, Katie, it's not important. Let it go."

"And you're not pissed off now?" Her laugh vibrated against him. "Could have fooled me."

"Oh yeah. I'm still at full boil."

"What changed between yesterday and now?"

*Seeing you,* he started to say. *Touching you,* he could have said. *Fearing I'd lose you forever.* "Listening to you remember everything that had happened, I guess," he said instead. "Coming here made the whole situation real for me in a way it hadn't been."

Her fingers tugged at the placket on his shirt, smoothed a wrinkle near his collar. Busy, busy little hands. "Before, it was only a puzzle."

"Yeah."

Kate wiggled her finger into the knot of his tie, and he felt the tiny tug all the way down his body. "But now it's real. And personal for you?"

"Yeah." If his body took it any more personally, he'd embarrass both of them. Interesting, in a wryly perverse way, this mix of desire and misgiving, adrenaline and caution. Like racing full speed with the brakes on. Put a real strain on the old engine, that did.

She tilted her head toward him, and a strand of her hair caught against his chin. "What are we going to do about this, Jed?"

For a second he thought the *this* she referred to was the press of his erection against her belly. His body reacted with a heavy surge, heat and blood pooling in his groin.

"I know I'm a walking target. But I *do* trust you in this, enough to believe that if anyone can protect me, you can. You will."

She'd said the same thing before, maybe not in exactly

those words. Maybe he hadn't heard it the same way. But something in the tone of her voice or in her eyes was different, and this time he heard the trust.

A balm, that trust eased something in his soul, made it easier for him to kiss the tip of her nose and set her aside. Made it possible for him to stomp on the brakes and do what he knew was best.

But he'd needed the words. He'd never expected that words would be so important.

And now he discovered they were.

"You know I'll do everything in my power, Kate. But I'm only one man. And I make mistakes."

"Really? I'll bet it grinds against your nature to admit that, doesn't it?"

"Damn right."

"And here I've been thinking you were perfect." Her murmur held a ripple of laughter.

"Oh, I am. I just make perfect mistakes. On the rare occasion that happens."

"Of course," she said in such a sugary voice that he was amazed her teeth didn't ache. "On that rare occasion."

"You're a pest, cookie." He ran the knuckle of his finger over the narrow bridge of her nose. "I'll bet you were a bratty little kid."

"Oh, yes. That was the only way to survive in my house. Daddy laid down the rules—"

"And everybody followed them except you," he concluded. "Right? That's why all the lectures from the colonel."

"Nah. I think Daddy just liked to hear himself talk."

"And you argued every time he crossed a *t* or dotted an *i*, I'll bet."

"Somebody had to. Mama and Sissy were too ladylike to fuss with him."

"Poor little bratty Katie." Touched by the image of Kate standing alone and taking the weight of her father's disapproval, Jed ruffled her hair. "Hard to wage guerrilla warfare when you're the lone soldier."

"That's not how it was." She stiffened.

"No?"

"I loved my father."

"I'm sure you did. But you fought him every step of the way, didn't you, Kate? Because it was the only way you could keep from being mowed down."

Her eyelashes fluttered down, concealing her expression. "I loved him," she repeated.

Her ramrod-straight posture told him he was right. Kate wouldn't give an inch of ground without defending it to her metaphorical last breath. And now he understood the source of the prickly independence she wore like a shield.

"But we were too much alike. Neither of us liked losing. For any reason." Kate didn't say anything else for a long moment.

Jed imagined the small defiant child and the rigid, by-the-numbers father, neither yielding, neither surrendering.

War.

"I'm sorry, Kate."

"No reason to be sorry, Jed. I loved him, you see," she repeated steadfastly. "We all did. In our own ways."

Jed did. He saw too much. He heard her protestation of love. He didn't hear her say the colonel had loved his headstrong daughter. Had the colonel loved her? Or had he only seen the determined, independent child as a threat to his authority?

Struck as one thought bumped into another, he studied her from the corner of his eye.

Whatever her relationship had been with her colonel father, Kate had resolved those issues.

Hadn't she?

She must have.

And if she hadn't?

He cleared his throat, started to speak, changed his mind.

As if by mutual consent, they silently returned to their search.

Twenty minutes later the far-off rumble of an evening storm penetrated the silence and made both of them move faster as they examined the minutiae of Patsy Keane's life, her secret vices and dreams revealed in such trifling ways. Her pleasures and failures.

The stash of M&M's in a coffee can. The bottle of expensive Irish whiskey. The bright red fingernail polish stuck in the refrigerator next to a moldy container of sour cream. An out-of-date bottle of salsa.

There was something sad, a touch pathetic about Patsy's treats and idiosyncrasies. But it was always like that when someone died, violently or not.

Jed stirred the mess inside a kitchen drawer, picking up several of the matchbooks. One was from The Last Resort. With a twist of his wrist, he spun the matchbook back into the drawer and examined the kitchen again.

*Here.*

No one came to a crime scene without leaving a trace of himself. Without being touched by the crime environment.

He should have found something.

He hadn't.

Frustration and this uncomfortable fear made Jed edgy. "Let's give the kitchen one more good toss, Kate."

"Sure." Weariness had begun to etch tiny lines in her face. She moved toward the sink.

The light coming through the glass patio doors had a greenish cast, and he felt as if he were swimming underwater. They walked once more around the kitchen, opening cupboards, drawers, and lifting cans and boxes of cereal. Peeling back labels.

Looking for the equivalent of the dog that hadn't barked.

Strange, otherworldly, this search with Kate in the dim, green light in a house where murder had been done.

They finished their second search of the kitchen, and by

the time they'd searched through the bedroom where Patsy had turned a corner into a makeshift office, Jed could see that all that kept Kate upright was determination.

There, too, they found nothing.

He opened a disc holder, checked the discs. He flipped through the open file-cabinet drawers, pulled out one and fanned out the pages of a thin file labeled with Kate's name. "Hey, cookie, what happened to the report Frank was supposed to pick up? Do the police still have it?" He shoved the file back into its drawer.

Kate carefully placed a glitter globe with pictures inside it back on Patsy's desk. Blue sparkles drifted inside the globe, clumped in blue snow heaps in the leaves of a royal palm. "The police didn't find it. Even after I explained why Frank was here and they searched through all of Patsy's papers, they never turned up the report. I don't know what Patsy had discovered."

"It was taken." Jed frowned. "We won't find it, either. It's gone for good." He raked his hand through his hair in irritation. "The police never had a chance to find it because the damned thing wasn't here."

With one finger, Kate pushed the globe back and forth on the makeshift desk. Sparkles spun and shimmered inside the silent world, lay against the brown hair of the woman in the picture. Patsy. Chin up, confronting him, Kate rested her finger on the globe. "You think the report was the reason Frank and Patsy were killed?"

"Only three people knew about the report. You, Patsy, Frank, right?" Hoping she would remember someone else, Jed challenged her.

She didn't blink. "That's right. As far as I know."

Picking up the globe, he shook it, watched the blue shimmer until it lay once more on the bottom and only Patsy's clear eyes, hazel like Kate's, stared back at him. Kate had asked him if he'd had a close encounter of the lusty kind with the detective. Kate had called it making love. Well, he hadn't done the horizontal bop with Patsy that lazy, rainy afternoon she'd shown up at the bar, but he'd been tempted with a sharpness of desire that had caught him unprepared.

But he hadn't taken her up on her offer. Shrugging it off with a laugh, he'd let the desire and the regret show in his eyes, let her know exactly how much he was tempted.

Now, looking into the glitter globe, Jed was glad he'd let her see the regret. He wondered, too, why he'd taken a pass on her offer of whiling away a rainy day in such an old, delightful pleasure.

Maybe because she'd reminded him of Kate.

Giving the globe a final shake, he placed it back on the desk, just as Kate had. "Okay, cookie. What are you leaving out?"

"Not much." She crossed her arms, rubbed them again.

"If you're not leaving anything important out, why do you think Patsy was mistaken for you and killed?" He leaned over the desk toward her. "Why not just break in and steal the report?"

"First, because I was the target. Second, because whatever was in the report was damaging to the killer." Arms still crossed, Kate walked to the window and peered through the wooden slats. "A storm's coming."

"If it's a gully buster, we'll pull off to the side. No problem, Kate. Go on," he said carefully, not wanting to disturb her flow of thought.

"Somehow the killer knew I would be here. It's happened before." She rubbed her arms hard. "That's the reason I hired Patsy. I've been followed almost as if someone could anticipate my plans the second I make them. Patsy said she was waiting for a call and might have to go out for a few minutes. She told me to come in and wait if she wasn't there. I think the killer knew that, saw my car here, assumed I was in the house by myself and broke in. But Patsy and Frank were there."

"You've had your office checked for bugs?"

"That was the first thing Patsy did when I hired her. She checked my home and the office. Heck, Jed, she even checked my car. But I still think someone has access to me. To my plans. I simply don't understand how. But you'll figure it out.'' She reached out and moved the wooden blind aside and stared into the increasingly murky sky. ''I believe murder was the intention from the beginning, but the killer expected to find me. By myself. And when his plans went awry, he made the most of what presented itself and left with the report, salvaging something of his plans. Or her plans. God—'' she shivered ''—I keep forgetting that their killer could be a woman.''

''Dangerous to forget, Kate. Forgetting could make you careless, you know.''

She let the blind fall in place, its clatter shockingly loud. ''Are we finished in here, Jed? It's stuffy. Hard to breathe with the barometer dropping and the air so still and heavy.''

''We're through,'' he confirmed. ''And it looks like it was a waste of time after all.'' He flicked off the light switch, leaving the room and its ghosts in dim, watery light. ''But I had to see for myself.''

''I thought you might find something,'' Kate said wistfully, her shoulders almost slumping as she walked ahead of him.

''Thank you, Katie.'' He followed her to the back door, setting the patio doors to lock as he pulled them shut.

They stepped out onto the patio. Jed glanced back at the aluminum frame. Summing up the scenario of what he believed had happened, he said, ''All right. This was where he broke in. Patsy heard the noise, came to investigate. He—'' Jed gave Kate a tight smile ''—or she killed Patsy. Hearing Patsy call out or make a sound, Frank came running to the kitchen. The table and chairs were probably turned over then. My guess is that he caught Patsy first, unprepared, and then, in turn, was surprised by Frank. I agree that the killer thought Patsy was you, waiting for Patsy to return from her errand. He didn't expect Patsy to be .there, but Frank was the real joker in the deck. There was a fight.''

''How do you know?'' she whispered, and her bottom lip

was bloodless with the force of her teeth clamping it. "This is the first I've heard about a fight."

"I looked at the death scene report, Kate. There were defensive wounds on Frank's arms and hands." Jed took a deep breath as she whimpered, a small, wounded sound that pierced him to the core of his being. "He fought. He did the best he could under the circumstances."

"The police never told me exactly what happened." Kate anchored a strand of hair caught by the fitful wind. "I didn't ask. Back then I suppose I didn't want to know."

Head down against the wind, Jed cupped her elbow and led her around the bushes and toward the corner where the air conditioner sat in rusted splendor. The crow cawed at them but didn't move. Flapping its wings aggressively, it stretched its neck, cawed angrily once more.

As they rounded the corner, a shaft of sunlight, low on the horizon, burst through the purple clouds and dark sky. The eerie light turned the edge of the sky yellow, cast a greenish tinge to the crow's glossy black head. Leaves whipped into a miniature tornado, whirling in the strange light and collapsing a foot away from their origin.

Kate stopped, her arm dragging against his.

"What is it? Did you remember something? We can go back inside." Facing her, Jed sheltered her from the buffet of the rising wind.

"No." Her hair blew wildly around her, and she reached both hands up to scrape it back, the lift of her arms catching the gleam of sunlight. "I thought I saw something."

"Where?" Jed pivoted, alert. "Who?"

"Something in the grass. Near the bush." The wind took her skirt and swirled it, wrapped it tight around her, pushed her forward as she moved toward the air conditioner. "Do you see anything?"

"Where the crow was?" Following her, Jed bent over, searching the ground.

"Yes, but I don't see it now. A glint. Jewelry, possibly? Something shiny, that's all."

Overhead the crow circled, landed in one of the trees near them. His squawks were loud and raucous as he scolded them for interrupting.

"Maybe that's what kept Mr. Loudmouth fixed in this spot."

The sweep of wind tumbled leaves and sticks end over end. The occasional flash of sunlight through the deepening purple clouds was disorienting as Jed looked where she pointed.

With the toe of his shoe he kicked at the brush near the air conditioner, dug at the ground. "We've been over this spot, but if you saw something—"

"There!" Kate stooped quickly. Her skirt snapped up with her movement and the rush of wind, wrapped tightly against her fanny and thighs, lifted, puffed with the wind as it died away. Silvery-blue material draped over one long, pale thigh as she scrabbled at the ground. "Look." She held her find up to him.

Stained with sandy dirt and leaves, her hand cupped a cracked rectangle of dark tinted glass toward him.

Taking it from her, he held it up to the flickering, lightning-lit sky. About fifteen or twenty millimeters in size, its edges were jagged, still sharp enough to cut. Turning the fragment this way and that, squinting, he looked through it. "I'll be damned."

"It's a bit of sunglasses, isn't it?" On tiptoe, Kate stood next to him, peering through the piece of glass as he turned it thoughtfully. Her hand rested on Jed's shoulder. "Where we decided the intruder had probably stood."

"Look, Kate." Jed held the glass up to the sky.

Like him she squinted, turned the glass back and forth. "It's a prescription lens." Through the exhaustion and weariness in her face, her eyes gleamed. "Someone broke a pair of prescription sunglasses here."

"Yeah." Jed threw the fragment up in the air, catching it one-handed as it tumbled back to him. "It was buried under this brush. We missed it in our original search. If the wind hadn't kicked up, if the sun hadn't come out just as you walked past, it might never have turned up. Luck, cookie.''

"That's what kept the crow coming back to the air conditioner.'' With the wind shoving her off balance, she beat one small fist against his shoulder.

He grinned, amused by the ripple of excitement coming from her. "Probably. The crow spotted the glass shining in the sunlight. He was attracted to the glitter. But now we're going to steal his toy." Jed tucked the piece of lens into his slacks pocket.

"This is important, right?" Snarled by the wind, her hair veiled her face. Through the tangles her eyes shone up at him. "The police didn't find this fragment. We did. We can use it, find out who stood here." Like the wind, her voice rose and fell with electrical excitement.

"It means what it means, Katie. And you found it." With both hands Jed smoothed her hair behind her ears. "It may be important. Or not. We won't know for a while. It may mean nothing. Patsy might have broken a pair of her own glasses out here on the patio while she was sunning.''

"Patsy didn't wear prescription sunglasses." Earnest and intent, Kate's gaze met his. "I think her killer made a mistake, Jed. That glass hasn't been worn away by weather. It's sharp. It hasn't been under the bushes long enough for the edges to smooth off, has it?" She gripped his arms where they framed her eager face. "We're going to find him." With a quick, decisive nod, she echoed his earlier comment to her. "And when we do, we're going to nail his hide to the wall."

"Don't get your hopes too high, Katie." He didn't want to see that blaze of eagerness in her face doused, but he had to prepare her for disappointment. "It's only a piece of glass. Who knows what it will tell us?"

"But we're going to find out, aren't we, Jed?"

He pressed his hands to her head, the vulnerable shape of it heartbreaking. Spunky, stubborn, she was fighting for her friends. For herself, too, but justice was the gasoline that fueled her. "Yeah, Katie, damned right we are."

"Because we're the good guys." She stretched up, planted a hard, fast kiss on his mouth, a kiss that curled his toes with its sudden heat and energy.

"Because we're the good guys," he repeated through the thickness in his throat as she turned away.

A crack of lightning stitched through the sky, and he felt the hair along his arms rise.

# Chapter 9

Inside the Blazer, Kate shook the rain out of her hair and clipped her seat belt. "I don't care what you say, Jed. I'd bet my life that broken lens is significant. And that, of course, is exactly what I'm doing, betting my life. But, oh, this feels like a break after all these months of confusion and fear." She touched his shoulder, wanting him to understand what a difference the find meant to her.

"It is what it is, Kate. Nothing more."

With a ground-shaking boom the storm had broken and they'd run toward the car and shelter. Soaked, they'd climbed into the car and wiped the rain out of their faces.

Kate's dress clung to her and she shivered, but she wasn't cold. Sparked by excitement, a furnace blazed inside her. She felt as if she might burst into flames any second. "Do you have a towel?"

Ruffling his rain-darkened hair, Jed motioned to the back of the Blazer, and she reached back for the box of tissues on the floor. "Thanks. You want a handful?"

He nodded, and she dug out a fistful. He swiped at his hair

and face. Bits of white dotted his hair and face. She reached over and brushed her fingers over the flecks, but they clung to the bristles along his chin. He jerked as she scraped at his face. His face was cool, rough, lightly stubbled. Her fingers tingled. "Sorry. I thought I could help." She picked one final bit of tissue free and let it drop.

Kate jittered. She couldn't sit still. She kicked off her shoes and slicked her hands down her legs. Twisting her skirt, she wrung out water and blotted the puddles with tissue.

The answer was in front of them. The terror would be over. She could go on with her life.

And the ghosts of Frank and Patsy would no longer haunt her.

"Are we going to the police? Right now? I think that's the best idea. They can send the fragment off for analysis, right?" She chewed the edge of her thumb. "No, they'd discount it because they didn't find it. It's not in the direct chain of evidence, right?" Exhilarated, she didn't wait for him to answer. "Okay. Let me think." She massaged her forehead, swiveled to watch the rain and then tapped the edge of the dash. "We'll—we'll take it to the optometrists in town. The opticians. They can identify it, can't they? I mean, after all, hey, the FBI can match paint chips from cars. Why couldn't we find a match for prescription lenses?" With both hands she beat a wild tattoo on the dash. Satisfaction raced through her. "They'll have records. With names."

Jed covered her drumming fists. "Slow down, cookie. This lens is only one small piece of evidence. And we were lucky to find it. True, our bad guy could have been wearing sunglasses. The sun would have been bright at seven o'clock in August. And I agree that the fragment *could* have come from the killer's sunglasses. Most likely, though, it didn't. Most likely, cookie, it means squat."

"Wet blanket."

"Realist."

"Gloomy Gus."

"Better to expect nothing—"

"And then you won't be disappointed." With a brush of her hand, she waved aside his comment. "Be a pessimist if you want to, but I have a funny feeling about what we found, Jed. Intuition. Instinct. Call it what you will." She unpeeled her skirt from her damp legs and fanned it up and down, letting the air dry her skin.

"I trust instinct, Katie. It's saved my life more times than I can count."

She hesitated, and then looked sharply at him. "You never talked about your, for lack of a better word, adventures."

"No reason to."

"I would have been interested in knowing about that part of your life. Wasn't that a reason?"

Jed snapped on the headlights with a frown and wiped the window where condensation fogged it.

Not quite a rebuff, but a clear signal that the subject was off-limits. Jed had always kept that part of his life separate from her. As mysterious and enticing as a lover, that part of his life compelled him in ways she'd only guessed at. And resented, she now realized in the aftermath of their shared discovery. "I'd like to hear about them. Sometime."

She thought he sent her a quick look, but he ignored her for a tick of time. Finally, his voice gruff as he avoided the opening she'd given him, he returned to the matter at hand. "But like I was saying, I believe in instinct, the primitive brain's alert system. I know how long a hunter has to sit in the deer blind, waiting, soundless. And that's what we're doing, Kate. We're on a hunt. Right now we're waiting to see what's coming through the woods. And I'll be ready for whatever does." He stared out through the streaming rain into the darkness.

She'd forgotten the way lines radiated from the corners of his eyes when he was focused on a problem. Or when he focused his formidable intensity on her, and nothing else existed except the two of them, cocooned in pleasure so thick that she'd sworn she could taste it for months after she'd left him.

"We're hunters, Kate. Patience is our strength. Quiet and hidden, we'll stay downwind and let the beast come to us."

"Nice metaphor."

"Comes from all that reading I mentioned."

"Sounded more like practical experience than second-hand."

"Sure. Hunting the human animal is how I made my living." He turned the windshield wipers to the highest speed. "But I had a lot of down time, and I spent it reading. A book can give a fellow an interesting perspective on where he fits into the grand scheme of things. Or doesn't. You sort of slide into someone else's head when you're reading, and it lights up your own world, clarifies things."

"Today changed my perspective," she said uneasily.

"How?" He slowed down and drove carefully through a dark, oily stretch of water that crossed the road. Water sloshed up the tires and spun back onto the road with a low, heavy sound. "What's different?"

She decided she wanted to tell him. Saying it out loud would help her figure out what had happened. "Jed, I don't believe in violence. I hate guns. I can't even kill a mouse. You can't begin to understand how much I despise violence." She kept her voice under control. "Fighting. All that posturing and loss of control. It's—sickening."

"And how did today change your perspective? Explain it to me, Katie." In the close confines of the vehicle his voice seduced her with its undertone of sympathy, a sympathy she rejected.

"It's been a confusing day. I can't explain it. I just don't feel like myself, that's all."

She was grateful that Jed let her comment pass, and didn't press her for an explanation.

The beating of the rain on the car roof blended with the hiss of the tires against the wet road as she sorted out her chaotic emotions.

Jed interrupted her thoughts. "I'm curious, Kate. Answer a question for me, will you?"

"Maybe." She preferred the silence. She didn't want to answer Jed's questions. She had too many questions of her own. Working together they'd established a certain equilibrium and in fairness, she couldn't hide behind her walls whenever it suited her. She expected him to be candid with her. "Go ahead, Jed. What do you want to know?"

"Did your daddy the colonel teach you how to shoot?"

"Yes."

"Are you any good?"

"Yes."

"Do you have a gun?"

"No." Feeling trapped, she tugged at the seat belt.

"You might need one."

"I don't want a gun. I won't have one."

"If I'm not around, or if something happens to me, and you're on your own with the person who's already killed twice that we know of, what then, Kate? How will you defend yourself? Or will you go meekly to the slaughter?" he asked her angrily.

"Not meekly."

"You're half my size, Kate. I outweigh you by over a hundred pounds. I'm a foot taller than you. How are you going to defend yourself against someone like me?" He spared her a long look, his hands steady on the wheel of the Blazer."

"I don't know. But I'd manage."

"The hell you would. You'd be dead, that's what. Think about getting a gun, Kate."

"Such concern," she mocked gently. "I'd think you cared after all, Jed."

"Just protecting my investment. And my reputation. Jedidiah Stone isn't known for losing a client." He flashed her a devilish grin, his teeth a gleam in the rain-darkened car. "I want to get paid, after all."

She thought again about The Last Resort, thought about the contrast between his clothes and where she'd found him.

"I know you're short of money, Jed. You'll be paid, even if something happens to me. I'll talk to my lawyer tomorrow."

"Damn, Katherine, that's a comfort. You've sure relieved my mind. I'd hate like hell to waste my time and not be paid."

"You're insulted."

"A little. Amused, too."

"You think I'm *funny?*" Insulted in her turn, she blew a whoof of air.

"Yeah, cookie, I do. And right now you sound like my dog, Booger."

*"Booger?"*

"He makes that same kind of annoyed woof. Anyway, you're so sure money's the answer. You're so damned determined to keep your account books balanced and even between us."

"I don't understand."

"I know you don't. But don't worry about it. Do think about my offer of the gun, though, cookie."

She sat stick-straight in the passenger seat as Jed returned his gaze to the road and peered through the sheets of slashing rain.

A gun.

Jed wanted her to have a gun.

Through the dark curtain of night and rain, she occasionally glimpsed the faint shine of an approaching car. The wipers were useless against the force of wind and water pouring over the windshield, their *thump-thump, whack-whack* on the glass an echoing beat to the pulse of excitement inside her.

Excitement, but anger, too, because that fragment of sunglasses was a link to the evil that had invaded her life and wreaked destruction.

Before finding that link, she'd thought she wanted justice.

She did. With all her heart and soul she wanted justice, and she was determined Frank and Patsy would have their due.

But with that small piece of glass in her possession, she was dismayed to discover she also wanted vengeance.

It was vengeance now that stoked the fire inside her, made her burn and chased the chill that had settled in her bones months ago.

Kate remembered the words. "'Vengeance is mine,' saith the Lord."

But she didn't want to leave vengeance to anyone. *She* wanted to smite her enemy *herself.* Leaving vengeance to God demanded a patience and a philosophy she'd lost with those deaths in the house behind her.

Untidy, shocking, this passionate hatred for someone Jed kept insisting she might know.

Unexpected.

She would never have guessed that she could hate so fiercely, so intensely.

But she did.

It was going through Patsy's house, her belongings. Seeing the details that added up to a life uncompleted that had aroused this ferocity.

She twitched in her seat again, rubbed her arms even though she felt as if she was going to burst into flames. If someone gave her the power to erase the killer's existence in that moment, she believed she could do it. No qualms. Happily. And that's what she was ashamed to admit to Jed.

That's why she didn't want to even think about a gun.

This thirst for vengeance was unnerving.

Was this ferocity her legacy from her father? Was she the colonel's daughter after all? In spite of everything?

She didn't recognize the Katherine March who burned with this need to wreak havoc upon another human being.

She wasn't sure she liked this Kate.

And she knew damned well she wasn't about to put a gun in *this* Kate's hands.

"Penny for your thoughts." Jed leaned forward and wiped the windshield again.

"Not for a million dollars," she said, and averted her face.

"Ugly thoughts, Kate?" Too much understanding in his seductive voice.

"Unbelievably." She tapped on the dash again. "All in all, this has been a peculiar, upsetting day."

Tugging at the hem of her skirt where it lay over her thigh, Jed drew her attention to him. His fingertips grazed her skin, and goose bumps skittered up her thigh, reverberated in private places.

Even now, even under these circumstances, her body responded.

Her instinct for self-preservation highly tuned, she shifted carefully away from the light, accidental touch.

"Don't worry, cookie. It'll all straighten itself out. And we'll check with the opticians tomorrow. We'll start the ball rolling and see what happens. One step at a time. Good enough?"

Kate nodded and focused on the driving rain.

The only thing in all the craziness that made sense was that piece of glass. That was real. Unemotional. Unambiguous. Something she could touch. A puzzle piece.

No wonder Jed compared what he did to solving a puzzle.

Water sprayed from the tires as the Blazer slid into the shadows of her office. Landscaped with old trees and high hedges to provide the illusion of privacy and privilege, the building wasn't visible from the road. As Jed drove into the circular driveway, the three-story building shone palely through the gloom, its creamy yellow muted by rain and darkness.

Close to the cream stucco structure, her car was the last one in the parking lot. Rain sluiced down on it from the overhanging banyan tree, collected in shiny black puddles on the brick paving of the driveway.

Leaving the headlights on, Jed parked the Blazer, front to back, next to her car. "Your keys, please."

She unsnapped them from her purse and held the smaller key out from the rest. "This one unlocks the door."

Reaching into the console, he fished out a large, thick flashlight. "Stay inside, Kate. I want to look your car over before you drive it home. I thought about leaving it here overnight, but that seemed like asking for trouble. Better to have it in your garage."

"You'll get—"

He flung open the door of the Blazer, and rain blew in, cold and needle sharp. "Wet."

He slammed the door behind him, and Kate leaned forward, her pulse galloping as she watched Jed vanish. The headlights pierced the darkness with bright cones of yellow.

Anxiously she watched until Jed crossed the path of yellow, stooped and disappeared once more.

She meant to stay inside. She knew it was stupid to get out into the rain. She knew Jed didn't need her help. He never had. He sure didn't now.

But the sight of his dark shape disappearing underneath her car sent her shivering into the rain, one hand on the cell phone in her pocket, the other on the screwdriver she'd found in the console.

As her heels sloshed through the puddles, Jed pulled himself out from under her car, the flashlight held with his hand curled around it, its beam spearing her in the face. "What the hell?"

Perhaps he wasn't as vulnerable under there as she'd thought.

"Me." She waved the screwdriver in his direction. "That's what the hell. In case you needed protecting."

He lowered the flashlight, and she blinked rapidly, trying to adjust her light-blinded vision. His voice came like a jungle cat's purr out of the night. "You don't want a gun, but you're ready to take on all comers with *that?*" The flashlight beam shone on the metal of the screwdriver.

"Sure." She wiggled it threateningly. "It's sharp. More or less. A Phillips would be better. Sharper."

He studied her for a moment before he scooted back under her car, shaking his head. She thought he muttered something under his breath, something that sounded like *bloodthirsty,* but it might have been only the rumble of thunder.

She didn't care. She *felt* bloodthirsty.

Her eyes straining to see between the flashes of lightning, the screwdriver held stiffly out, Kate swiveled from side to side, watching the twist of tree and bush in the darkness.

One hand braced against the driver's side of the car, Jed popped out and stood up. Flattened by the rain, his hair shaped his skull. Rain dripped into his eyes. Mud or oil streaked his cheek and washed away with the rain. Kate kept her attention on Jed and the parking lot. He moved around the car, checking the bumpers and opening the car door to access the hood release.

Partially hidden by the hood, he bent over and ran his hand over the engine. His slacks, already splattered with mud from Patsy's and now irredeemably stained, were plastered against his thighs and butt. As he twisted and ducked his head under the hood, the light worsted fabric outlined the shape of his boxer shorts.

And other things.

Kate couldn't look away.

She had stroked those lean flanks with wet, soapy hands once, following the shape of those long muscles. The memory came out of nowhere, and her hands curled, almost as if she sensed those strong muscles flexing against her touch.

A sharp, metallic sound had her looking into the darkness again, and then Jed slammed down the hood.

Clicking off the flashlight, he raised his arm and glossed a strip of hair out of his face. ''Well, cookie, your car passes muster.''

''Am I going to have to check my car every time I want to drive it? Or sit in it?'' She hopped from foot to foot, working off adrenaline and that surge of longing to touch him.

He slicked back his hair with the hand holding the flashlight. ''No. You won't have to check your car.''

"Good." Rain snaked inside the back of her dress. "I'd do it, of course, but—"

"I'm your driver until this is all over."

"Oh." She hadn't expected this kind of togetherness. She should have. "You're going to pick me up every day and drive me to work?"

"That, too." He stepped toward her. Stopped.

Rain curtained between them, a silvered blackness separating them. She was drenched from head to foot, exhausted, exhilarated and buzzed.

"What do you mean, 'that, too'?" She didn't move.

He took another step through the rain toward her. "I mean, Kate, that you're not going anywhere without me."

"Of course I am, Jed," she said, quite reasonably she thought as her mind whirled with the possibility of Jed's presence in every aspect of her life. She should have foreseen that likelihood. She hadn't, not consciously at least, and now she couldn't wrap her mind around the idea of Jed in her car, her house, her *life*. For days. For however long it took. "Look, Jed," she said, a tinge of desperation in her voice, "I have my life to lead. I'm not going into hiding, for heaven's sake."

Fat raindrops plopped into her face from the banyan tree as she looked up at Jed, who was suddenly in front of her, toe-to-toe.

"Of course you're not going into *hiding*," he said. His eyelashes were beaded with rain, and his shirt was dirt-streaked and translucent with water. A curl of dark chest hair edged his collar. "In fact, you're not going to change your schedule one whit."

And then she got it. "You're changing your schedule."

"That's what you hired me for, cookie." He tipped her chin up. "Remember?"

She did, too. She remembered *everything*. The touches, the taste of Jed's skin, the musky scent of him after loving. Oh, yes, she remembered.

She'd never forgotten.

Never.

Rain splattered onto her from his face, from the tree, from the sky, and she was drowning in heat and freezing in the slash of cold rain, and her body fizzed and hummed and she was so confused, and hungry for the taste of Jedidiah Stone in the cold rain that she reached up and wrapped her arms around his neck and hung on with all she was worth while the rain poured down on them.

Hunger poured into her, from him. The taste of his mouth was hunger. The feel of him against her was want. And she rejoiced in it. *This* was what she needed, this hunger. This heat that burned her from the inside out and sizzled her brain, this heat that told her she was alive. Every time she touched him or he touched her, she came alive.

And that sensation was what she *craved*.

Not the passive kiss of a gentleman lover. Not the careful touch of a man who asked permission.

She wanted a hunger that answered her own need. She wanted aggression that matched her own.

No tenderness now.

She wanted to forget the ugliness in this rush of *life*.

Jed gave her kiss for kiss, his mouth covering hers and flashing heat down to her curling toes. His palm swooped down her rear end and cupped her forcefully to him, his pelvis bumping her, hard.

This, too, she wanted. This rawness.

She raked her hands down his back. His wet shirt bunched and rippled under her hands, and she yanked it free of his slacks, sliding her own palms into the gap of belt and skin.

Jed planted his feet and lifted her, wrapped her legs around him and strode to the hood of her low car. Her dress rucked up and the slick wetness of the hood chilled her heated skin.

Nothing passive about the bite of his teeth on her lower lip. Nothing passive about the drag of her hands against him. Freeing one hand, she yanked at his tie, pulling him to her. He bent forward, one hand balancing on the hood, the other gripping her head.

Rain beat on her face, her arms, her bare legs. Wet and heavy, his slacks slapped against the outside of her thighs. Between them, hot and heavy and hard, Jed strained toward her. She reached between them and pressed against him. At the jolt of him against her open palm, she gripped and stroked that heat that drew her.

"Easy," he muttered, his voice a growl under the thrumming of the rain and the rattle of leaves around them.

"No," she said, "I don't want easy." She curled her other arm around his neck, holding him to her as her fingers shaped him again and again, frantically. "I want you, Jed, in me, around me. Now." Through his slacks she coiled her hand tightly around him, moving tip to long length, taking the weight of him in her palm.

He stilled her hand. "Too fast, Kate. Too fast." Rough, compelling, his voice rasped along her nerve endings and set them to vibrating. Clipping her ankles around his waist, he stepped into the open V of her thighs, leaving no room for her seeking hands against him, so she slipped both arms around his neck and clung tightly.

"Please, Jed, please." She lifted herself up to him, seeking peace, pleasure, release from the pain that bound her so tightly inside that she hadn't been able to take a good, deep breath in months. "Now. Fast. Hard. Not easy. Not gentle." Fast and primitive and mind numbing, that was what she wanted, *needed.* "For God's sake, don't give me gentle, Jed." Her throat closed with the urgency of her need.

"Ah, Katie, girl." He nudged the neckline of her dress aside, worked at the buttons at the back, and raindrops from his hair, from his face, dripped onto her as he nuzzled the corner of her neck, inhaling. "You smell like rain and sunshine and yourself, all mixed together. I could get drunk on the scent of you, Katie. On the texture of your skin." He ran one hand down the line of her throat, his thumb rough and callused. "But not this way. Not now." Still, though, he moved his cupped palm over her breast, thumbing the nipple turned hard with cold rain and heated need.

"Yes," she said. "Now. *Now* more than ever." She angled her neck, seeking that shivery graze once more, but he buried his face against her breasts, his bristled chin scraping her skin into long, rolling shivers that convulsed the muscles of her thighs and belly and made her tighten her ankles around his waist. His mouth closed around the hard nub of her breast, and she jerked, yielded to the coiling heat. Shameless in her need to soothe where she ached, she pressed her hips into his pelvis, moving to the internal tide within her. She didn't recognize her own voice, soft and insistent, but she recognized the hunger in it as her own as she urged him, "Jed, don't leave me like this."

He closed his teeth lightly against the cord at the side of her neck, tugging, and she shivered with heat and pleasure while the rain drummed on the hood of her car. "I want you so much I hurt with it and tonight, while you're sleeping, I'll be mentally kicking myself." His pelvis bumped her and she pushed back eagerly, need demanding an answer. "But Kate, I'm not going to take you on the hood of your car in the middle of a thunderstorm." His laugh was tight and breathless. "I'm not that big a fool. This is wrong."

"No." She slid forward, her skirt bunching up behind her, and she worked the wet buttonholes of his shirt with trembling fingers. "This is right, Jed. Right, when everything else has been wrong. You said I should be grateful I'm alive. I am. I am, but make me *feel* alive." She shoved back his shirt and kissed the midline of his broad chest, brushing aside the drops of rain that shimmered in the nest of hair disappearing into his slacks. She rested her hand against the satin ridge of muscle and blood that pulsed against her hand. "I want you, Jed. Now. In the rain, on the car, on the ground. I don't care."

"And what about tomorrow, Kate, what then?"

"I don't give a damn about tomorrow." She didn't, either. She wanted Jed to fill the emptiness gnawing inside her, she wanted Jed with an intensity she'd never had in all her lonely dreams. She took his hand, flattened it against her where she ached. "Too much death."

"Too much death." He cupped her, hard, his hand moving to the rhythm of his hips, to the rhythm of her hand on him. He slid his finger under the edge of her panties. "I can do this for you, Kate. But tomorrow you'll wish I hadn't."

"No, I won't. This is what I want." Tomorrow she would pay whatever price she had to, but in the vast loneliness of the world, she needed Jed tonight. She believed that the needing and wanting had nothing to do with a rational decision, but, rather, something to do with the life force bursting free, demanding satisfaction. Like a seed sprouting through a crack in the sidewalk, that power wouldn't be denied. She rested her face in the crook of his shoulder and the thick muscles of his neck. "It's only sex, Jed. Nothing more."

"Yeah. Only sex." His fingers parted her, sent her shivering and shuddering against their seeking touch, her body softening and dampening with each long stroke against her. "That's my Katie," he murmured. "Come on, sweetheart, go with me," he whispered while his hand moved over her and his mouth took hers, taking her breath into him.

"Only sex," she repeated, lost in the scent of him, the rich fragrance of his arousal enveloping her. She touched the tip of him lightly, delicately, feeding his hunger as she fed her own. "An impulse, desire, nothing more."

"Desire," he said, helping her anxious fingers undo his buckle, "will do. For the moment."

The metal rectangle was cold and slippery, and she worked it free finally with his help, edged the waistband button out of the waterlogged buttonhole holding it captive. She pulled too hard, and the button made a tiny, barely perceptible pop as it hit the ground. His mouth and lips sang against her wet skin, slipped in the rain down her breasts, and his hands, ah, his knowing, skillful hands, ratcheted her higher and higher into a place where nothing mattered except this pleasure beyond explaining.

Impatient, she slid down the zipper tab of his slacks, caressed him as he caressed her, met his rocking hips with a matching rhythm, gave to him as fiercely as he gave to her here in the pounding rain and darkness. She met him touch for touch, taste for taste, not surrendering, not yielding.

And yet...

No winner in this game, only this dark pleasure riding her higher and faster until she wanted to cry out. To keep from keening into the wind and rain, she bit her lip until she tasted blood. Pain. Pleasure.

All around her the rain slashed against ground and car and filled her mouth and pebbled against her closed eyes as her head dropped back in that final moment when life and death seem one and surrender has no meaning.

# Chapter 10

Boneless, drained of tension, of energy, Kate rested against Jed. Reluctant to open her eyes, she let the rain beat onto her, a baptism, a cleansing of the ugliness of recent weeks. So much sadness and grief, but gone for the moment. Peace curled through her with each beat of the rain, with each beat of Jed's heart against her.

Astonishing this urge to stay under heaven's black, rain-spangled curve with Jed, amazing this need to lean against him, to close her eyes and rest, wondrous this peace seeping inch by inch through her. A blessing in the darkness and rain and terror.

With the back of her finger she stroked the springy hair of Jed's chest, curled her hand into that soft fur, burrowed closer and inhaled the scent of him.

She knew she should feel guilty.

She didn't.

She should be embarrassed that she'd lost all awareness of time and place. She should be dismayed that she hadn't once thought of the possibility of danger.

She wasn't.

She rubbed her cheek against him. The texture of his hair on her skin, the springing softness—a miracle of DNA and cells. Catlike she spread her fingers over his chest and twined them through the curls over his heart.

This was what she'd needed, this journey into a mindless place of touch and feeling.

Life, in all its mystery, rearing up and taking what it would. Spitting in the face of death, that's what it was. And she'd do it again.

She pressed her hand flat over his heart and felt the rhythm there speed in response to her touch. She liked that feminine power over him. She always had. And now, well, if she'd been selfish in her demands, she'd given to Jed measure for measure, equally.

No, she didn't regret what she'd done. What *they'd* done. He'd made his own demands, taken his own pleasure.

A fair exchange, and if her heart argued otherwise, well, she could silence that unruly organ once more as she had so many times over the past years. Over the past months.

If something in her heart bled for what might have been, for what should have been, she could bandage that wound, too, and move on. Wounds healed. Life rolled on. If the heart yearned, ached for what it could never have, well, the world didn't end, no matter if it felt that way.

A woman could do what she had to.

And she felt no guilt.

"Katie, sweetheart," Jed said, his bare chest vibrating against her, his heart still pounding under her hand, "I don't know about you, but I wouldn't mind continuing our tête-à-tête under a roof. A roof has a number of advantages, you know." Slicked flat by her hands and the rain, the soft, damp hair of his chest tickled her mouth as she surrendered to the need to taste once more. Avoiding the hoop of her earring, he nipped the lobe of her ear. "For one thing, it's dry under a roof. A person might even find a bed there." He nibbled thoughtfully, and her toes curled. "And we'd have privacy. I like privacy, Katie."

"Me, too," she murmured, not in any hurry to move, not with his chest warm against her and his arms giving her all the privacy she needed at the moment. "Sometimes."

"Naked Katie in the rain." He smoothed the dripping strands of wet hair from her face, and his hands were gentle. He touched her nipple where a drop of rain trembled with her breathing. Taking the drop to his mouth, he licked his finger, tasting the rain, her, and her insides coiled in response to the concentration in his face as he touched his finger to her mouth. "The prettiest thing I've ever been privileged to see. A gift. Thank you." He stooped and brushed his mouth so gently, so gently she wanted to weep, across her bare breasts. "Not just sex, sweetheart. Don't kid yourself. Or me."

It took her a moment more to translate that richness of sound back into words. When she finally did, when she finally understood what he was asserting, what he wanted from her, she straightened, looked him straight in the face and lied. "Sex, Jed. That's all."

His eyes glittered in the darkness. The lines around his mouth tightened. In the fitful light his face was harsh. For a second she wondered if she'd made a mistake. His voice, though, was soft on the wind, as soft as the skim of his mouth across her skin. "Sure, Katie. If you say so. Just sex. I don't have a problem with that." He scooped his hand across the back of her neck and kissed her hard, skillfully, his tongue splitting the seam of her lips, diving in, the flavors rich and dark.

Stirring her hunger, her need. Proving the truth to her lie.

Even as his mouth and tongue demanded a response she couldn't hold back, Kate recognized what he was doing. But she softened her mouth, felt his soften in return, the kiss translating into tenderness that could have broken her heart if she'd allowed it to. Instead, ruefully, gently, she smoothed his hair off his forehead, brushed the rain from his face.

"You forget, Kate—" he held her face still between his palms "—how well I know you." He stepped back, releasing her.

"So you say."

"So I say." An undefinable confidence in his hip-sprung stance, amusement in the twist of his smile.

The hood of her car was cold against her skin, and she shifted uncomfortably. She raised her arms to fasten the buttons at the back of her dress. The soggy gauze clumped and twisted, and she couldn't force the tiny pearl buttons through the buttonholes. "Ah!" She threw up her hands in frustration.

"Here. Let me handle button duty." Even rain-chilled, his fingers brushing the slope of her upper arm, her nape, felt warm as they moved swiftly over the five buttons, sliding each into place smoothly. "There. Done. But you look like the cat dragged you through a knothole backward." He patted the last button flat.

"I can imagine." Grimacing, she tried to slide off the hood, stuck, her skirt rumpling and bunching beneath her in heavy wads. Jed stabilized her on the ground as her knees buckled.

"And, Kate, in case you're wondering, I didn't forget where we were. You weren't in danger."

Oh, but she had been, danger of a more subtle, seductive kind, a danger that lured and called and invited her soul. "I didn't wonder," she said. She had been lost to the world, lost in that richness of scent and taste and touch. And Jed hadn't been? He'd been able to keep some part of himself distanced?

Or like a wild creature, did some primitive sense telegraph to him the presence of danger, alert him to the rustle of the snake in the underbrush no matter what the circumstances? Some tang of evil in the molecules of the air?

Odd, how much she preferred to believe that explanation, even if it meant self-deception. She didn't want to believe that she had been in that sparkling darkness by herself. Too lonely.

Her experience might be limited, but every female instinc
she possessed told her Jed had been as enthralled as she.

Jed held her elbow and gathered up shoes, flashlight and
keys. Scudding clouds and rain shrouded the parking lot. He
glanced warily around the dark lot. "It's dark as hell back
here."

"I know." She surveyed the empty lot, seeing it through
his eyes. Seeing the hidden places, the shadows where a killer
could hide. "The lighting's nonexistent. But until I thought
I was in danger, I wasn't afraid to stay at the office and work
late." She shrugged. The events of these past months were
still incomprehensible to her, that such cold perversity could
occur here, in her town. "You know something, Jed?"

"What's that, cookie?" He touched her forehead gently,
carefully traced the line of her eyebrow.

"I *resent* the loss of that fearlessness. Someone stole that
from me, stole that sense of my town as a place of sunlight,
not of darkness and evil." This anger was clean, pure, a flame
of heat uncomplicated by remorse. She wanted satisfaction
on this point for herself. Wanted to see the killer's face and
know the person who had robbed her. "My world's turned
a hundred and eighty degrees. I wonder if I'll ever walk down
a street again without looking over my shoulder. That's not
the world I want. I won't be that kind of person, a person
who looks at everyone and everything with suspicion, looking for the hidden agenda, the secret motive, the knife concealed behind a smiling face." She shuddered. "A world
where I can't trust a stranger. What kind of world is that?
Where I can't trust a friend?"

"Well, Kate, unlike you, I've never seen any place as in-
nocent. I can't change that, can't fix it. I can't give that back
to you. I can protect you. I can shine a flashlight in the
darkness, keep the tigers at bay. That's all." His laugh was
tinged with bitterness.

She touched his arm carefully, wanting him to understand.
"Jed, I'm not afraid of the dark. I'm not naive. I don't leave

ny doors unlocked the way my parents did when they were kids.''

She didn't mention the drills her father had put her and Sissy through, his attempts to turn them into tiny soldiers prepared for combat, taught to see an enemy behind every corner. In her father's world there was no such concept as ''fight or flight.'' Fight. Never surrender. That was what he'd taught and she'd deliberately rejected. Now she was being forced down that path.

As Jed's expression remained unchanged, she shook her head, insisted, ''Look, give me some credit, will you? I'm careful. I didn't worry about coming to the parking lot by myself until Patsy and Frank were killed. And even then I felt prepared.''

''Thus the confidence?'' In the dark, the gleam of his smile was feral. ''You are woman, hear you roar?''

''I can kick delicate male areas with the best of them. And I won't hesitate to kick and gouge if I have to.''

Before she blinked, he had her up against him, her rear snugged tight into his front, his arm braced against her throat. ''Jed!''

''Run away, cookie. Throw me on the ground with some of those slick moves you learned. Show me I can't rape you. Or kill you. And remember, Patsy had more training than you do,'' he whispered in her ear. ''Come on, Katie, I'm not even trying,'' he taunted in a raspy voice. ''Show me your stuff, so I can see how tough you are.''

Even knowing he wouldn't hurt her, she felt the strength, the implacable control of muscles and tendons, and knew he wasn't using a tenth of his power. Furious that he could use his strength so casually, so effortlessly, and hold her captive, she stomped her foot on his, but he held her up just high enough that she couldn't leverage herself, couldn't swing her heel back against his shin, his groin.

''Aw, Kate, come on. Give me your best shot,'' he encouraged. ''Make me work. Shoot, my pulse hasn't even speeded up.''

No matter how she twisted, how she reached for his throat
his eyes, he countered so easily that his breathing remained
slow and easy in her ear, and she could believe all her strug
gling hadn't changed his heart rate. Squirming and wriggling
in his grasp, trying as hard as she could to use the moves
she'd learned, she swung helplessly until he lowered her back
to the ground.

"All right. You proved your point." She was annoyed to
discover that her pride was dented. "But you surprised me."
The comment spilled out of her mouth, increasing her an
noyance.

"That's the point, Kate. If the killer gets his hands on
you…" Jed ran the back of his hand slowly up her throat
and she shivered with pleasure, not fear. "If that happens,
it's survival of the fittest."

"You're preaching to the choir, Jed. I know that." It was
all she could do not to turn her mouth to his knuckles where
they rested at her chin, irritation changed into this purring
delight.

"You need an edge, Kate. I'm the only edge you have. If
I'm not there when the killer comes for you, and he will
don't kid yourself about that, what's your edge then? If
you're on your own?" He flicked her chin casually.

She rubbed her eyes. "I don't know, Jed. I can't think
through that scenario right now."

"I don't want you helpless, Kate. If—"

"If something happens to you." She closed her eyes and
lifted her face to the sky, let the rain wash over it.

"If that happens, yeah." He shifted in the rain, a barely
perceptible movement of hips and shoulders, his movements
easy and slow. "I want to know you'll be okay."

She gripped the flapping edges of his shirtfront, pulled
them together. "You're my protection, Jed. So take damned
good care of yourself." The thought of Jed mangled, bloody
*dead,* slammed the air out of her lungs. She took a deep
breath, and the smell of wet pine and earth filled her. She
pressed her face against his chest. Her breath fluttered the

wiry hair there that filled her nostrils with the scent of the rain. The scent of him. "Have faith in me, too. If I'm on my own, if you're not with me, I'm not going to behave stupidly." She nuzzled against him once more, then lifted her face. "I need to go home. What do you plan to do after you follow me home?" She wrung out the skirt of her dress and took the keys of her car from him.

His hand closed around hers. "Oh, I thought you understood, cookie. I'm rooming with you."

She blinked. And blinked again, raindrops splashing from her eyelashes. "I missed that little detail," she said faintly and pressed the remote key opener.

The chirp of the remote was cheerfully loud.

"I don't need a bed."

She figured he meant his smile to be reassuring. It wasn't. *Safe* had a whole different meaning when she thought about Jedidiah Stone in her house twenty-four hours a day. For the duration.

Bad miscalculation on her part.

She couldn't move. It was one roller-coaster swoop too many.

He continued in that soothing voice that only ruffled the hairs along her arm and did nothing to soothe her. "I don't need caretaking. I can bivouac on your floor." His hand resting on the top of the driver's door, he waited for her to fold herself into the car.

"You won't have to make do with a hard floor. I have room." She stuck the key into the ignition. The mornings would be tricky. "I have a guest room. With its own bathroom. You can sleep there. You'll be comfortable."

"Comfort isn't the issue. If someone came crawling through your windows, I'd be too far away. I'm going to be closer than your shadow." He bent over the door, swinging it back and forth as he shifted his gaze from her to the bushes surrounding the parking lot. "That won't be a problem, will it? No reason we can't share space, is there?"

*Yes.*

He must have seen the unspoken word in her expression. His eyes narrowed thoughtfully and he went very still.

She made her comment slow and casual. "None at all." Focusing on the steering wheel, she fired the ignition, curved her hand around the gearshift. "I'll see you at my house, then?"

"I'll be the tailgater in your rearview mirror." He shut the door with a quiet *snick,* expensive metal guided by male control. "You all right to drive home?"

"Absolutely." She nodded and controlled her anxiety. It would be stupid to roar out of the parking lot, leaving him behind. She'd find a way to keep her privacy. But her foot pressed the accelerator hard and the engine whined, revved. "The address is—"

"I know where you live, Kate." Pivoting on his heel, Jed strode back to his Blazer. "And you don't want to have a race down the Trail at this time of night."

"No." She lifted her foot from the accelerator, and the engine slowed. "I'll wait."

"Of course you will. Because it's the smart move." His shadowy form disappeared behind the bulk of the Blazer. He started the car.

All the way home, down the rain-slicked roads where puddles gleamed in the dark and wind snapped against her car, she planned her strategy, tried to anticipate what would happen with Jed, as he'd promised, sticking to her like her shadow. If she were careful, she could keep her secret from him.

If she were very lucky, she'd be able to maintain her charade.

Because Jed *saw* everything. Observed every flicker of expression, every small twitch and flinch. Every blink.

She'd noticed his subtle awareness of her reactions several times already. He couldn't have figured out her secret. But Jed was so damnably clever. Still, not even Jed could have added up the few signs— Could he? Her breath hitched.

Surely he wouldn't sleep in the same room? Maybe she'd misunderstood?

But if she hadn't... One long spell of throwing up in the bathroom, and he'd figure out pretty damn fast that flu wasn't her problem. She ran her palms over the cool leather covering of the steering wheel, forcing her brain to face reality. All right. Suppose he did mean he was sleeping in her bedroom.

If Jed discovered that she was pregnant, she wouldn't give a snowball's chance in hell that he would continue to help her. Not Jed. He would see it as an unforgivable betrayal.

Perhaps it was.

She banged the wheel. All right. She would control the nausea, the gagging. She would just damn well make herself face the day like Pollyanna, smiling all the way. Easy. No problem.

She could do it.

She had to.

With grim determination she took the last curve into her street too sharply and skidded around the corner, straightening the car easily and nosing it into her driveway.

She tapped the garage door opener and the door groaned upward, the light shining into the night. She scowled. The entrance to her house, like the parking lot of her office, was dark and shielded by too many mature bushes and trees. Where the driveway curved toward the back of the house, the tall purple bougainvillea at the corners of the garage effectively hid the entrance from her neighbors and from the street. Hibiscus hedges and oleanders transformed seclusion and privacy into menacing shadows and unknown shapes.

A jungle, filled with formless predators.

She hated, *hated,* this unnaturally heightened wariness. Reasonable caution? Sure. She took a breath. But not this poisonous suspicion casting its shadow on everything in her world, making her afraid to enter her own home, making her suspicious even of Calla.

Looking at the shadows, paralyzed by uneasiness, Kate bit

her lip and gripped the steering wheel. No, this wasn't the world she wanted.

For the time being, though, it was the one she would have to inhabit. If she wanted to live.

To protect those she loved, she had to protect herself.

She glanced in the rearview mirror.

Behind her the warm glow of Jed's headlights bounced into view, bathing the shadows with yellow, momentarily chasing away ghosts and fear. Freeing her from the paralysis.

She pulled in to the garage, and Jed parked next to her. In the silence of the garage as the heavy door rattled shut, she shook her keys in her hand, took a deep breath and said, "I'm glad you're here, Jed. I didn't think I would be, but I am."

"Doing my job, Kate. No big deal." With a casual glance, he checked out the garage, motioned her toward the house. "Mind answering a couple of questions for me after I reconnoiter your house?"

"No. Ask away. What do you want to know?"

"First, why you hired Patsy. Second, I want to go through a list of people who might benefit from your death. Third, you need to tell me how your business is structured financially."

"My business? Why?"

"You know, money and passion. Power. Best motives going, since I don't think either of us believes you're being stalked by a serial killer."

"Where's the money, the power? Jed, I don't have a lot of liquid assets. Everything comes from the business, and right now I'm dealing in paper money. Lines of credit. Calla and I have earned a very nice life-style for ourselves, but I don't have a lot of liquid cash. I don't think Calla does, either. Her new husband helps, I suppose, but she's not extravagant."

"Smoke and mirrors, Kate. I have to see what's behind the illusions of the people in your life. Someone wants you dead. And until I can figure out why, that someone is relatively safe. Unless he makes a mistake. And since that mistake could involve your dead body, I highly recommend that you put your loyalties aside and look at the facts.''

She shuddered. ''All right. We'll go through your questions. Even though I don't like them. You're focusing on people close to me, and I hate that.''

He touched her cheek. ''I know you do, Katie. I know. But the questions have to be asked. And answered.''

''But not tonight.''

''They can wait,'' he agreed. ''But not for much longer.''

Punching in the security codes, she waited, opened the door and canceled the alarm. ''Are you hungry?'' She brushed her still-damp hair away from her face and wearily surveyed the kitchen as he followed her into the large room lined with pickled pine cabinets. She opened the refrigerator door. ''Ham? Cheese? Leftover egg rolls?''

''Nothing.'' He circled the room, much as he had Patsy's kitchen, his gaze flicking from one area to the next, taking in her lemon-yellow place mats, the brass-and-wood ceiling fan. He opened the pantry door where her few canned and packaged items lined up in soldierly, alphabetical order. ''Wait. I'm having second thoughts. Maybe that sandwich?'' He shut the pantry door and covered the distance from the hall to the front room in the time it took her to blink twice. ''If it's not too much trouble?''

''Not at all,'' she said faintly, the sound of Jedidiah Stone moving through her house troubling her, stirring her in some undefinable way.

The sound of his shoes on her pine floors, the *feel* of him in the atmosphere of the old house, his energy disturbing the still air. She pressed her hand against her belly and fought the urge to cry.

The reverberations of his steps from above carried to her, moved through her as if he were touching her. Holding the loaf of bread in one hand, the jar of brown-speckled mustard in the other, she listened as he opened closet doors, stepped out onto the gallery off her bedroom, and then returned down the back stairs that led from the end of the upstairs hall back to the kitchen.

"Don't see any sign of intruders. You have a pretty good security system. Should have wired the upstairs windows, though. Anyone could climb up the oak tree and swing across real easy to the balcony off your bedroom." He peeled a slice of Virginia ham from the stack she had in front of her. Rolling it into a cylinder, he caught her eyes and asked, "That is your bedroom, right? The one with the picture of the Outer Banks in the bathroom?"

The loaf of bread folded between her fingers. She'd forgotten about the picture.

"Yes."

"You kept it." He ripped open the plastic encasing the cheese.

"Obviously." She slathered a squashed slice of bread thickly, the mustard smearing onto the sides, onto her fingers, onto the counter. "It's an important work. I liked the way the artist used sunshine and shadow."

"Yeah." He handed her two slices of cheese, and she plopped them on top of the ham. "When we bought it, I thought it was an interesting picture, too."

He'd bought the painting, with its moody blue-and-purple ocean underneath a yellowing sky, for her after a brief weekend on the Banks. They'd made love on the beach, in the ocean, in the sandy bed that never got remade. She'd kept the painting. And one of his old shirts. Nothing else.

While she returned the ham and cheese to the refrigerator, he wiped the counter and then poured two glasses of milk into her green tumblers, tapped his against hers. His shadow loomed large and dangerous on the wall behind him. "Cheers, cookie. It's been a long day, hasn't it?"

"Yes." Kate clinked her glass against his and gulped down a mouthful of skim milk. She didn't want to think about the long night ahead of her.

The morning to come.

She didn't have to wait for morning.

Showered, shampooed, the scents of her lotion and soap drifting into the dimly lit bedroom where Jed had made a pallet near the door, she stooped, straightened an edge of the spread that dangled off the bed. The hem of her heavy T-shirt slapping against her plaid cotton sleep shorts, she turned to him and started to ask if he had enough blankets and pillows, to ask if he really wouldn't prefer to sleep in the guest room two doors down, to ask if he *really* thought it was necessary to stay in the same room.

She didn't have a chance.

He closed in on her, his bare feet silent on the uncarpeted floor. Backing up, one step at a time as he moved in inexorably, Kate felt her heart speed up, skip, race with panic.

No expression softened the planes and ridges of his face. Distant, as if he looked at a stranger, he regarded her. And then, with an intentness that sent ice down her spine, he reached out to her.

"Don't," she said, her voice catching in her throat. She took another step back and backed into the wall.

"Why not, Katherine? It's not as though I haven't touched you before. Why, if memory serves, I think I had my hands on you just tonight. And yours on me." His voice was hard, aggressive. Sliding his open palm under her T-shirt, his fingers brushing her shower-warm skin, he placed his hand carefully on her belly, smoothed it over the barely-there curve. "So this is the secret you didn't want me to know."

Heavy, hot, his hand rested against her and she felt herself drowning in the hot gray of his eyes. "When were you going to tell me you were pregnant? Or were you going to skip over that detail?"

At his words, she jerked. Her arm brushed the light switch on the wall, plunging the room into darkness, and his disembodied voice, no more than a harsh whisper in the oppressive blackness enveloping them, came to her like a scorpion's sting, fast and deadly.

Unforgiving.

# Chapter 11

Jed didn't think it was possible to hurt so much and still draw breath. To be so confused and furious. The tiny swell of her belly under his hand, the miracle of what was in her ripped through him.

Kate would never have told him she was pregnant. She'd been guarded from the first minute she'd walked into The Last Resort, and he'd registered the clues, known she was hiding something, but it had taken him until now to understand what they meant.

She'd walked out of the bathroom, weariness in every line of her body and face, and he'd known. Maybe it was the unconscious lift of her shoulders under her T-shirt, the way she faced him with her hands crossed in front of her, reminding him of the times she'd kept her hands protectively in front of her earlier. Maybe it was the lift of her chin, as if she was preparing for battle. He didn't know.

But observations had simmered in his subconscious, weaving together with other details until the pattern emerged.

And the truth had slammed him in the gut, rocking him back on his heels.

He hadn't needed the stricken look she shot him when he confronted her to know she was pregnant.

Cautious, careful Kate, who'd walked out of his life telling him that she wouldn't have his baby if he was the last man on earth had chosen to bear Frank's child. *Chosen.*

Somehow that simple choice shouldn't have the power to tear a man to pieces. It was her choice after all, and they'd been apart three years, but Jed felt like everything inside him was shattering into a million pieces.

He shook his head, trying to erase the reality of Katie in her outlandish green T-shirt and green-and-yellow-plaid shorts, everything thick and loose and deliberately concealing. Not thinking, not even knowing what he intended, he took another step, crowding her, driven by a fury and torment so deep he didn't recognize himself.

"So whose baby is it, Katherine?" Tentatively, barely touching her, he traced the outward, imagined shape deep inside her. *Hate* was too simple an emotion for what he experienced in that instant as his fingers moved delicately across her smooth, still-flat abdomen. He wanted to lash out, to make her feel some of the pain crushing him. "The wonderful Frank's, I assume?"

"You know it is." Defiant, anxious, her huge eyes met his.

"Well, now, how on earth would I *know* that?" He leaned forward, and the sweet, clean scent of her enveloped him, the minty fragrance of her shampoo teasing his senses, tormenting him.

"Whose baby would it be if not Frank's?" She didn't move, her body still and vibrant to his touch.

"Silly me. To wonder." He bent closer, not willing to let her go, the darkness stripping him of his veneer of civilization and reducing him to his most elemental self, a self where pain scoured him down to the bone. "Frank was your fiancé.

And you've always been admirably loyal. True blue Kate. So of course this baby is Frank's.''

He thought she flinched, but Kate wouldn't, not Kate with her eyes steady on his face, not this Kate who didn't move, no, she wouldn't flinch. He couldn't hurt her. He'd never had that power. She'd never cared enough for him to hurt her the way she'd destroyed him.

''You'll have to forgive me. A momentary lapse. That's all.'' Holding her in place with his body, he placed his other hand at her neck, his thumb resting at the base. Her skin was satin to his touch, and her pulse, belying her calmness, jumped against him. ''Tell me, was it a difficult decision, to have Frank's baby?'' He felt her swallow. ''When you wouldn't make a baby with me?''

''No, Jed, it was easy. The easiest decision I ever made.'' A drop of water slipped down her cheek, and he wondered distantly if she was crying. ''I wanted this baby. I *want* this baby,'' she corrected.

''And that's why you came to me, sweet Katherine? To help you protect Frank's child?''

''Yes. I told you I needed your help.'' She swallowed again, her throat moving under his light press as he stroked the skin.

''But you didn't tell me everything, did you?''

Her chin angled up. ''No.''

''Why not? Were you afraid I wouldn't help you?'' He brushed the dampness away from her cheek, took the final step toward her, the step that brought his body against hers. Jed knew the baby was not much more than a speck, its imperceptible movements deep in that interior, protected ocean, but he believed he felt the presence of that infant stirring as Kate's belly bumped against him. A child, but not his. The baby she'd chosen to have with Frank, not him. ''You don't think that's a little, oh, I don't know. Perhaps *duplicitous* is the word I'm looking for?''

Her hands hung at her side, but not in surrender, no, never in surrender. Not Kate. ''I didn't know where else to turn. I didn't think you would help me if you knew." No excuses, just a flat explanation of why she'd done what she'd done. Strands of wet hair slapped his hand as she turned her head away from him and then back. "Would you have?" she asked bluntly.

"You didn't give me a chance, did you? You didn't trust me to help you. You had to keep your secret, didn't you?" His heart ached, each slow thump an actual pain, as if iron bands wrapped it, squeezing tighter with each breath he took, with each beat of his wayward, breaking heart.

"It was my secret, Jed."

He paused, his hand lying still and flat on her, his thumb ceasing its restless stroking of the base of her neck. "Ah. *Your* secret. Frank didn't know? You didn't tell him either? Katherine, Katherine," he chided. "All those secrets. Must have been hard to keep them all straight. One more strain on top of everything else. So Frank didn't know you were expecting." Jed wondered why that information gave him no pleasure.

"He was killed before I found out." Her voice in the dark was weary, exhausted. "He didn't know about the baby."

"A shame." Pity fluttered the edges of his anger.

"It was, in fact." Her head rose and now he heard how deep her exhaustion was. "We both wanted this child." She took a deep breath and her breasts, her belly, her *womb*, moved against him. "Now, unless you have any more questions, Jed, I'm going to bed."

He admired her no-quarter-asked attitude. He always had, and never more than now when she was so much in the wrong. It was one of the many qualities that had drawn him to her. She wasn't going to win this battle, though. He wouldn't let her walk away unscathed this time.

"Oh, I have a lot of questions. But one more will do. For the moment. Did the ever-estimable Frank know you make the softest sounds when you come, Katherine? Did he know all your secret places, where to touch, where to kiss?" Jed ran his finger over the fine ridge of her collarbone, the fragile bone covered by all that satin-soft skin. "Did Frank's touch turn your skin to fire, Kate? Could he make you cling to him and beg for more? Could Frank do that, Kate?"

"Never ask a question unless you want to know the answer. Do you really want the truth, Jed?"

He raised his hand and flicked on the light switch. He wanted to see her face, her eyes. He wasn't going to allow her to hide in the darkness. She blinked, her pupils contracting quickly. Her eyes were clear, unafraid. She would give him the truth.

"Yeah, Katherine, I damned well do want the answer."

Her arms still hung at her sides, surprising him. "No, Frank didn't know me that way. I was a different person with him. One I liked. Frank was my anchor, Jed. He was *there*, no matter what. And I wanted to have a baby with him, to make a family with him. He was a good man, and I knew he would be a good father. He would have been, too. And I'm more sorry than I can say that he's not alive to know about his child. There's the truth for you, Jed. Make of it what you will. I don't give a damn. But I'm going to bed."

Stepping back, he flung his arms away from her, releasing her. "Sleep tight." Then, some devil lashing him, he caught her arm and pulled her back around to face him. "But you're going to dream of me tonight, Kate. Not him."

Knowing her better than she knew herself, he reined in his anger and hurt, let his mouth touch hers fleetingly, gently, as if he had nothing better to do than to explore her inch by inch. Nothing better to do in the whole wide world than to take his time giving her pleasure. She could resist passion. She couldn't resist tenderness, and he gave her tenderness in the butterfly flicker of his mouth at the corner of her eye. He gave her tenderness in the bend of his body over hers. He wrapped her in his arms, bringing her close to him. Slipping his hands under her shirt, he cupped her fanny and stroked, his thumbs gliding into the dimples on either side of her spine. She gasped, sagged into him, and as she swayed, her skin warming under his touch, he slid his hands to her belly, let them rest against the presence of the child.

Some sound escaped him, one he didn't recognize.

She grasped his wrists, stopping him. "Don't do this to yourself, Jed. I was wrong not to tell you. Causing you pain was never what I wanted. Not that, believe me. But we weren't right together."

"No? Funny. I thought we were. I liked the way we were together. In all ways. I liked coming back to you, holding you in my arms. Loving you."

"It wasn't love, Jed. You know that." Her voice was so soft, filled with an emotion that made no sense.

Scarcely hearing her, he let his palms support the imagined weight as he said, "This should have been my child, Kate, mine and yours. Nobody else's. Think about that when you fall asleep." And with that, he deepened the kiss, his tongue swooping inside her mouth, tangling with hers, anger and passion mixing and taking them both to a place where nothing mattered.

Not pain. Not the past. Only the sigh of her breath into him, the need of his body for her. For *her*.

He wanted to waltz her backward to her bed piled with pillows and thick comforters, to lay her down on those exotic sheets and make love to her slowly, sweetly, while moonlight and clouds flickered on the bare white walls of her chaste bedroom, a room where she'd surely lain with Frank. Made love with him. Created this child. Jed wanted to make her forget those moments, to erase them from her body, from her mind, from her soul.

He could.

He didn't.

Instead, not understanding what moved him, he called on every ounce of discipline at his command and lifted his head. "Now go to bed, Kate. We'll talk tomorrow." He couldn't swallow past the lump in his throat.

He walked away from her toward the pallet he'd made on the floor near the doorway into the bedroom. Standing at the doorway with his hand on the dual switch that controlled the overhead light from there or by the bathroom, he said, "I'm not leaving. I told you I'd keep you safe. I'll honor my word." He stared out into the hall, noticing the red pin dot gleam of the security system. "Nothing's changed."

It had, of course. Everything was altered, the tenuous rapport building between them shattered by the fact of the child, by the fact of Kate's lie—

No. She hadn't lied. She was right, it was her secret, none of his business, but it *felt* like a betrayal. He couldn't sort out the conflicting emotions and thoughts pulling him one way, then the other. His anger was hot, disturbing, out of control inside him, and he couldn't find the distance to lessen the corrosive pain biting through him.

Her bed creaked as she climbed onto it, the springs squeaking and rattling. He didn't turn around. He couldn't. He didn't want to see her among the pillows and sheets. Wouldn't let himself think about the sight of her there, her still-damp hair in strands on her pillow, the shape of her under those expensive sheets.

"You can turn off the light."

With a quick, impatient movement, he plunged them into darkness and crawled between the sheets of his pallet.

Her careful breathing didn't fool him. She was no more asleep than he was. Rolling onto his side, he thumped the lump of quilts beneath him, trying to find a more comfortable position.

The rustle of sheets from her side of the room was rifle-shot loud in the silence. At his insistence, Kate had turned on the air conditioner so that they wouldn't need the windows open even in the cool October night, and he was aware of the fan drone only viscerally, the drone just below hearing level.

The rhythm of her breathing altered. Bedsprings rattled. A rustle of sheets again as she turned toward him. "Jed…"

He jammed the pillow under his head. "Tomorrow, Kate. We've talked enough tonight."

"I'm sorry, Jed. I thought I had no other choice. To protect my baby."

"Yeah, well, go to sleep, Kate." He rolled over onto his other side, facing the door and the dim red glow from downstairs. He knew he wouldn't sleep, not this night. Instead, drawing on years of experience, he made his mind a blank. Emotions were dangerous. They made a man vulnerable. Lives were at stake here, and he was responsible for Kate. For her child.

He let himself drift away from the pain, drift away from the anger that he now understood came from that false sense of betrayal, drift into that white cave of consciousness where he was aware only of the physical, every sense hyper-alert and on guard.

He sensed everything. The moment when Kate's breathing slipped into the slow rhythm of deep sleep. The sudden crack of a tree branch against the side of the house as the wind blew hard toward morning.

And with every breath, the scent of Kate, of her room, that powdery, citrus fragrance that was Kate, filled him.

In the morning over dry toast and ginger ale, her face greenish-white from a round of nausea, Kate told Jed about the incidents that had led to her hiring of Patsy.

He'd made scrambled eggs for both of them, but Kate took one look, headed to the bathroom and left him to consume his eggs and bacon in solitary splendor in the shiny white kitchen. When she returned, he handed her the plate of toast without comment.

He observed her dispassionately, focused his attention on what she was saying. He could deal with the problem. He couldn't deal with his feelings. To hell with getting in touch with his softer side. To hell with sensitivity. Right now he felt about as sensitive as a grizzly bear tormented by whips. So, to do what he had to do, he stayed in a mental cave, an animal observing the wilds, preparing for the hunt.

"Start from the beginning. Tell me everything," he said.

Breaking off bits of toast and crumbling them into a pile of brown specks, Kate said, "The first time I noticed anything peculiar was on a return trip from the Port of Tampa." Scraping the bits off to one side of her saucer with the side of her finger, she didn't look at him, her concentration furrowing her forehead. "I'd gone up there to talk face-to-face with one of the captains in charge of our shipping orders. I'd been unhappy with the quality and condition of the fabrics on several of the last deliveries. I hoped if I talked the situation over with him, I could figure out what had happened."

"Why didn't Calla go with you?" Question, answer. Check out the facts. Keep the emotions locked safely away. Deal with the job at hand. "Anyway, seems like you made a big deal out of something you could have handled with a phone call."

Ordinarily she would have glared at him. That she didn't told him she was still chewing over what she intended to say to him about the way she'd handled the news of her pregnancy. Ordinarily he would have been amused.

Today he wasn't.

"Checking the shipping arrangements was my area. My job. And I like going up to the Port. I like having an excuse to get out of the office."

Jed clasped his hands together. She'd said it was her *job*. Funny, her word echoing his like that, as if their thoughts were in sync. He let that thought slide away. Dangerous to think of her now in any terms except that of client. "What was the difficulty?" He slid the blue tumbler of ginger ale in her direction.

Something in his voice caught her attention, and she shot him a glance from the corner of her eye before returning to her careful demolition of the toast. "Some of the bolts of cloth were waterlogged. I thought the packing was shoddy. Then, too, the delivery count was off. That happens. It's not a situation for major concern, but I don't like loose ends. Details are important." She sipped slowly, cautiously, from the ginger ale.

"In my line of work, too." The detail that caught his eye was that she couldn't keep her fingers still. She fidgeted, drummed them on the table, twined them together. But he didn't want to think about her feelings. If guilt nibbled at her, fine. So be it. "I have to notice the little things."

"Yes, of course." Her face paled. "Naturally."

For a second the cave vanished as he saw the tremor in her hand. Maybe she deserved to feel guilty, but she wasn't having an easy pregnancy. Ruthlessly, he resurrected his cave. "Did the ship's captain threaten you?"

Hesitating, she pressed her fingertip into the hill of toast crumbs, mashing it flat. "No, nothing so simple." She frowned. "I was running behind schedule—I know, I know. Anyway, it was late afternoon, almost evening before I left the docks. Nothing happened there to make me edgy. I took State Road 60 home, intending to pick up I-75, the way I always did. No problems for most of the way." Abruptly she stood up. Wrapping her arms around her waist, she paced from one end of the kitchen to the other. "I was almost home. There had been an accident on I-75 near the Ellenton over-pass, so I exited, planning to loop around and hit the Ellen-ton-Gillette Road. I'd noticed a car in my mirror sometime earlier." She stopped at the sink, ran the water and splashed her face.

"Why?" Jed was surprised. "It was dark. What made the car stand out?"

"The shape of the headlights. And one flickered as if it were shorting out." Running her hands over her face, she stayed at the sink, one long, bare foot resting on her knee like a flamingo. The red scratch that went from her knee down her calf, a souvenir from their exploration of Patsy's grounds, was puffy.

He pointed. "Better put some iodine on that."

"Iodine?" She rubbed the scratch.

"Betadine, then. It looks infected."

Her eyes met his, slid away. "Thanks. For mentioning it."

He cleared his throat. "No problem. Go on. What spooked you?"

"Oh, that part's easy." Her laugh came out almost as if it surprised her. "You know how that road is?"

Jed nodded. "Pastureland mostly, a few residences with long, winding driveways. Canals along the road. Yeah. Not a road I would have taken if I thought I was being followed, though."

"I didn't realize the car was following me. Not at first. Not until I noticed that it was still behind me when I passed that food storage depository. Then I started getting uncomfortable. I couldn't believe I was being followed. I kept telling myself I was overreacting."

"What did you do?"

"Almost as soon as I realized I was being trailed, the damn car passed me and slowed down in front of me on that flat stretch through the woods north of Sabal Palm. You know where I mean."

"Yeah. There's a little grass airport not far from there. No road traffic. No streetlights. A nice, lonely bit of highway. A swell spot to plan a bit of mayhem if that was what a person had in mind."

She touched the scratch on her leg, plucked at the edge of her shorts, her hands in constant motion. She didn't look at him as she muttered, "At that point, I still wasn't really spooked."

"Of course not." He let his sarcasm show, and she glanced quickly at him from under the shadows of her curling eyelashes as he continued. "You were probably ready to challenge him to a game of chicken and leave him choking on the dust from your car."

Her eyelashes lifted, and a spark of antagonism shone at him before she dropped her gaze. "I wasn't scared," she insisted. "But I was cautious."

"Of course you were. You made a clever decision to bypass the accident, found yourself out in no-man's-land with an idiot who'd apparently followed you from where? The

Port? Somewhere outside Tampa? That would be my guess. With everything that's happened since, it's not likely the jerk was picking out random women to harass. No, cookie, he was hot on your tail, and you made it easier—''

"Don't get rude—"

He glared at her.

She stopped. "Maybe I'd been followed from Tampa. I can't say how long I'd been followed. Or from where. But I went to pass, and the driver edged over toward the center, wouldn't let me by. Finally, I gunned my car and tried to pass one more time. The other car sideswiped me, forced me off the road. I was lucky I didn't hit a tree head-on. I bounced into one of the canals, halfway out and up the bank and slammed into a fence post.''

He could see impetuous, impatient Kate on that lonely slice of highway, and cold seeped over him. She'd been more vulnerable than she realized even now. That road wasn't Alligator Alley by any means, but it was as empty and long a stretch as parts of the Alley were. Anything could have happened to her out in those woods.

"Did the driver stop? Did you see the driver? Any identifying marks on the car?"

"No, no, and no. The police asked me the same thing. They took paint samples, ran them through their computers, went through all the steps. Nothing.''

She began pacing again, picking up table mats, putting them back down, touching vases, salt and pepper shakers, almost as if she needed to ground herself in the moment. With his foot he angled a chair toward her as she neared the table. Caught up in her narrative, she didn't even see the chair. She skirted it and looped around the kitchen one more time, nervous energy propelling her in erratic swoops and glides.

Watching the pale flash of her legs, the flex of muscle and sinew, he rocked back and balanced in his own chair. She was too thin. Too strung out. All this tension and exhaustion couldn't be good for her or the— His chair legs smacked against the floor. He laid his hands flat on the cool surface of her table. "Okay. What did the police do?"

"I'd called for help on my cell phone. Thank heavens I'd charged the battery, or I'd have been sitting out there for heaven knows how long in the dark. Anyway, a couple of weeks later, the police found an '87 automobile abandoned near the old dolomite pits near the new civic center. The paint samples matched. The car had been reported stolen. No fingerprints matched through AFIS. No leads. Dead end. I didn't think too much about it myself. I mean, I just figured I was in the wrong place at the wrong time. It happens." She shrugged, and the lift of her shoulders under her T-shirt was almost unbearably moving, the narrow shoulders rising as if nothing more than her will lifted them.

He studied his hands where they rested on the table, rubbed his thumb along the thin white line of an old scar that curved from the back of his hand over the wrist and into the base of his palm. "The police report I looked at yesterday said you'd reported two other incidents before the murders. What happened?"

"A week or two afterward…I don't even remember clearly anymore—" she rubbed her forehead "—I was running along the beach just before sunrise. Fog had rolled in and you really couldn't see much. Shapes. Everything gray. Blurry." She rolled the hem of her shirt around her hand. "For a few minutes I thought someone was following me, and I started running faster, but the other person's pace picked up, too. That quiet thump, thump of his shoes on the sand unnerved me. I started looking around me for anything to use in case— Well. In case."

"The report said you weren't attacked." He unclenched the fist he'd formed unbeknownst to himself as he listened to her story. "Nothing happened. Right? Or did you leave some facts out?"

"I told the police everything. I'd scooped up a handful of sand. I thought it was better than nothing if I needed a distraction, but a group of early-morning shell hunters came out of the gray. Somehow the runner following me vanished into the fog. I wondered for a while if he'd been one of the shellers who'd wandered off on his own and then rejoined the group.''

''You sure couldn't be accused of rampant paranoia. Sheesh. I would have thought the first incident would have been enough. Much less the attempted break-in here off your patio. I don't have to tell you how similar that incident was to the entry at Patsy's, Kate.''

''Up to then, the whole situation seemed too bizarre. Too dramatic. I mean, why would anyone follow me? What would be the point?''

''Ah,'' he said quietly, ''that's the point, isn't it? Because we know someone *has* targeted you. We don't know why, and the *why* is the key.''

''I hired Patsy after the attempted break-in here, but I have to tell you that some part of me doesn't want to know the who or the why.''

''We've been over this, Kate. You have to do this.''

She wrapped her arms around herself, and her shirt stretched tight over the soft slope of her breasts, pressing her nipples flat. ''I'm absolutely terrified by the idea that I'll look into the eyes of someone I know, someone I love, and discover a murderer looking back at me. I dream sometimes about faces with no eyes, no mouth, blank masks. And then a hand reaches up to remove the mask, and I wake up. I never stay asleep, even when I can sleep, long enough to see that face. I don't want to, not really.''

Jed didn't want to hear the plaintive softness in her voice, didn't want to see the droop of her shoulders. He glanced out the window where sunlight splashed across her terraced patio.

In the months to come, she would sit out there, her belly round and firm, her eyes sleepy with feminine knowledge. And he would be... Where? Still at The Last Resort? Sweating in some unnamed jungle again? Wherever, he would be alone. As he'd been all his life.

He tipped the chair in her direction. "Sit down, Kate. You're worn out. You didn't sleep much last night either."

"How could I?" She sank down, bowed her head in her hands for a second. Then, abruptly, she shoved away from the table. The chair clattered behind her as she stood. Her eyes filled with misery, her mouth soft and pink, she looked at him. "Jed, forgive me. Please. I should have told you."

He rose slowly, like an old man, carefully uncoiling his length from the chair. "Yeah, Kate, you should have. But you didn't. And now you want me to forgive you? You ask for a lot."

He saw the lift and billow of her hair as she nodded, and a faint scent, mint and citrus and *her,* drifted to him, the scent of Kate. He remembered it from the night before, from years gone by.

In that moment he wondered if he'd ever forget that elusive fragrance.

# Chapter 12

"Oops. Hey, there. You surprised me." Calla's orange-and-pink caftan billowed as she whirled to face Jed and Kate, a sheaf of papers in her hand. Her bright cheerfulness and sideways glance at Kate set Jed's teeth on edge. He was in no mood to humor Calla today.

"Did we?" Jed held open the door to Kate's office.

By his side, Kate bumped into him, her chin smacking against his outstretched arm. "Sorry, Calla. I didn't mean to startle you. The door was closed. I wasn't expecting to see you in my office."

"I didn't hear you in the reception area." Calla's breathy explanation grated against Jed's raw nerves, though for the life of him, he couldn't have explained why the woman's cheerfulness was making him long to strangle her. Calla laid one hand over her heart. "Gosh, you gave me such a start."

"I can see we did." With an all-encompassing glance, Jed skimmed Kate's office as she brushed by him to sit in her desk chair.

Fanning her flushed face with her hand, Calla said, "How nice of you, to chauffeur Kate to work."

"Yeah, well, I'm a hell of a nice fella."

"Oh. I…" Orange and pink blazed a sunset in the corner of the room as Calla drifted toward the door, the sheaf of papers still clutched in her hand and lost in the folds of her brilliantly colored caftan. "Kate, when you have a chance, I'd like to talk with you about some of the bills. I think we can cut a couple of corners on the reproduction costs and grow our profits a bit."

"Do you want to go over the bills now?"

More a perception than anything, Jed sensed the look Calla sent his way, her hesitation before she spoke. "No. Later will be fine."

Making a note to ask Kate if she was missing any papers, Jed strode to the window with its view of the parking lot below. Anyone looking out this window could have seen Kate and him last night. Could have seen the hunger in the way he held her to him, the passion between them.

"Whenever you have the time, Kate, all right? But soon?" Backward and forward, the furls of pink-orange moved through his peripheral vision.

"I may not have another chance for a few days, Calla. Jed's visiting with me this week." Kate spoke in the same flat voice she'd used since what had passed for breakfast. "In fact, I won't be in the office long today, and I'm booked fairly tightly for the rest of the week. In fact, Jed's going with me while I pitch our fabric line to that new boutique on Palmetto Key, and then we're headed over to Bonne Fete's headquarters."

"Really?" Calla stopped at the doorway, eagerness lighting up her round face. She slid her glasses back up her nose, hesitated. "Another surprise, Kate? I didn't know you'd talked with them."

"Briefly. A couple of weeks ago." Kate's fingers flew across the stacks of papers on her desk, sorting them by instinct. "I have an appointment with the chief buyer and

Bonne Fete's design crew. With their stores in Orlando and Miami, Bonne Fete is a terrific opportunity for us. If their designers take us on, we could double our business by next year.''

In the brief glance he spared her, Jed caught Calla's puzzled look, the air of relief quickly suppressed. ''Really?''

Kate nodded.

''That would be wonderful. I like the sound of higher profits. You do, too, I'm sure,'' Calla added hastily. ''After all, that's been our five-year goal. But I didn't know Bonne Fete was interested. That would really put Bowen and March on the map.''

''I hadn't mentioned it to you yet. I wanted the accountants to run the numbers first. I didn't want to get your hopes up and then have everything fall apart.''

Even under the circumstances, Jed admired the smoothness of Kate's lie. Or maybe she was telling the truth. Hell, how was he supposed to know? She'd pulled the wool over his eyes. Why wouldn't she feed Calla a line, too? He jammed his hands into his pockets irritably and listened to nuances, read body language as Kate and Calla continued.

''By the way, have you seen the cost estimates for the Guatemalan fabrics? I wanted to review them.''

''Here.'' Calla thrust out the papers in her hand. ''I'd pulled them to go over the numbers myself. Great minds run in the same channels, right?''

''Right.'' Kate tapped the edges of the papers on her desk, glanced at them and then returned them to Calla. ''But don't let me interrupt. You go ahead with whatever you were working on.''

Calla fanned herself with the papers but didn't leave. ''Is everything all right, Kate?''

Kate flashed a smile. ''Sure. Don't worry about me, Calla. I'm back in the saddle and ready to carry my share of the load again. Anything happen between yesterday and now that I need to deal with?''

"Not really. We ran short on another shipment, though. This month's delivery from Haiti."

"I'll take care of it."

"Sure. If you want to. Or I can."

"Calla, I said I'd take care of it." Soft but firm, Kate's answer closed the subject.

Bracing his shoulders against the wall, Jed studied Calla. Clearly Kate's abrupt manner was unexpected. He thought Calla looked hurt. And something else. Uneasy?

"I guess I'd better get back to work. Since you're tied up, this isn't a good time to visit."

Kate whirled her chair around and sprang out, covering the distance to Calla with several quick steps. Hugging her, Kate said, "Calla, just ignore me, okay? I'm cranky and tired and in a funk. Leftover flu symptoms, probably. Don't take it personally."

"Of course not." Calla's smile wavered for a second. "I was taken aback that you hadn't told me about the Bonne Fete deal. But it doesn't matter," she said, floating to the door in streamers of orange and pink. "It's a wonderful opportunity. It's just, um, usually we do the pitches together."

"I know," Kate said gently. "This fell in my lap so fast."

"Sure." Calla paused. "Nice seeing you again, Jed."

Still studying her, he nodded. "Absolutely."

When Calla shut the door quietly behind her, he sat down in Kate's chair and picked up an unusual piece of silky material. "Nice." He let the sample slide against his arm.

"It's a Philippine fabric, made from banana leaves."

"Banana leaves. Hemp. Guess you can make anything wearable." Playing with the swatch, he thought for a moment. "So, Kate. What was that conversation with Calla really about?"

She took the swatch from him, dropped it into the basket beside her desk. Settling on the edge of her desk, she looked down at him. "Simply doing what you asked, Jed. Checking out my friends. Making sure Calla wasn't sneaking off with some secret business papers. Perhaps she was figuring out a way to embezzle from the business. Oh, and, you know, seeing how my best friend stacks up as a potential murderer. That's all. Routine stuff.'' She shifted, and the skirt of her suit, the color of a vintage port, rippled in the light.

''How much of what you told her was the truth, Kate?''

''All of it, of course.'' She smiled cheerfully, with a brightness to rival Calla's.

The weariness in her eyes betrayed her effort, and Jed could see now what he'd missed the first day she'd sought him out, the lines raying out from her eyes, the strain he'd misread as confidence. ''You had those appointments all set up?''

Amusement lent a sparkle that momentarily vanquished the weariness. ''Why, Jed, you didn't think I was lying through my teeth, did you?''

''The thought crossed my mind.'' He flipped through one of the stacks of papers piled on her desk. Consignment lists, shipping dates, fabric attached to sketches. ''Do you have to see those people today?''

''Why?'' The burgundy fabric shimmered with her movement as she stood up, shoulders back, spine straight.

''I want to head out to The Last Resort and check with Ben. Run some things by him.''

Her eyes darkened, and she nodded. ''All right. I'll call and reschedule for next week. Whatever you say.''

''I like this new attitude. Such a delightful change, this agreeableness.'' He knew he was being a bastard, knew it and couldn't stop himself. Worse, didn't want to. For the first time in his life he couldn't seem to stay in his assigned role as the hired gun. He swung his feet to the floor. ''Can you pull the shipping files, your supplier lists and your account deposit statements and bills for the last five months? And employee records. Especially anyone you've fired.''

''People I've fired?'' Her face tightened.

''Yes, Kate. Anyone you've fired within the last year. Any employee anywhere along the line who might have reason to hold a grudge against you or your business. Save those records to a disk or let me have hard copies. I'm going to have Ben run through them and see if anything hinky pops up.''

"Give me an hour." Kate motioned to the couch. "Make yourself at home. Amuse yourself."

"I will." He stretched out on the couch and shaded his eyes, watching her. "Take your time. Ben and the Bonne Fete guys can wait."

Retreating into stillness, he watched her as she opened the files on her computer. For a while the occasional click of the keyboard, the whir of the computer hard drive and the muted hum of voices outside her office cocooned them. Copying files and moving through spreadsheets, she worked smoothly and quickly, occasionally throwing him a sideways glance.

He knew the minute she forgot he was there. Her shoulders slumped, she sighed and massaged her back. A small sound escaped her as she twisted in her chair and kneaded her lower back. Eyes shut, she rested her forehead on the rim of the computer monitor.

This was the Kate behind the expensive clothes and don't-mess-with-me bravado, the Kate he'd glimpsed yesterday. Frightened and overwhelmed and hiding her terror for all she was worth.

Kate, terrified and pregnant.

And alone.

He sat up suddenly, his shoes banging on the floor. "Done?"

Her head snapped up. She reached for the mouse, clicked it. "Almost. Another fifteen minutes."

She was finished in ten. Dumping the disks and files into one of the baskets on the floor, she covered them with fabric swatches, shooting him a troubled glance as she did. "I don't like this—"

"Deception?" he drawled, watching her as her face flushed. "You don't like deception? Now there's a surprise, Kate, darlin'."

Scooping up her purse, she marched ahead of him to her door and opened it, letting it slam back toward the wall. It would have smacked him in the face if he hadn't reacted first, catching the edge of the door. "I'm not in the mood for games, Kate."

Her hand rested above his near the glass pane. "Guess what, Jed? Neither am I. I've told you I'm sorry for what I did. I don't know what else to do, to say. If I could change the last few days, if I could make things right—"

"Some things can't be made right, Kate. Can't be fixed." Looking down into her face, which seemed even thinner and paler than two days ago, he found himself reaching out to smooth away the lines in her forehead. He let his hand drop. "You came to me to do a job. Let's get on with it."

"Are we going to talk about this?" Kate placed her hand lightly against her belly.

"No, Kate. I don't believe we are. That's personal. And I'm merely working a job. You did what you thought you had to. Nope, sugar-plum, I truly don't believe there's anything else to be said on that subject." Carefully taking her elbow, he ushered her out of the office, throwing Calla a genial smile as he shut the door behind them. "But you haven't told me yet how you and Calla structured the ownership of your business. Why don't you amuse me by telling me what happens to the business if you die? Suddenly or otherwise?"

"It's fairly simple," she said tiredly. "We're partners. Everything is divided equally. We have an insurance policy on the firm. It's an executive life/key man life insurance policy."

"The policy covers each partner's contributions if the other dies?" He didn't see how Calla could benefit, not really. But there had to be an angle. "The surviving partner does what?"

"The policy is structured so that if I died, for instance, the policy would yield proceeds that would enable Calla to buy my portion of the business. She would have the first option to buy out my portion. Or vice versa. The premiums are paid out of the business accounts, not personally. And Calla could use the benefits only to purchase my half of the firm. Mom and Sissy wouldn't receive the proceeds of the executive life policy. Oh, they'd inherit what was left of my estate after all the firm's bills were paid, but right now that wouldn't amount to much. I have a small personal insurance policy, and Sissy and Mom are the beneficiaries, of course. But, again, Jed, even if I adopt your point of view and look at all these people as bloodthirsty sharks, I'm worth much more to them alive than dead."

"No hidden offshore accounts?"

"Are you serious?" She rolled her eyes. "Oh, sure. I have buckets of money parked in the Bahamas. No, Jed, I don't cheat. I don't lie on my income taxes. I'm about as straight-arrow as they come. Come on, Jed, you know me better than that."

"No, Kate, I don't. I don't think I know you at all." He meant the words to sting.

"You're getting perilously close to my personal line in the sand, Jed," she said quietly. "I know I was wrong, but you only get so many shots at me."

After that he didn't ask any more questions, retreating once more to the safety of silence.

In the absence of his questions, Kate slept the rest of the way to The Last Resort, her head resting in the gap between the seat and the window. Stopped at a red light, he managed to ease his wrinkled jacket under her head without waking her.

When he braked at the back entrance to The Last Resort, Sparks was standing in the frame of the door, looking out, Booger draping over his feet as Jed stepped out of the Blazer.

"Huh. What's a body to think when another body don't call? Don't show up all night? A body might worry."

"And a body might have plans of his own that some nosy body shouldn't concern himself with," Jed said, stooping to scratch Booger's floppy ears.

"Folks worry." Sparks slowly retrieved the ever-present cigarette from behind his ear, rotated it between his fingers. "Oh, hey there," he said as Kate walked into view.

"Hey yourself, Mr. McGarrity." Her cheek was sleep-creased and pink, vulnerable.

Jed looked away.

"Sparks'll do, Ms. Kate. You and this scoundrel goin' to have lunch here?"

"I'm...not sure." Kate tried to catch Jed's eye, but he deliberately fixed his attention on Sparks.

"I want Ben to work on something. Is he up yet? Or did he spend all night playing cyber-spy again?" Jed turned to Kate. "Ben's a real smart kid. Too smart for his own good."

"Why?" She glanced from Jed to Sparks and back.

Sparks's chuckle was phlegmy. "Oh, young Ben's kind of an inquisitive youngster. He doesn't like secrets."

Jed rescued Kate. "What Sparks means is that Ben Jones is a computer hacker. His curiosity landed him in prison for a few years."

Bewildered, Kate looked back to Sparks. "Prison?"

Sparks fired a match and puffed on his cigarette. "Yep. Me, too, Ms. Kate. Arson." His slitted eyes watched her absorb the information, and, amused in spite of everything, Jed waited to see how fastidious, play-by-the-rules Kate would react.

She blinked twice, smiled and said, "Thus your nickname?"

"My family and friends used to call me Jimmy Jack McGarrity. Before I took to my line of work. But I'm no pyromaniac, Ms. Kate. I didn't burn down buildings for fun."

"No." Jed choked back a cough as Kate's eyes widened. "Sparks was a very careful worker. A career man, you could say. He made sure no one was ever hurt when he torched a building."

"Damn straight," Sparks said proudly. "When I did a job, I did it right. I gave a dollar's work for a dollar paid. I had my principles. The insurance companies took a hit, and I know that was wrong, but hell's bells, I paid my debt to society. Even took to reading the Bible in prison. Anyways, I figured I was doing my bit in a way to clean up some blighted areas. But I've retired from that line of work," he concluded with a nod of satisfaction. "Working in the service industry now."

"The prosecution concluded Sparks was a menace to society, a professional arsonist, but Sparks envisioned himself as an urban environmentalist," Jed said solemnly. "Clearing out abandoned buildings. Making way for new growth and construction."

"Ah." Kate nodded. "Improving the scenery, so to speak."

"Exactly." Sparks nodded and blew a blue vapor skyward. "I knew you'd understand. Anyways, like I said, I'm a Bible thumper now, and I invest regularly in my 401K."

"I see." Kate shifted, and a genuine smile spread across her face, piercing Jed's heart.

When had she last smiled like that at him?

"Planning for your future, are you?"

From behind a wreath of smoke, Sparks grinned back at her.

Watching both of them, Jed felt the band around his heart squeeze even tighter. On the outside, looking in once more, he was the dog at the campfire, prowling near the warmth in the dark, edging close, but always outside that bright circle.

For a while Kate had made him believe that he could come in from the cold and warm himself at her fire.

"So where's Ben?" he asked gruffly.

"Got a burr under your saddle?" Sparks tamped the cigarette out, shredded it and placed it carefully in his pocket. "Go on in and give a holler. He'll show up. He's probably upstairs in his room."

Jed hollered.

Kate wondered for a moment if she'd fallen down the rabbit hole.

A bushy-haired, round-faced man, not much more than a teenager, surely, opened a window at the back of the building and peered out sleepily at them.

"Come on up, Jed. I bought a new toy. It's way cool. Hey, Ms. March."

"How does he know who I am?" She addressed her question to Sparks since Jed had already headed for the porch.

"Ben has his ways. He probably knows how much you spent on your last vacation." Sparks coughed. "Around here we try to ignore Ben's little idiosyncrasies."

"I don't blame you in the least." Kate frowned. She'd seen enough television shows on what kinds of tracks people left through credit cards, catalog orders, even grocery store purchases that she believed Sparks.

Young Ben probably did have his ways. The thought disturbed her. Ben could be useful in their search for a motive linked to her business, but she felt uncomfortably like a Peeping Tom.

Leaving the warm sunlight behind, they entered the dim coolness of The Last Resort.

"Back here." Picking his way through a warren of small rooms and storage areas, Jed led her to a back stairway leading upstairs. Still carefully keeping his distance from her, he pointed in the direction of the room in the middle of a dark hall made narrow by boxes of computer manuals and computer parts. "Ben's not the neatest camper," Jed said sourly as Kate bumped into a stack of cardboard cartons.

A blinding-white smile appeared on the round face of the young man waiting for them. The shape of his face and the blue-black of his hair hinted at Seminole blood. "Neat? No way. Waste of time and energy to put everything away and then drag it right back out. Besides, you never know when you might have a need for something, so I save." He waved his arm exuberantly. "Y'all have to see this."

Kate was willing. She was able. She just couldn't figure out where to step. The room was packed floor to ceiling with electronic gadgets, gizmos and God-only-knew-whats. A tangle of cords spiderwebbed across the floor and in back of monitors, scanners and printers. Books and magazines walled the mat on the floor, and a large, very expensive leather chair held the place of honor in front of a computer screen with mermaids singing a ribald sea chantey.

"This way." Shoehorning a path, Jed went in front of her. "Ben, I'm not kidding. This is dangerous. Either you clean it up, or I'll bring in the backhoe. I'm giving you two days. Tops."

Ben looked blankly at the room. "But I know where everything is, Jed." With a wave, he encompassed the room. "It's organized. Really."

"It's a firetrap, that's what it is." Jed shoved aside a stack of magazines so that Kate had a place to stand. Pages fluttered. "Two days, Ben."

"Okay, you're the boss."

To her side, Kate thought Jed turned her way, but then Ben elbowed a place on the L-shaped desk that filled one wall and part of the next. "See?" He pointed proudly to an object that meant nothing to Kate. Rectangular and gray, its cords drooped from it to one of the computer terminals. "I can do some power-hopping now with this baby. It'll add juice to the system."

Jed pivoted toward her, and dust particles whirlpooled in the air. "All this is Ben's creation. He raids old computers. Puts together bits and pieces of electronic gear and comes up with machines that virtually think for themselves."

"Someday machines will think," Ben said darkly. "Wait and see where you are then, Jed." Ben rubbed his chin. "I can't make Jed understand that he's a dinosaur. He has to learn about computers, and he won't."

"I reckon I'm doomed to the tar pits." Jed laid a hand on Ben's shoulder as Ben headed for a laptop computer Kate had only just noticed. "Hold on, cowboy. I need your help. *We* need your help. Kate's had some business problems—" Jed scowled at her as she started to speak, and Kate clamped her lips together "—and I want you to work your magic on these copies of her records. See if you notice any peculiar patterns, any figures that look doctored or not what they should be. And I'm going to give you a list of people to run through your databases. I'm interested in any financial short-ages, any unusual expenses. Anything that stands out. You know.''

"I want to see that list, Jed." Kate held out her hand, and looked at the sheet of paper with the names handwritten in Jed's angular scrawl. "My *mother?* Sissy? Mom's gentleman friend? She's only recently met him. Why on earth would you have his name down here?" Kate's stomach knotted. Jed had listed everyone she'd mentioned to him. "You even have Calla's ex-husband on this list. *Hal?* And Sissy's boyfriend as well? I've met him once, maybe twice." She'd heard him say everyone was a suspect, but seeing the names written out and understanding what Ben was about to do, she was ap-palled.

Jed remained silent, watching her. Finally he shrugged and said, "Everybody has a motive. That's what we're trying to identify. Remember? Cui bono.''

"And as I've said several times, not one of the persons on this list derives any good from my death."

"Whoa, mama!" Ben swiveled to face them. "I don't like the sound of this conversation. What's up, man?"

"What's up, Ben," Jed said slowly and clearly, "is that Kate's fiancé and a private detective were murdered. The police are sympathetic but unable to move forward with the information they have. Kate hired me to investigate further. Because of my—" he shot her an enigmatic glance "—spe-cial skills."

Ben shook his head. "This isn't good. No wonder you came to me. I won't let you down, boss. Promise."

Avoiding Kate's eyes, Jed punched Ben in the shoulder. "I know you won't. But don't leave any tracks in your cy-berworld, okay?"

"You underestimate me, Jed." Ben's expression turned endearingly earnest. "I owe you. Big time. Don't worry." His grin was lopsided as he gave Kate a sly look. "I'll use *my* special skills. Jed may be the brawn, but I'm the brains of this operation, no matter what he pretends."

"Smart aleck."

"Dinosaur." Ben winked at Kate.

His goofiness charmed her. "Thanks for your help." Following Jed's lead, she rapped her knuckles against Ben's shaggy head. "We'll go out to dinner when this is all over. My treat."

"I like pizza."

"I thought something fancy?"

"Hard to beat pizza. Have to dress up for fancy restaurants. We could order pizza with lots of garlic, we could sit out on the porch in our jeans, and Booger could keep us company."

"Pizza it is," Jed said. "Go to work, Ben, and be careful with the disks."

Ben rolled his eyes. "You're talking to the master, Jed. Like I'd accidentally erase a disk. Ha. You would, but not me. Now go away and let me work my magic."

"Boss?" Kate trailed her hand over the worn banister on the way down the steep stairs. "You own this place, don't you, Jed?" She'd caught his discomfort as Ben called him boss, and had decided it wasn't merely a title of respect.

"Yeah." In front of her, he stopped and turned to look at her. "And, yeah, Ben, Sparks and Tuba Tony are all ex-cons. You uncomfortable with that, Katherine?"

"Are *you?*" she shot back. "Because the way I see it, Jed, you're the one sleeping here, living here, intertwining your life with theirs. If you're not *uncomfortable,* why on earth would I be? Do you think so little of me that you'd imagine I'd hold their mistakes against them when they're so clearly working their rear ends off to earn your respect?"

Expressionlessly, he stared back at her. "You're pissed."

"Yes, Jed, I think I am. I told you you were getting awfully close to my line in the sand, and I think you just crossed it. Give me some credit for decency and humanity, will you? Even though I've been unforgivably cruel to you?"

In the gloom of the stairwell, Kate couldn't see his expression. "Now let me by, and I'll go visit with your other ex-con while you play investigator. Frankly I prefer his company to yours right now.''

Jed took a step upward, his face dark and unreadable. ''Do you?''

She nodded once, hard. ''Sparks is straightforward. Uncomplicated. No games. His company appeals to me right now. Yours doesn't.''

''By all means, go. I'm not keeping you.''

''Then don't take up all the room on the staircase.''

An edgy energy pulsed from him, and for a second she thought he might not move, might confront her and they would finally talk about her pregnancy. She wanted him to challenge her, wanted him to rip loose from the tight rein he held on his control. Anything was preferable to this cold politeness.

But then, very carefully, his eyes never leaving hers, Jed backed to the wall. ''Pass.''

Kate turned sideways and squeezed past him. At the bottom, though, she turned to look at him. He hadn't moved. One foot still resting on the step where she'd stood, his hand on the banister, he filled the stairwell with his presence.

He'd made this chintzy restaurant/bar his. He'd brought these outcasts of society here and given them work. He cared about them and had given them part of himself.

Given them a home. Created a home and family for himself whether he realized it or not.

The Jed she'd known three years ago had lived in cheap motels, staying only long enough to turn her world upside down before heading out again to save the world, or at least some small part of it. That Jed had never needed a home. Had never wanted one.

Or had he, and she hadn't known? Hadn't been able to see past the soldier to the man? Had his choice of occupation reminded her too much of her father?

Thoughtfully, she walked outside and found Sparks leaning against the rail along the porch. His glance was inquisitive, but he didn't say anything.

"Ben's working on the papers we brought." Like Sparks, Kate leaned forward onto the railing, looking out at the parking area and the trees beyond. "You know he's looking for reasons why someone might be trying to kill me, don't you?"

"Anything there to find, he'll locate it. The boy's damned smart."

"He's lonely."

"I know. But he wouldn't admit it. Not even to himself."

The shrewd look in the old man's eyes made Kate wonder if, indeed, they were both talking about Ben.

"Nobody has to be alone unless he chooses to be." She picked at a splinter along the railing. "We make our choices. We have to live with them."

"That so?"

"Isn't that what you did, Mr. McGarrity?"

"Sparks," he reminded her.

"You lived with the consequences of your choices. You served your time in jail. But then you changed. You chose a different kind of life."

"Yep. But I had help. I kept butting my head up against the same old wall and getting a headache. I didn't know no other way."

"What made the difference for you?"

"My parole officer hooked me up with Jed, said he was looking for some help at this little Podunk restaurant and was hiring ex-cons. Said Jed might give me a chance. I showed up, Jed asked me two questions and then hired me. That was that."

"What did he ask you?" Kate couldn't imagine what one question cynical, mistrustful Jed could have asked that would have caused him to hire Sparks. Jed's mantra was trust no one, and he'd let no one past his guard, not even her.

But he'd given Sparks, Ben and Tuba Tony jobs, given them hope.

Sparks tapped the railing. "He asked me why I'd never gotten married. Not real politically correct, but I answered him. 'Mr. Stone,' I said, 'I never found anybody I loved enough to lay down my life for, so I didn't see any reason to put my name on a piece of paper.' Jed laughed, and then he said, 'You tired of living on the run, McGarrity? Or do you still get a rush from being an outlaw?' I looked him straight in the eyes and replied, 'Hell, yes, I like the rush. But I'm getting too old to sleep on park benches.' He laughed again, and that was that. Like I said, he hired me and I started work that afternoon. Three months later he offered to let me buy half of The Last Resort with sweat equity. I did, and we've been partners ever since. Even-Steven. And, yes, Ms. Kate, I'd lay down my life for him. Not that he'd ask. But I would, and I'd count it a small price.''

She didn't know how to reply to the old man's declaration. Jed had gambled on Sparks. She lifted her chin and let the light breeze touch her face. Or was it the other way around? The idea worked its way into her consciousness. Had Sparks taken the gamble on Jed that she'd never had the courage to? The idea made her heart lurch. "Jed's very lucky."

"Nope. I'm the lucky one. You see, people can get so used to walking down the same path that they don't see there's another road. Unless somebody hands them a map. Or points out a signpost.''

"I don't know, Sparks. I think most of us make our choices subconsciously and they reflect what we want at our deepest level.'' That was what Jed had done. His behavior had made his choice clear a hundred times. He hadn't wanted roots, stability. Only when he thought he'd lose her, had he offered everything she wanted. An empty promise because it wasn't his choice. Not meaning to, not wanting to, she'd boxed him in. A choice made under those conditions sure couldn't be considered a free choice. Not in her book. Staring somberly at the ground, she laughed awkwardly and returned her attention to Sparks. "Deep thoughts for such a beautiful afternoon. Let's change the subject.''

"And what do you want, Ms. Kate? What kind of bad choices you been making to put such a sad look on your pretty face?''

Startled, she looked up, looked past Sparks right into Jed's shuttered gray eyes.

''Interesting question, Kate. I'd like to hear your answer, too.''

# *Chapter 13*

"I can't think of a single, solitary choice I regret." Meaning every word, Kate stared Jed straight in the eyes. "I'm sorry for some of the consequences of decisions I made. And sure, I made some dumb decisions as a result of ignorance, lack of experience, youth, but given the same circumstances, I'd make those same dumb choices again. Can you say the same, Jed?"

Sparks cleared his throat, murmured "See ya" and vanished, leaving Jed and Kate alone in the sunshine.

When Jed didn't respond, she brushed her hands together briskly, trying to ignore the tiny hurt of his silence. "Well, so much for philosophy," she said.

"'Adversity's sweet milk, philosophy.'" As she frowned, he added, *"Romeo and Juliet."*

"Poetry now?" From her point of view, his quote seemed one more way of achieving distance between them, of not talking about the elephant in the living room.

"Why not?" Dropping the duffel bag he carried, he looked back at the restaurant as though he wished Sparks were back with them, a buffer. "Good old Will had a way with words. And he's right. Having a construct to plug life's ups and downs into does help make a little sense out of all the random, meaningless stuff coming down on us. So good for you, Kate, if you can look at your life and not feel regrets. That makes you damned unusual in my book, that's for sure."

So much for her assumption that he was using his quote to keep her at arm's length. Any distance was effectively made nonexistent by the acid in his low tone.

"You have regrets? Things you'd change?" Tentatively, testing the water, she tiptoed in.

Chilly gray eyes held hers. "Not a damned one, sugarplum. Like you, I'm just happy as a pig in mud with my life."

Kate swallowed. "Of course."

What had she wanted him to say, anyway? That given a second chance he'd be a different man? That he wouldn't have let her walk away from him three years ago? That he would have tried to change, to become the man she believed she needed? And if he had, if he'd been different, would she have loved him as desperately, as hopelessly?

No, she'd loved him for his flaws as well as his charms. And, ultimately, was it his fault that she'd needed something from him he wasn't able to give? He was what he was, a man of action and danger, while she was who she was, a woman who needed routine and stability, all the boring, tedious elements of domesticity that would have made Jed feel like a caged animal. A white picket fence kind of woman, she'd been the wrong woman for him as much as he'd been the wrong man for her.

Too bad for her that being with him had felt so right, so perfect.

Perfect as long as she hadn't looked too far into the future. The inevitable end was present the first day they met.

That, of course, was the tragedy, the loss.

They'd never had a chance with each other. Both of them

so dratted stubborn and unyielding, it was a wonder they'd lasted as long as they had.

In the heat of battle, as her father would have said, all the submerged yearning of those lost days was bubbling up, but it didn't mean anything.

People were who they were. They didn't change. Her throat closed with regret, regret for what could never have been, could never be.

So close to heaven, so near, and the gate slamming in her face.

Booger ambled in her direction, collapsed with a huff onto her feet, and Jed stooped to tug at the animal's ears. "Good dog."

As Jed rubbed the dog's belly, his long fingers tangling in the matted fur with such tenderness, tears came to Kate's eyes. She looked off in the distance so that Jed wouldn't see the shine of tears. "How's Ben coming with his Net surfing?"

"He'll be a while. You gave him a lot of files. After you left, he muttered something that sounded like 'Go away, leave me alone until tomorrow.'"

"Are we?" She cleared her throat, hating the weepiness that was so foreign to her nature. "Going to leave him alone, that is?" She sensed Jed's abrupt glance in her direction.

He spoke slowly, his attention split between her and the dog. "Might as well. Ben has his job. Neither of us can help him. We're through here." As Jed scratched Booger's belly, the dog moaned, a ululation of bliss. "You okay, Kate?"

"Of course." She widened her eyes, fighting the sting that wouldn't go away. Pregnancy hormones, that was all. And she'd be damned if she'd let him see how close she was to dropping in a heap on the porch and squalling simply because he was sending a droopy-eared hound dog into ecstasy with nothing more than a touch. When she was sure Jed's attention was completely on the delighted hound, she half turned toward him. Afraid that he would ask more questions, afraid that in her drizzly mood she would disgrace herself with tears, she didn't meet his sideways glance.

She rubbed her nose. "All right. What are we going to do? Where are we going?" She didn't want to go back to the office, and she sure as heck didn't want to stay enclosed inside her house with Jed in his austere, businesslike mode. He'd push, she'd react, and if she cried in front of him, she'd never forgive herself.

Continuing to torment Booger into squirming delight, Jed said, "There's enough to do. I want to take the piece of glass to some local optometrists. I thought I'd give another sweep through your office and your house to double-check for bugging devices. Patsy might have missed something."

"I suppose I shouldn't be surprised, should I? You can't let yourself trust that she handled her job competently, can you?" Defensive on behalf of her friend who could no longer defend herself, Kate couldn't help the sharpness that escaped.

"I trust myself. After all, I only talked with her for an hour or so. Why would I trust her? She hadn't proven herself to me. Somewhere along the line she made a mistake that got her killed. Of course I'm going to do the job myself and not depend on what someone else did or didn't do. At the very least, Katherine, you ought to know that about me." Shrugging, he looked at Kate as if he scarcely knew her, as if he'd never made love with her, as if there were nothing but business between them.

His studied coldness betrayed him, though.

No matter what he pretended, she'd hurt him, badly.

Even so, even being in the wrong, she'd reached the end of her tolerance. She'd made the awful decision to keep her pregnancy a secret from him. As a result, she'd done Jed a grievous injury. She couldn't change that.

She'd acted to protect that tiny scrap of life. She would make the same decision again. She owed this child protection, safety. Security.

She couldn't defend her actions, couldn't excuse them. An

apology would never cover the enormity of the choice she'd made.

But she wouldn't endure Jed's insistence on avoiding the subject they were going to have to face, on keeping her at his distance that reduced her to nothingness.

Regardless of the fact that a murderer was lurking in every shadow, in every face she looked at, she couldn't, wouldn't, go another twenty-four hours like this, with this politeness between them that chilled her to the marrow of her bones.

He didn't like to talk about difficult subjects, about his feelings. That had been the source of the uneasiness she'd always felt with him, the core of their problems. Her problems, anyway, because she'd needed more from him than mind-numbing passion. But that was all he'd given her, their time together like Brigadoon, a magical place that disappeared when they left the protection of its boundaries.

And if she still yearned for that breathless wonder, well, she was learning to live in an everyday world where magic was merely a myth. Frank had taught her that much. Her obligation to his child, *their* child, had forced her decision concerning Jed.

So, one way or the other, Jedidiah Stone was going to talk with her. Today. Tonight. But not a minute later. Enough was enough. He wasn't going to raise the drawbridge and retreat.

"You ready?" Jed stood up, leaving Booger in doggy paradise on the porch, legs splayed to the sides and tongue lolling happily and damply on the boards.

"Sure. Let me say so long to Ben and Sparks." Pride made her avert her face as she walked past him.

Entering the restaurant, Kate was grateful for the dim coolness of the interior. If Jed had looked at her for longer than a nanosecond out in the bright sunshine, he would have seen the gleam of tears, the strain.

Calling up the stairs, she made her farewells to Ben, whose grunted reply almost made her smile. Sparks nodded, his eyes knowing and shrewd.

He waved a spatula in her direction. "You take care now, Ms. Kate, hear?"

"You, too." She chucked him on the shoulder. "See you later. Don't inhale too much grease."

"Huh." He banged the spatula on top of the hamburger oozing juices and grease on the cook top. "Grease is good. Gives flavor. And one of these days, you're going to get lucky and get to sample one of my burgers. You'll think you died and done gone to heaven, Ms. Kate."

"I'm sure I will." Her stomach bounced northward from the smell of frying meat. Taking a gulp of mellow fall air, Kate let the door slam behind her on the sounds of Sparks and his hamburgers.

Jed waited on the steps of the porch, his duffel slung over one shoulder. Side by side they walked to his car, the duffel bumping her arm. He lifted one shoulder and let the bag thump carelessly on the floor in the back of the Blazer. "Change of clothes, shoes. Underwear. Since I'm staying at your house."

"Naturally."

"Actually, I'm stupefied Sparks didn't rag me about wearing yesterday's shirt and slacks. He's slipping, I reckon."

Without comment, Kate waited while Jed slid into the driver's seat. She would bide her time.

Uneasily, he glanced in her direction, but when she remained silent, he started the engine. "I have an optometrist friend I'm going to let take a look at the broken sunglass lens. We'll start there. Unless you're not up to it? Or, if you have a better plan, we'll start there," he said, exquisitely polite.

Politeness could cover a multitude of feelings, and Jed was a master of concealment.

"Fine." She snapped her seat belt into its lock.

With one more assessing look at her, he pulled the car out of the parking lot and onto the highway.

Michael's Optometry was in a small, exclusive mall on the outskirts of Sabal Palm, not far from the Sarasota-Bradenton

Airport. A creamy orange stucco building stood alone at the edge of the mall, its glassed entrance flanked by two enormous and expensive potted palms. Bordered by terra-cotta tiles, the nubby beige carpet was five steps up from the usual indoor-outdoor carpeting of most shops. As Jed walked ahead, she lingered next to an artfully displayed arrangement of glass frames.

"Kate, who wears glasses besides Calla?" Jed had halted next to an elegantly slim man in a beautifully tailored light gray suit.

Carefully Kate returned the three-hundred-dollar mottled tortoiseshell frames to the mannequin's blank face. "Besides Calla? My mother, Sissy's boyfriend. Perhaps Calla's new husband. I don't know for sure." She went to stand beside Jed as he held out the lens to the man in the lovely suit.

"We can make it easier for Michael to eliminate prescriptions that are obvious non-matches for our fragment."

*We.* Somehow his use of the plural touched her. In spite of the coolness between them, Jed apparently continued to think of them as a team.

Had he used the word deliberately for his own reasons, a message to the man in front of them, or had the word slipped out, an unconscious revelation of his true attitude?

Knowing Jed, she assumed the *we* hadn't been a slip of the tongue. Evidently there was more to the history between these two men than seemed possible at first glance.

Still, the word had warmed a tiny, cold place inside her.

"Kate, meet an old friend, Michael Arroyo. Michael, this is Kate March, another...old friend."

Michael's smile was an expensive flicker of orthodontia as he looked from Jed to her. "Hello, Kate March. A pleasure." His slim hand was cool against hers, with a deceptive strength beneath the elegance. "Jed and I have spent many an entertaining hour conversing in boîtes around the world."

"About philosophy?" Kate murmured, and allowed her gaze to flick in Jed's direction. "Occasionally Jed's expressed an interest in philosophy."

"That, too." He smiled again, but the intentness in his golden-brown eyes reminded her of Jed. Michael Arroyo was more than the elegant clotheshorse he seemed. "Among other things, of course."

"Of course." She had the sneakiest suspicion that the boîtes were, in fact, probably under a jungle canopy or under a desert palm's rattling branches in some hellhole of the world.

"Okay, Michael, here's the deal." Jed placed the lens in Michael's hand. "What can you tell us about this? And how fast can you give us the information?"

"Life-or-death matter, I take it?" Michael rubbed a well-manicured finger along the splintered edge.

Jed merely grinned. "Is it ever anything else?"

"I have a splendid Pinot Grigio in the back. Why don't you both sit down, have a sip and give me a few minutes?"

"Tea for both of us. And how about five minutes?"

Michael shook his head mournfully. "The things I do for...old friends." He sauntered into the back of the store, returned with two tall glasses of iced tea in crystal. "Twenty minutes, and that's only because of Ms. March's beautiful eyes. A man could never resist a woman who looked at him with those eyes." His manner was the next best thing to a bow.

Warmed by his appreciation, Kate smiled sunnily back at him. "Thank you," she said, taking the glass and napkin he offered and taking a sip. "Ahhh. Two glasses of this and I'll take Michael home with me," she muttered.

"Michael isn't housebroken," Jed said dryly. "In spite of what he'd like the fine citizens of the Sabal Palm area to believe."

"Never mind, then." Kate let another mouthful of raspberry tea tantalize her taste buds.

Ten minutes later Michael returned, his manner subtly altered. "Here's the deal. I neutralized the prescription—read it," he explained, looking at Kate. "I can give you the long explanation or the short." As Jed lifted one eyebrow, Arroyo said, "Short it is. What we have here—" he held the fragment in front of them "—is a compound prescription for someone with presbyopia complicated with astigmatism. The diopters of measurement and the high cylinder reading indicate greater distortion."

"Naturally," Jed said ironically. "I should have seen that for myself."

Arroyo scarcely paused. "In other words, this farsighted, astigmatic patient would have trouble functioning without glasses. A break for you. Everything would be distorted, blurred. The material of the lens is CR-39 plastic resin, and my best guess is that the original lenses were fitted into small, round, rimless frames. The old-fashioned kind."

"This is part of an old pair of glasses?" Jed bent closer to stare at the lens. "If the piece is from an old pair of specs, we're not going to be able to find out anything, are we?"

"No, no. Wrong path, my friend. Everything old is new again. Retro's with it, the happening look." Arroyo clicked his fingers. "This fragment isn't old, but the frame for this lens was one of those retro styles. See the holes drilled into the side here?"

Kate, too, bent forward, Jed turned, and his chin bumped her mouth. "Sorry," she said, her mouth tingling from the bristly brush of his chin against her lips.

Jed lifted a hand toward her face, touched the fragment instead. "I don't see the holes."

"There." Handing Kate a magnifying glass, Michael touched the edge of the fragment with a delicate silver pick.

Kate squinted. Now that she saw what he was pointing to, she could see the holes without a magnifier. "Why are the holes important?"

"They were the means for mounting the lens, but they make the plastic easily breakable. People think of plastic as indestructible. It's very hardy, but it can shatter, and sometimes without much force with this kind of mounting."

"So whoever dropped the sunglasses could have stepped on them?" Kate liked the idea that whoever had murdered

Patsy and Frank would be caught perhaps by careless vanity. The notion satisfied her at a deep level. If, as Jed kept reminding her, they were lucky, a murderer might be found through his or her desire to have a "happening" look. "Even though they're made of plastic, they would break if they were stepped on?"

"Certainly. Or if the glasses hit a hard surface, they might have cracked. Not an unlikely scenario at all."

Jed straightened. "Any chance you can track down the owner of this particular prescription?"

"Me? I don't know. Is it possible?" Arroyo grinned, a hungry catlike stretch of facial muscles. "Definitely. The axis where the cylinder is ground into the lens is specific to each eye, to each patient. It's not exactly a fingerprint, but a prescription of this nature is very individualistic." Michael motioned for them to bring their glasses with them and follow him to the back. "Here's what I'll do. I can send a flyer around the area and see if anyone's filled this prescription. Your person would need replacement glasses. How far out do you want the notice to go?"

"As far north as the Georgia border, south to the Keys. Is that possible?" Jed's mouth was a thin, white line. "We need the answers soon, Michael."

"I'll flag it for immediate attention." Michael laid a piece of paper with a list of names on it beside the lens fragment. "You want these checked against the prescription, and I can do that. Do you want the names mentioned in the flyer?"

Kate raised her hand and let it rest on Jed's arm. She didn't want her mother's name, Sissy's, on some flyer circulating around the state.

"Yes."

She let her hand fall to her side.

"Discreetly. Write a nice flyer, Michael. You can do that."

"This isn't police business, then?"

"It is."

"And?" Arroyo adjusted the knot of his tie.

Kate kept silent. Arroyo and Jed had their own communication line established. She wasn't about to interfere with whatever unspoken agreement they were headed toward.

"I only ask, you understand, because usually the police handle this sort of thing. I'd prefer not to interfere with their business. But..." Not looking at them, giving them time, Arroyo ran his hand over the length of his silky tie and waited.

Jed didn't miss a beat. "They're not moving fast enough. For one thing, they can't."

Kate had no way of knowing how much of what he said was the truth, but this was Jed's "old friend," his arrangement. She was an observer in this elegant room with its whiff of secrets and danger.

"Hmm." Arroyo waited. "I've found the ladies and gentlemen of the force to be fairly territorial. They move forward at their own pace."

"True, and we're going to give them the lens. Eventually. Since the police didn't discover the lens with the initial search of the crime scene, they have a chain-of-evidence problem. So, Arroyo, I'm in the nature of an information gatherer, that's all. The police position is that the fragment is tainted evidence."

"But not for you?" In spite of the orthodontic miracles, Michael's smile wasn't in the least bit civilized.

Desert and jungle, Kate decided, suppressing a tiny shiver. Two of a kind, Jed and Michael were.

"Nope." Extending his hand, Jed retrieved the lens and shook Arroyo's hand. "Thanks. Give me a call as soon as you hear anything."

"Perhaps Ms. March would prefer the call?" Michael's smile at her held an unspoken question.

Before Kate could answer, Jed smiled companionably back at him and draped an arm casually over her shoulder. "Call me, Michael. When you have a name."

"Of course," he said smoothly, an air of regret in the tiny, teasing glance he shot Kate, in the small smile that curved his mouth.

As Jed shoved open the polished glass doors to the outside, Michael's silhouette glimmered behind them.

His lean elegance with its underlying hint of power was appealing at a very primal level, much in the same way Jed's was. Except Jed was power in jeans and boots, a rawness that swept her away. "I like your friend."

"He liked you, too. How nice for all of us. A regular set of musketeers, I reckon. Next thing I know, Arroyo'll be setting up club meetings."

Ignoring his scowl, Kate climbed into the Blazer.

Jed didn't want to wait for Michael's flyer to make the rounds. It became a long day as they visited one optometrist's office after another, checking to see if any of the local offices had filled the particular prescription that Michael had written down for them. No one had.

Late in the day, Kate's phone rang. Flipping open the ends that expanded the three-and-a-half-inch expensive accessory into a functioning tool, she spoke into the pinhole dots of the speaker. "Yes?"

"Whoo, Kate." Dyan, the receptionist, spoke through breathy spurts. "Sorry, let me catch my breath."

"Is there a problem?" Kate mouthed the word *office* to Jed.

"Probably. Maybe. I don't know for sure." Dyan panted. "A package for you. I thought you might want to know about it, so I rushed back with it to your office. That's where I am now, in fact. I put the package on your desk, Kate." Dyan's breaths were coming in more evenly spaced spurts. "Listen, Kate, I can't tell for sure, but I think the package is from that Miami decorating firm. You might want to take a look ASAP. You know we had that letter from them complaining about the dyes in the fabric they ordered?"

Kate tugged at the seat belt. She knew. They'd had problems with each order for that store. If she'd had her way, she would have scratched them off and taken the loss. Calla, however, had pushed to keep the store because of its high-end clientele. "I'm coming in for a short while tonight, Dyan. I'll take a look at it then. Calla hasn't seen it?"

"No, she left early with Hal. She had a meeting out on the island with some people from the Chamber of Commerce. Said to tell you she'd see you tomorrow. Anyway, the package came after she left. Looks like it was a courier delivery."

"Interesting. That must have cost the store a bundle." Kate frowned. The Miami firm must be really annoyed to pay courier costs. Heaven help Bowen and March's Import Imprints if Miami intended to sue. She sighed, and Jed's eyes caught hers in the mirror. She made a face, mouthed *problem*.

"Hey, Kate, I gotta go. My ride's waiting. Bye." The phone clicked at the other end.

"Two birds with one stone, huh? My chore and your problem?" Jed guided the Blazer into one more parking lot.

Wire eyeglass frames above an entrance door announced one more optometry shop, one more run down a blind alley.

She'd been so certain that the shattered lens would pay off with information, especially after their visit to Arroyo's store, but so far, none of the other optometrists had been able to supply them with even the most remote link to a name.

For the past hour, discouragement had settled over her with an exhausting weight. Wilting, she looked dubiously at Jed, whose unflagging energy was beginning to annoy her.

"Four more stops, and we'll take a break. Unless you need to quit?"

Tension in the offer, and she could only guess at the cause. The baby. But he'd offered. That was a recognition of the embryonic person inside her, she supposed, even if he wouldn't discuss the situation.

"I'm fine," she lied, damned if she'd let him know how tired she truly was. "The drive-through salad was enough, and I don't have an appetite anyway. We don't have to stop on my account." Deliberately she brushed her stomach.

"All right. We'll hit these last stores, then."

"You know, Jed, I never realized that you have a bit of

the sadist in you." She clambered out of the car and followed his broad back.

"Doin' my job, Katie. That's all."

"I know," she said glumly. "I know." If he'd looked as tuckered out as she felt, she'd be happier. Even wearing the same clothes he'd gone through yesterday's events in, he should have looked ragged, disreputable, unappealing.

He looked very disreputable.

And irritatingly appealing.

In clean clothes, shampooed hair and makeup, she was the one who felt as if she'd slept for a week in the same outfit. She hoped to heaven she looked better than she felt.

At this point, she wouldn't have the energy to confront Jed. He'd make mincemeat out of her attempt. Kate brushed her hair back from her face and plastered on a smile as the bell over the door ding-donged their entrance.

After the final fruitless stop they headed toward her office.

Jed had saved the return to her office for the last stop, planning, he said, to sweep the offices after everyone had left for the day.

By the time they arrived at her building, Kate was so tired that she would have begged Jed to take her home if she hadn't promised Dyan she'd check out the Miami package.

The lights from the lawyer's office above hers shone from the building. Except at the entrance, the rest of the lights had been turned off by the cleaning service. Leaning silently against the back of the elevator, she kept her eyes shut until the elevator shuddered to a halt.

"Come on, Kate. I promise I'll be fast." Jed guided her forward, and the press of his hand on her back gave her the energy to move forward, out of the elevator, down the dim hall to the doors of her office suite.

In her exhaustion she imagined that his touch was gentle, that the distance between them had narrowed. In her exhaustion she wanted the fantasy to be real.

Jed stopped in the reception area. A staleness in the air swirled around them with his movement. His black bag of electronic equipment swung in his hand as he opened her office door, stepping in front of her, his glance sweeping the empty space.

Inside her musty-smelling office, the butterflies danced across her monitor screen.

"You leave your computer on all the time?" Jed pulled out a sensor from his magic bag and began searching the room.

"Sure." She collapsed into her chair and stared at the package on her desk. "I hate this account, I hate it, I hate it."

"Dump it." Jed was examining the light fixtures, the baseboard. "It's your company. You get to make decisions."

"Calla wants to keep this account."

"Oh?" Jed stopped. Frowned. "Hold on, Kate. Don't unwrap that package yet."

"Oh." Her hands hovering over the package, Kate froze. "Oh," she said, slowly pushing her chair away from the desk. "Of course. A package could be a bomb."

Jed slid the metal wand under the string and lifted the package, holding it straight in front of him as he moved swiftly out her door and down the hall to the bathroom, Kate right at his heels.

"Get back inside, Kate." His tone left no room for discussion. "Now, damn it."

Her brain quit functioning.

She knew she was behaving stupidly, she knew he was competent, more than competent, but there had been too much destruction, too much death, and she couldn't possibly think of letting Jed walk down that hall without her.

She followed, the need irresistible, even as he tightly ordered her back into her office. Followed him right into the men's bathroom where Jed dunked the box into the urinal and flushed.

Soaking the package, water gushed, foamed, softened the cardboard. Jed flushed again. And again.

Slushy cardboard peeled away from one side.

Dangling from the box, a waterlogged corner of purple-and-acid-yellow cotton swirled in the water, dipped, sank.

"Well, Kate, looks like I just drowned a load of cotton for you."

She laughed.

"Yeah." His grin split his lean cheeks, lightened the saturnine cast of his face with hellish amusement. "Damn all, ain't it?"

"Never ran into this kind of enemy in the jungle, I suppose?" She giggled again as she watched the drift of fabric in the water.

"Killer cotton?" His laugh matched hers. "Nope."

"I told you, I hate that account. Good riddance, is what I say." She leaned against the wall, weak with amusement. "I'd give you a medal any day for this act of courage, Jed." She giggled, choked and wiped her eyes. "You're my hero."

The laughter faded from her eyes as she realized what she'd said.

Jed's eyes locked with hers, held, a bleakness in their gray that puzzled her and left her melancholy even on the tag end of laughter. "I'm nobody's hero, Kate." Turning, his back to her, he ripped a wad of paper towels from the cabinet and fished out the cardboard and its contents. "Let's get back to work."

Back in her office, she decided to run through some accounts. Her brain grew foggier and foggier with fatigue, the numbers and words beginning to blur into nonsense while Jed continued to search every inch of the room, Calla's office, the reception area and the closet kitchen behind it.

"Interesting." He gestured to the picture hanging on the wall near Calla's office.

In her foggy-brained state, she thought he looked confused as he stared back at her and then again at the picture with its flashes of black in a lowering red sky. Brilliant yellow streaked through the sky, and beneath it, a vermilion house with a twisted doorway, as though torqued at the corners, squatted, its tilted roofline bleeding into the black-and-red sky.

"I know," she said stupidly, forgetting the rest of the sentence.

"You have blue lips, Katie." The confusion deepened in his eyes. "Blue lips."

"I'm not cold." She touched her arm. "No, I'm not cold." The fogginess wrapping around her made her lean forward and cross her arms on her desk. "Sleepy. Not cold, Jed."

Jed shook his head. "Wake up, Kate," he said, his speech slurring. "You can't go to sleep. There's a gas leak in here. That's why your lips are blue. Wake up, Katie. And don't…" He stopped, thinking, and then continued, "Don't touch anything electrical." He walked slowly toward her, his face blurring in her vision as she turned her head from its resting place to look at him.

"Okay," she said, and shut her eyes.

He scooped her up in one hand and made his way to the outer door of the office, tried to open it. "Did you lock this door?"

Sleepily she forced her eyes open. "I don't remember."

"It's locked now." He lowered her to the floor with her back against the door. "Is there another exit, Kate? A way out? Concentrate."

Her head flopping forward, she said, "No." She lifted her head, yawned, yawned a second time. "The window in my office. No. You can't break it." She blinked. "There's a small window in the kitchen. It opens. I think." Her eyes drifted closed.

She remembered floating through the air, remembered the tinkling, crackling of glass, the clean smell of the night rushing in at her.

Later Jed would tell her how he'd broken the window and let the office's air out. Later she would remember the low voices of the detectives, the same ones who'd investigated the murders at Patsy's house, Mark Roberts and Dennis D'Amico. The old brass connector on the gas stove in the cubicle kitchen had corroded. Gas had leaked into the office suite. Apparently the leak had occurred shortly before their arrival, or they would have caused an explosion when they flipped the light switch.

If she'd been there by herself, she would have drifted asleep and died. Without Jed's careful observation, without his physical strength, they both would have died. That was the realization that seeped through her consciousness during the hours with the police and in the emergency room, where she and Jed had been taken for observation, Jed grumbling and arguing the entire time, but never moving from her side. Escorting her into the cool, predawn dimness after they were released, he checked the Blazer that the police had brought to the hospital.

That she remembered very, very clearly.

And in that dim twilight of morning before sunrise, he was at her side when the cramps began, when the tiny child she'd tried so hard to protect fought its desperate battle against the lonely darkness.

# Chapter 14

As faint as a kitten's mew, the smothered wail slashed through Jed. He charged through the bathroom door off her bedroom, slamming the door so hard against the wall that it ricocheted back onto his shoulder.

"Kate!"

Huddled on the floor, white-faced, she stared at him. Her arms were wrapped around her middle, her legs curled underneath her. His heart rapping wildly against his rib cage, he scanned the room, finding nothing, only Katie hunched on the floor. No intruder. No threat. Mystified, he returned his attention to her. Dry, burning hot, her eyes were so desolate that he knew in that instant what was happening.

"Oh, Katie." He knelt in front of her. Helpless, he could only repeat, "Katie, Katie." He reached out for her, wanting to comfort, wanting to make her misery less, wanting to do *something*. "The baby?"

She swallowed, nodded and curled tighter into herself, away from him.

"We're going to the hospital." He lifted her into his arms,

tucking her close to him, her frantically beating heart pounding through him. He'd resented this child, focused his anger on it, maybe even hated it, he no longer knew, but now, now as it fought for life, he sensed a will like his own, stubborn, determined, strong. Katie's baby needed him.

*She* needed him.

She shook her head. "Too late. There's nothing to do. Not now. Go away, Jed. Please. I don't want you in here. Not now. Please, please, go away."

"Can't do that, Katie," he said, and stood up with her in his arms. He'd never seen her so defeated, all her bright energy and defiance crushed.

Carefully he carried her back toward the bedroom, a faint voice in his head urging him to action, insisting that he not give up. For one mad moment he believed it was the voice of Katie's child calling him, and Jed knew he would face a firing squad sooner than he could ignore that fading whimper.

Katie's baby was not going to go gentle into that good night, not if he could do anything about it. No surrender. Not now. Not ever.

That thready, tiny voice inside him wouldn't let him accept that it was *too late*.

Bundling Kate into his Blazer, he drove through the dim streets where mist and fog blurred his vision. Or maybe it was the burn of his own eyes as he caught glimpses of Katie's terribly pale face. Skin tight against the bone, she was reduced to the most elemental look of tragedy, a marble statue of grief.

"It's going to be okay."

Looking away from him, gazing into the mist streaming past them, she didn't answer.

False hope was no hope. He knew that, but he'd needed to reassure her. He had nothing else to give her, nothing else he could do. Banging the steering wheel once, he swore and slammed the accelerator down hard.

Over the river and one hard turn into the emergency room. Through the double glass doors and into a surprisingly quiet room where nurses came and went, taking a history, checking Katie's vitals. And all the time she lay silently, passively. Waiting to hear the verdict she'd already accepted.

They tried to shoo him out. He stayed. The look on his face dared them to try to throw him out. They didn't, their sympathy obvious in the looks they shot Kate. Him.

He finally understood. They thought that the baby was his.

Her doctor kept her for observation. They all waited through a long afternoon and into a twilight that seemed only a continuation of the morning's dim light. And then they waited some more, trapping Kate in the web of hospital policies and procedures.

Late in the evening they finally released her, giving her medications, instructions to take it easy, and, ultimately, hope.

Kate's baby was fighting a good fight.

Jed carried her up the stairs and back into her bedroom, expecting her to speak, to say *something,* to show relief after the awfulness of the past hours. But she didn't.

Yanking back the bedcovers with one hand, he settled her between the sheets as carefully as if she would break.

Too late after all, he thought, sorrow chilling him as he saw the despair in her eyes. She'd already shattered. But she wouldn't cry in front of him, and the hot gleam of those unshed tears burned into him as she looked up at him from the pillow.

"Go away, Jed."

Husky and scratchy, the words pierced him to the depths of his soul. He shook his head, and her eyes blazed. "You keep saying that, Kate, but you're asking the impossible. I'm here. I'm not leaving. Deal with it. We're going to get through this." The *we* was automatic. He, Katie, her baby— they were in this battle together.

"There's no *we,*" she said, her voice as faint as the voice he'd imagined crying to him earlier. "Just go away and leave me in peace, Jed. If you have any mercy, leave me alone."

"Mercy?" He sat beside her on the bed, his weight tightening the covers around her. "What you need—"

"You're the expert on what I need?" Almost imperceptible, that note of anger.

"What you need now," he repeated slowly, "is someone to look after you, to feed you. To do whatever has to be done. Mercy isn't the answer. So, bottom line. I'm not leaving. Believe me." He stared back at her, saw the sheer force of her will, a will as strong as that of the child she carried. Maybe, somewhere, his Katie was fighting.

Silent, holding her hand in front of her face, she turned on her side away from him and shut her eyes, closing him out of her desolation.

He waited a moment, willing her to open her eyes, to look at him, to let him comfort her and tell her that this, too, would pass. In time.

When she didn't open her eyes, he strode into the bathroom, rummaged through her medicine cabinet and found an analgesic the doctor had indicated she could take. Filling the plastic tumbler with tap water, he returned and tapped her on the shoulder. "Take these, Kate. For pain. They're only a nonaspirin analgesic."

When she didn't respond, he placed the tablets gently in her hand, closed her fingers around them and left the tumbler of water on the nightstand. She wouldn't take the tablets while he was there any more than she'd let him see her tears.

For long, silent moments, Jed studied her pale face, as pale as the pillowcase next to her skin. She'd never been more beautiful to him. She was curled so tightly into herself that the shape of her under the sheet was nothing more than a slight rise, fragile, infinitely precious.

It was a miracle her baby had survived. A miracle Kate had. Despite the appearance of the gas leak, it had been no accident. Both detectives had agreed with him. The cold eye of evil had fallen on Kate and her child.

It was time to see someone blink.

But taking care of Kate came first.

Silently he left the room, walked down the stairs and put a kettle of water on the stove to boil water for tea. Flipping out the card from the emergency room, he placed a call to Kate's physician, then waited impatiently for him to return the call. Catching the phone on the first ring, Jed gave a terse update, explained that there continued to be no bleeding or spotting, and spooned herbal tea into a pot, listening tight-lipped to the doctor's reassurances while the tea steeped.

Basically, Kate needed sleep and rest. If she were to show signs of hemorrhaging, he was to take her immediately to the hospital. Wait. Rest. Sleep. Otherwise, since it was such an early pregnancy, there wasn't much else to do at the moment.

He'd promised her that he'd protect her and the child, no matter what. He'd promised her he'd keep them safe.

He'd almost failed.

He took the pot of tea and some saltines to her. She'd swallowed the tablets, and her balled-up fists were under her cheek. She'd turned over to face the door.

Moving the empty tumbler, he laid the tray on the end table. "Sit up if you can, Kate. Drink the tea. Eat a cracker." He pulled the chair beside the bed, rubbed his hand across the smooth sheet. "I called your doctor."

She closed her eyes for a moment, opened them, and the gleam of tears shone like jewels. One by silent one, teardrops ran down her cheek, soaking the pillowcase.

"Aw, cookie, you're breaking my heart." Jed shoved the chair away and climbed into the bed beside her. Wrapping her tightly in his arms, he tucked her head beneath his chin. Her tears soaked through his shirt onto his skin, a scalding lash he knew he deserved.

Words were hollow, meaningless. No one could guarantee the future.

"I want this baby, Jed." Forlorn and lost, the small sound. "For me. For Frank."

"I know, Katie. I know." He sat up, lifted her onto his lap, pulled the sheet up around her and braced himself against the headboard. "I'm sorry Frank never knew about the baby, sorry he'll never have the chance to hold his child. I'm sorry for both of you, and I wish I could fix this, Kate. I can't.''

The admission came easily. He *was* sorry, and the realization raked him. He'd been so envious of a *dead* man, so angry with Kate for what he saw as a betrayal, and all along the child had been swimming in that amniotic sea, growing and becoming.

Frank's child, *his?* What the hell did it matter whose baby Kate carried? It was *Kate's* child. Kate's. Whatever that tiny miracle of cells would become, whatever wonder of laughter and stubbornness, all that was now at risk, and he couldn't do a damn thing about it.

He would have bartered with the devil himself and sold his soul to keep Katie and her child safe.

He tightened his arms around her while her body shook with hard, wrenching, noisy sobs.

And all through the night he kept her close to the beating of his aching heart, a heart that wept silently with her and would have taken her pain from her. But this was Katie's fight. She would have to fight it on her own terms.


The next day Kate protested once as Jed insisted on taking her to her doctor's office. Her silence speared him. She seemed shrunken and dimmed, not a Kate he recognized.

Over the next three days she remained withdrawn, suffering in a place to which he had no access.

Jed called Calla and said that Kate was still ill from a combination of the effects of the gas leak and the flu. He brought her hot tea and toast. He made her eat, preparing soup for her and broiling chicken in her fancy kitchen. He sliced mangoes, peeled oranges and spread the orange segments on one of her crystal service dishes, alternating the gleaming orange stripes with bright green lines of grapes. Listless, she picked at the food. She didn't eat.

The last straw had finally broken her. She needed time to come back to herself. To rest. To heal. And they were terrifyingly short of time.

Each night Jed held her in his arms through the long hours of darkness while she wept, her thin body racked with sobs.

Even if he made her as mad as a wet hen, Jed was ready to drag her out of the house and into the brilliant October sunshine. An angry, spitting-mad Kate was preferable to the thin, pale Kate drifting around her house like a silent ghost.

On the morning of the fourth day she awoke in his arms, her eyelashes spiky with tears. "Why are you still here, Jed?"

"Because you are."

"I didn't want you to stay."

"I know you didn't." He rested his chin on top of her mussed, silky hair. Her bones were sharp against him, her eyes red rimmed.

"You should have gone. Why didn't you?" She curved her palm over his T-shirt, her fingertips pressing lightly into him.

"Because I couldn't go." He sighed, and her hair fluttered with his breath. "I had no choice. I couldn't leave you. I told you, Katie. You asked for the impossible."

For a long moment she was silent. Then she stirred, her breasts soft at the edge of his arm, her pebbled nipples hard little bumps. "I'm going back to work, Jed."

"Good." Reluctant to release her, he shifted, and his thigh bumped hers, hers smooth against the furred length of his.

She inhaled, exhaled, her breath feathering across his chin.

He took a deep breath. "I wish I could have protected you both better."

She curled her fingers into him. "It wasn't your fault, Jed. Yours, least of all. I thought I could control what happened. I did everything I could to protect my baby, and my everything wasn't good enough. But this baby—" her hand pressed against her abdomen "—is going to survive." Her body shuddered as his hand joined hers. "With each passing hour, I'm more and more sure of that."

The green numerals of the clock on her nightstand flashed the passing of the minutes as she lay against his chest, their joined hands resting on the slight rise of her belly, on the shape of her child.

He needed to give her more, to atone for what he saw as his unforgivable failure. His nature demanded more, but this nonsexual holding was the closest she came to accepting comfort from him.

Finally she sat up, her legs dangling over his toward the side of the bed. "Even if the person who tried to kill us the other night, the person who killed Frank and Patsy and almost made me lose this baby, is someone I know, I don't care anymore. I can't believe my mom or Sissy would be so monstrous. Or Calla. But I just want the person caught. Whoever it is. I want the evil stopped." Resolute, her thin face resembled bone china, fragile, translucent.

A strength shone in her eyes, a strength that would carry her through the coming days.

Brushing her hair back from her face, Jed kissed her forehead. "We will, Katie."

He went with her to her office and stayed while she forced herself to face the waiting paperwork. He admired the discipline that enabled her to face her friends and co-workers as they exclaimed over the accident, over her thinness. Gracefully she acknowledged their concern, their curiosity about the gas leak.

Since none of them knew about her pregnancy, no one thought her calm out of the usual. She schmoozed the Miami firm, whose manager disclaimed any knowledge of the package that had been on Kate's desk. Kate laughed, told them that they would be receiving a discount on their next order and apologized for her error.

Kate was a good actress. She would have convinced him if he hadn't known better.

Someone else had sent the package.

The package had been part of a setup.

Jed didn't have to spell it out for Kate. Her startled glance at him when the manager clarified that, no, their shop hadn't returned any fabric, told him she, too, understood someone knew they would be in the office and had prepared a nasty trap for them.

A death trap, as they learned a week later when D'Amico and Roberts showed up with the metal door stopper that had been found in a garbage dump at the construction site two blocks down from Kate's building. "A likely hiding spot," the detectives said. "And good detective work." They'd grinned as they told Jed and Kate that metallurgy tests matched its metallic scrapings with those on the door. The detectives had pulled in favors to rush the tests.

The door hadn't been locked. It had been blocked from the outside so that Jed couldn't open it.

Kate had talked about feeling that her very thoughts were monitored, that someone was privy to her every decision, but Jed couldn't find any listening devices when he searched a second and a third time. He'd seen nothing that remotely resembled any kind of listening apparatus following them. He would have recognized repeat cars, vans, trucks. He was looking for familiar faces where they shouldn't be.

One more frustrating dead end.

Jed needed action, not this tedious checking of details when he sensed time racing past. His extraordinary ability to outwait the most patient foe had deserted him and left him in uncharted waters. The anger inside him boiled until he wanted to knock down a cement wall with his bare hands. He hoped Roberts and D'Amico found the killer before he did.

His version of swift and sure justice wouldn't meet their approval.

In the meantime, from Kate's office, Jed checked with Arroyo and found that an ophthalmologist in Gainesville remembered a similar prescription. Arroyo was narrowing his inquiries to the Gainesville area and had found an optometrist who believed he'd filled that prescription. Not on a computerized system, he would have to hand search his records for a specific name, but understanding that it was a matter of some urgency, he'd agreed to give the search priority attention.

Kate almost smiled when Jed told her that news. In repose, her face remained too solemn, too sad. To look at her unawares was to torture himself with remorse, and he redoubled his efforts to follow the elusive trail of dead ends and possibles.

Jed checked in with Ben, who said he thought he'd have some information soon, that some of the invoices from one particular ship consistently seemed to be off, and Jed should come pick up the papers and see what he thought.

Jed lowered his voice so that no one in the outer office could hear his question. "Have you run the financial checks on Calla's present husband or her ex? Or Kate's mother's boyfriend?"

Nothing there. Ben had cleared the boyfriend, and Calla's ex-husband seemed so far to be on solid financial ground. He had some more checking to do, though. "When you coming to see us, boss?" Ben concluded with a plaintive note in his voice. "Booger's lonesome. Whines a lot."

"When will you have the rest of the information for me? Kate and I will come then."

"Tomorrow night, most likely. The joint's closed tomorrow, so I'll have time to go over these invoices with you. I could sure use your thoughts on this stuff I found, Jed. Not bitchin' you, boss, because it's weird. I can't make heads nor tails out of what it means."

"Tomorrow night it is, then. Kate and I'll see you sometime after nine."

No moon or stars shone in the cloudless sky when Jed pulled in to the parking lot the next night. The smell of onions and cheese filled the Blazer. Kate had insisted on celebrating with Ben, and made Jed stop for a stuffed pizza at Papa Angelo's.

Against the darkness where gulf and sky met, only the

lights from Ben's apartment upstairs at The Last Resort gleamed like a lighthouse in the tropical pitchiness.

"I need half an hour," Ben shouted down at them. "Go somewhere for a while. Take a walk down the beach."

Kate nodded. "The pizza's going to be cold if you take too long," she called upstairs.

"Nah. Stick it in the oven. Thirty minutes, that's all. Guys, you're slowing me down, and I'm starving. Go away," Ben pleaded.

Kate shrugged and followed Jed to the flat, hard sand still damp from the outgoing tide. She kicked off her shoes and left them above the tide line near The Last Resort. Jed followed suit, throwing his light jacket across her shoulders. "It's chilly, with the night wind blowing across the water."

Her eyes were mysterious and dark as she nodded. The wind flattened the jacket against her as they walked farther and farther down the sand, the bar's shape disappearing from view with the curve of the shoreline.

Near a sheltered stand of sea oats, Jed motioned for her to sit. He thought she looked tired. They still had the walk back, but he knew better than to ask if she needed to rest. Kate would always tough it out. So, not waiting for her, he hunkered down on the dry, still-warm sand near the secluded sea oats.

Under the black sky, black water rippled, crumpled toward land and shushed against silver-gray sand.

"Come here, Kate," he said finally as she continued to stand looking out at the gulf, her arms wrapped around her waist. "Sit in front of me. You'll be warmer that way." Jed tugged at the jacket until she stooped and sat down in the space he made for her between his legs.

Caping her with his arms, he looked out at the water with her, felt the moment when the tension eased out of her body, felt the sag of her straight spine as she relaxed into him and lay back against his shoulders, her head resting on his chest. He could have held her all night against him like this, the two of them quiet under heaven's canopy.

"I love this view."

"Me, too." He looked down at her, at the supple shape of her breasts under her light poplin jacket, the gleam of her thigh as the breeze flirted with her loose skirt.

"Is the view the reason you bought The Last Resort?" Half-turning toward him, her profile broke the darkness.

"No." He scooted her closer, and her rear end bumped the notch of his slacks, pressing the hardness that he couldn't help whenever he touched her, saw her, thought of her.

Kate wanted to be closer to him. She was so tired of being alone.

She knew what the ridge pressed against her fanny meant. She knew he wanted her in the way they'd always wanted each other. Nothing had changed that power. As he'd held her during the sad, lonely nights, even then, even lost in sorrow, she'd been aware that his chaste embrace had been anything but for him. He'd directed all his energies toward comforting her, but she hadn't been able to accept his comfort because of her guilt over the deaths of Frank and Patsy, her betrayal of Jed, the near loss of her child.

She hadn't believed she deserved comfort, and certainly not from Jed.

But the morning he'd told her he had no choice except to stay with her, his words had wound down deep inside her, like a seed sending roots into the dark, biding its time.

His presence had kept her sane during those dark hours.

Now, in a darkness that reminded her of those nights, of the unspoken comfort he'd given her, his low voice mingled with the booming surf. "Kate, if I could, I'd give you your Frank back and put his ring on your finger myself, if that would make you happy."

"Would you do that for me, Jed?"

"Kate, you have no idea what I'd do for you."

She raised her arm and cupped the side of his face. "But you couldn't love me."

He stopped the slow movements of her fingers. "Kate, I told you I had no regrets. I lied. If I could change anything about the past, change anything I've done, I would figure out what went wrong between us. I never understood why we couldn't make it work. Because I would do anything for you. Except leave you. You took my soul with you when you left me." He wound his fingers through hers. "Why did you walk out on me, Kate?"

The darkness invited truth, clarified what she'd only lately begun to understand.

"You overwhelmed me, Jed. You only let me into your bedroom and closed off all the rest of your life. There was no room for me in your world."

"I didn't want you there, Kate." Harsh, that low voice, absolute in its brutal frankness.

"I needed to be with you, though. Why couldn't you make room for me in your life, Jed?"

He drew her closer, rested his chin on her head as he had during the long nights when he'd lain with her and held her, taking her sobs into himself. "I didn't want the violence of my life anywhere near you, even secondhand. The blood and ugliness. Every time I came back to you, Katie, it was like coming to a safe, clean place. A place where there was the possibility of innocence and goodness. You were my safe place." He touched the curve of her ear, a skimming touch that shivered through her. "I couldn't talk to you about that other world. I didn't want it to touch you."

"And so you shut me out." She felt him nod. She understood the silences now, but not the lack of trust. "But why couldn't you trust me enough to know that I was strong enough to handle that part of you, too? Why close yourself off entirely?" She moved her hand in his grasp. "Except sexually, I never felt important to you."

Behind her, he shifted and brought her around to face him, his dark face above hers. "How could you believe that? You were everything I'd ever wanted. I was so damned scared I'd get you pregnant and wind up killed during one of my assignments. There you would have been, alone with a baby to raise by yourself. I couldn't even think about you when I was gone. If I had, I wouldn't have been worth a damn. I would have been so cautious that I would have gotten myself or my men killed. My life with you was separate, special.''

"But where was *I* in all that worry, Jed?" She held his stubborn, narrow face in her hands, making him look at her. "Why couldn't you trust me to handle whatever life threw at me, at *us?* Why didn't you give me a chance to share the burden? To make my own decisions about our life together?"

"I had to protect you." Determined, hard, the shape of his cheekbones and chin beneath her hands, unyielding. "That was my job. To keep you safe."

Her heart turned in her chest with the regret she'd sworn she hadn't felt. "Ah, no, Jed, that was never your job, never what I wanted or needed."

He drew her up onto her knees. "I didn't understand then. I don't understand now. What did you need from me, Kate? Explain it so that it makes sense to me."

Her palms still cradling his lean face, she peered through the darkness, trying to see his face, but like the night in the rain, knowing him only by touch, by instinct. "Jed, I needed you to trust me to be your *equal,* to be capable of making my own decisions. I never wanted to be an accessory."

"An accessory? That's what you believed you were to me?" He placed his hands on her shoulders. "How could you think that?"

Edging closer to him on her knees, she let her palms slide down the strong column of his neck. "What else was I to think? You made all the decisions, arrived on my doorstep at your convenience, or when you wanted sex, and never shared your life with me. How was I supposed to believe I was anything more to you than your version of the sailor's girl-in-every-port?"

"I wanted to protect you, to take care of you," he insisted, his nose bumping hers as he leaned into her, pulling her against his chest so tightly that her breath left in a whoosh.

"I didn't want to be protected, Jed. I didn't *need* to be taken care of. I wanted you to love me enough to let me be your partner, to let me take care of you once in a while. To love me enough to let me make my own decisions and take responsibility for myself, not be reduced to a child who couldn't take care of herself.''

''That's not how I saw you, Kate.'' He rubbed her nose gently with his. ''*I* needed to protect you. I always considered you my equal, though. Nobody ever argued with me, stood up to me the way you do. You've always been as strong in your way as I am in mine.''

Soft and damp, filled with the smells of salt and gulf, the air moved over her. ''I think,'' she said hesitantly, ''that in some ways your strength reminded me of my dad's. He never left me room to maneuver. Everything had to be done his way. Maybe I pushed so hard against your strength because that's what I did with him. If I hadn't, I would have been destroyed.'' She tried to focus on that stubborn child who'd fought and resisted, no matter what. ''Maybe I was afraid I'd be lost in the sheer force of your personality.'' Carefully she traced the line of his mouth. He inhaled, turned his mouth into her palm, imprinting the warm shape of his lips onto her skin. ''You are larger than life, you know.''

''I'm just a man, Katie, a man who wanted you so fiercely that I was terrified I'd scare you away. I thought if I gave you what you wanted, marriage and a baby, you'd stay with me. I gambled. And lost. You left me anyway.''

A faint glimpse of the truth shimmered in front of her. ''I wanted predictability, ordinariness.'' Her laugh was shaky. ''You have to admit, Jed, no one would describe you as ordinary.''

''I made a good living. Even if it was an unconventional occupation.'' The shape of his mouth thinned against her palm. ''I would have taken care of you. I *needed* to take care of you.''

''But fulfilling your need diminished me and made me feel like a child incapable of taking care of myself, of being a responsible adult.''

''I'm sorry, Kate. That was never my intention.'' His arms

were so tight around her that she inched forward into the harbor of his arms. "When you told me you wanted a family, I offered to marry you, to make babies with you."

The bleakness in his voice saddened her. "But you wouldn't have been around, would you, Jed? Would you have been there for our baby's first step, first words? I wanted a father for my child who wouldn't drift in and out of our lives. You needed the adrenaline rush. Oil and water, Jed. Our children and I would have been—" she rested her forehead against his "—on the sidelines of your life, not an integral part. And there's the loss, mine and yours. Because a marriage is like a braid, interwoven lives, not railroad tracks moving along parallel lines except for the occasional intersection every now and then. I didn't want to follow in my mother's footsteps, Jed. I wanted a different kind of life, a different kind of marriage." Tears came to her eyes and she rubbed them away on the heavy linen of his shirt. "And the saddest part is that I loved you so much that I felt as if I couldn't take a deep breath without you. I just couldn't live with you."

"Katie, you color my world. Didn't you know that? *Everything* is sharper, clearer when I'm with you. When you walked out on me, I felt like someone had cut me in half and left me bleeding on the ground. I hated you for a while back then, Katie, because I wanted you back and you weren't there."

"Oh, Jed, I wish—"

"Shh." He buried his face in her hair and she thought his arms trembled. "Me, too. I wish." He anchored her to him with the slide of his hands around her fanny. "Wish with me, Katie, one more time."

She stroked the smooth cap of his hair and listened to the surf, its insistent, eternal rhythm. The rhythms of her body, of her heart, moved toward this man. Impossible, their coming together, impossible to keep apart. She sighed and turned her face to his seeking mouth. When all this was over, he would walk away, of course he would. Her doubts, her reservations, what did they matter? Whatever drew them together was as powerful as the pull of the moon on the tides.

If he left, so be it.

Security, after all, was an illusion. Maybe she hadn't understood that three years ago, but she did now. She'd done everything she could to achieve the kind of life she thought she wanted. All her efforts had meant nothing, not in the face of fate's whims. Where was her security now?

Jed had stayed with her. He could have left when he'd discovered her pregnancy. She wouldn't have blamed him. But he hadn't. He'd protected her and saved her life. He could have walked away when she almost lost the baby. She'd wanted him to, had begged him to. He hadn't.

"What about the baby?"

Her ear tingled with his warm breath. "Shh, Jed, don't talk. The baby is fine. Just love me."

"Bossy." His tongue dipped into her ear.

She'd wanted security and stability, but, ironically, Jed was the one who'd been there for her, every time. Later she would have to figure out what that meant.

But not now, not under the dark bowl of a starless sky where the thumping of the tide on the sand echoed the pulsing of her heart, where Jed's touch in the darkness took her out of her self and transported her to another place, a better place, a space free of sadness and loneliness.

## Chapter 15

Jed made love to her there, a slow, gentle loving that spoke of healing, of regret, of hopeless wishes. Like the tide moving out, his touch had an easy power that took her with him, a floating toward a moment unlike any she'd ever known. He told her she was his heart, his soul.

He shifted her slowly, turning with her on the cooling sands so that she was above him, his face tense with need beneath her. "Sand, sweetheart," he murmured, "and never a bed in sight." But he didn't speak of permanence, of tomorrow.

He reached up under her skirt and pulled her to him, letting her set the pace. "Are you okay, sweetheart? Am I hurting you?"

"No, never," she murmured, taking him slowly into her deepest self, a rightness that shattered her even as he withdrew and entered again.

He was the magnet to her most feminine self. How could she have ever thought of anyone else? How could she have imagined that her life would be good without him? All the reasons that seemed so powerful in the light melted in the darkness with his tenderness.

He simply loved her, coming into her so slowly that she wept with a pleasure so exquisite that she felt as if she would splinter into a million stars.

His actions spoke of care and protection. And love, she realized. Jed loved her. Whatever he was, whatever she needed, in this moment of dark brilliance they fulfilled each other in a way she'd never known with anyone else, would never know again without him.

He cupped her breasts, rose to kiss them. "Is this okay?" His teeth scraped so lightly over her nipples that she shivered, and shivered again, her head thrown back to the sky, darkness and light filling her as her heart and body wept with her love.

And in the final moment he waited, his body rocking and rocking, the patience he showed speaking of an infinite tenderness and control until he reached between them and touched her.

He was with her then, tumbling into the abyss. Together.

Collapsed onto him, Kate only gradually became aware of the red glow in the sky, the pungent smell of smoke. Bewildered, she raised herself up and looked past the sand dune that gave them privacy toward the leaping flames coming from The Last Resort.

"Jed! The bar. Oh, good God!"

"Hell." Pulling her up with him, he leapt to his feet. "I told Ben to clear away that firetrap outside his room. Damn, damn." His shirt flapping behind him, he raced down the hard, packed sand where the footing was more reliable, faster.

"Call the fire department." Those were the last words he spoke as he grabbed his shoes and vanished into smoke and flames.

Hands shaking, Kate grabbed her cell phone and dialed the island fire department. Still clutching her phone, she was halfway to the porch when sirens shrieked through the night. Turning toward the lights and noise, she screamed, "Inside! Two men! Upstairs!"

Flinging her phone through the open door of the Blazer, she ran back toward The Last Resort, to Jed.

Off to her side, cloaked and helmeted figures leapt off trucks, unrolled huge hoses and wrestled them into position. Water bucked forth as she ran, spraying the roof and the porch, but still fire blasted from windows, from the walls in a fierce upward surge.

She couldn't see Jed, couldn't see him coming out of the smoke.

"No, ma'am, you can't go in there." A burly arm snaked around her waist, jerked her back and thrust her into another set of yellow rubber-covered arms.

"I have to! Jed and Ben are in there!"

A goggled face peered at her. "Upstairs?"

She nodded.

Arms gestured, deep voices called incomprehensible commands as she struggled futilely against the arms chaining her to safety.

Through the smoke a shape emerged—Jed, holding Ben over his shoulders and dragging him out of the crumbling structure.

Sobbing, Kate ran to them, sandspurs piercing her bare feet, heat roaring at her from the remains of the building even as the hoses tamed the fire. "Jed?"

"I'm okay," he choked out. His face was soot and smoke blackened, his voice so hoarse she could scarcely make out what he said. He sank to his knees on the sand. "I don't know about Ben." He coughed.

Kate knelt on the sand and took the tip of Ben's fingers in her hand. His face and torso were charred, shreds of cloth hanging from his body. His eyebrows were burned off, and patches of scalp, black and burned, showed through his hair.

"Ben, you're going to be all right." Her tears slid down her face. "You *have* to be, hear? Because we didn't have that damned pizza. So—"

Emergency medical technicians shoved her to one side and lifted Ben onto a gurney. He struggled to speak, and she leaned forward, trying to decipher the words croaked through his swollen lips. "The computer, Kate. Computer. Check it, that's why they know—"

With swift movements the EMTs carried him into the van, and sirens wailed his journey to the hospital.

Hours, centuries later, Mark Roberts and Dennis D'Amico made their appearance.

"You're a lightning rod for trouble, Ms. March." Roberts took out a narrow notebook, began writing. "We'll get the final report from the fire investigators later, but the boys are saying this was arson. Kerosene all around the foundation. Looks like someone doused it good and then tossed a cigarette onto your place. Whoosh."

"Whoosh," D'Amico repeated with a grimace. "If the boy makes it, he'll be damned lucky. You were fast, Stone."

"Go ahead and fill us in." Roberts poised his pen above the page.

Kate did. Jed did. And Kate told them Ben's final words as he was carried away.

"What does that mean?" D'Amico frowned.

"Don't have a clue." Jed coughed again, but his words were less scratchy as he gulped air and cleared his throat and lungs.

Leaning against the Blazer, Jed told them how he'd found Ben trapped upstairs and kicked his way through black smoke and boxes.

Just before dawn when the sun gilded the sand and Jed and Kate were stupid with fatigue, Roberts and D'Amico left, shrugging their shoulders.

By dawn's light, the devastation was appalling. Smoke still drifted skyward. Shaking with fear, Booger slunk out of the patch of woods, tail between his legs. He shoved his nose under Jed's hand and wouldn't leave him.

Kate felt the same way. She didn't want to leave Jed's side either. In an instant he could have been lost to her forever. They might not have a future, but she needed to know that he existed somewhere on the face of the earth. From that moment of tenderness on the beach to nothingness. All the force and power of his being could have been reduced to dust, Jed only a poignant memory. "I didn't think—"

His tired grin split the sootiness of his face. "I'm a tough old bird, cookie." In the gold morning his smoke-blackened face became terrifyingly savage. "And I haven't finished my job." He gripped her arm. "You're all right, though? The baby?" He pulled her into his arms and held her tight to him as she nodded.

Inhaling the smoky smell of his shirt, of his skin, she nodded, her brain finally shutting down. "I'm so sorry about your place," she muttered, her breath stirring the singed hair of his chest.

"Me, too, Kate." He tucked her hair behind her ears. "I can rebuild it. It's only a place. But Ben—"

"Ben," she agreed, holding on to Jed for all she was worth as she thought about the boy who had been rushed to the hospital, the EMTs giving each other looks and shaking their heads.

Later that morning, Sparks was arrested.

He was the logical suspect, and a witness had placed him at the scene shortly before the fire. A cigarette butt matching Sparks's usual brand had been found near the emptied fuel containers. Kate watched Jed's face become more and more grim, his eyes narrowing to slits as he listened to the police. She waited for him to defend Sparks, to insist that Sparks wouldn't have done such a thing.

But Jed didn't say a word.

Dizzy with fatigue, cleaned up but her hair still reeking with smoke, Kate went with Jed to the police station.

Behind bars, Sparks regarded them silently. Finally he shrugged, heaved himself off the narrow bed and came to the bars. "You want to ask me anything, Jed?"

The two men stared at each other, neither breaking eye contact. Finally Jed touched the bar Sparks was gripping so tightly that his knuckles were white. "Don't reckon I do."

Sparks nodded, and Kate saw relief wash over his face.

"Okay, then." He bowed his head and then glanced up at Kate and back to Jed. "I had a message. Don't know who left it. I was supposed to come back to the bar after hours to help you unload a delivery."

"I didn't leave a message." Jed frowned.

"Figured out you didn't once I wound up here. Anyway, I didn't see you, and I left. But I don't have an alibi, Jed. That going to be a problem?" Sparks hunched his shoulders forward, waiting, Kate thought, for the blow.

"Not a problem for me, old man."

"Okay, then. Good." Sparks's face collapsed inward.

"I'm posting bail. We'll get you out of here as soon as we can."

Kate patted Sparks's gnarled hand. There was nothing she could say. In a few words, Jed had said everything. Three years ago he wouldn't have given Sparks the benefit of the doubt, not without concrete evidence. Once more she sensed that Jed had forged bonds at The Last Resort and made a makeshift family without realizing it, without intending to do so.

No matter how heroic the image, men with bonds didn't walk off into the sunset. They stuck around for the dirty business of everyday life. No glory in day by day living, no medals except in a woman's heart, in the glow of a child's eyes looking at a father.

"You trusted Sparks." Stumbling into the sunshine, she shaded her eyes.

"Sparks always, *always,* fieldstrips his smokes. He wouldn't have left any evidence. He was set up. By someone who knew we were going to be at the bar."

Kate felt an urgency she couldn't explain, and Jed's hard-eyed grimness affected her. In critical condition, Ben wasn't allowed visitors. Remembering Ben's last words, Jed went back to her office and looked at her computer, turning it every which way.

Although it was Monday, Kate had asked Calla to shut down the office, and no one was there to interrupt them.

"Damn." Jed slapped the top of the monitor. "The boy's right. I'm a dinosaur. I don't have a clue why he mentioned the computer. And it had to be yours, not his. He knew his stuff was destroyed by the fire. All right, this sucker's out of here."

Ripping the cord from the wall, the phone connection coming with the terminal as he lifted it, he gestured toward the door.

Kate opened it. "Where are we going?"

"To a damned computer shop where I'm going to find someone to tear this baby apart."

As they left the office suite, Jed's gaze fixed on the picture near Calla's office. "Strange picture. I remember it from the other night."

"Calla likes it, too. She framed it for the office. A lot of people comment on it. Can you believe Hal was only nine when he painted that?"

"Colorful," Jed grunted as he elbowed through the door.

The straggly-bearded child-man at the computer store was happy to take the computer into his possession, intrigued with the puzzle they presented him. An hour later he came back into the area where they'd waited.

"Neat," he said. "The computer has a voice-data modem, right?"

Kate nodded. "Sure. I think."

"Well, you do. And here's the deal. Someone installed a duplex speaker phone on it. You've been monitored—" he chuckled at his joke "—by someone who accessed your computer, activated the modem and speaker phone. Dialed you up. As a result, whoever was listening in heard everything within microphone range."

Kate felt the blood rushing from her head. "Hal," she whispered. "Hal set up my computer at the office and at home. He set up all the office computers. But he doesn't wear glasses, Jed. He doesn't."

Back in the car, Jed said, "I'll call Roberts and D'Amico. They'll check his alibi."

Her hands were shaking. Hal *couldn't* have been that devious, not the charming boy she'd known for years. Not possible. She kept shaking her head. She didn't want to face Hal and know that his was the face of evil. "There must be some explanation. Calla's husband has the same access Hal does."

"And so does Calla," Jed reminded her somberly. "Maybe the three of them worked together. After all, the business would become Calla's if you died. That's a strong motive."

"I want to talk to Calla. Face-to-face. She's my friend. I owe her that much. I have to do this."

"Absolutely not. I won't let you put yourself at risk like that."

"It's not your decision." She reached for her phone, punched out Calla's home number.

Jed whipped the phone out of her hand, snapped it shut before the connection was made. "Kate, don't fight me on this. The attacks have accelerated. We're facing a desperate and dangerous killer, whoever it is. You'd be walking straight into the lion's den."

"I have to give her the benefit of the doubt, Jed," Kate repeated, despairing of making him see that she had to give Calla the same kind of trust Jed had found for Sparks.

"Call, then." He handed the phone back to her, drummed his fingers on the steering wheel. "D'Amico and Roberts will be talking with the Bowens anyway. And you're with me. I don't like it, it feels wrong, but go ahead if it's so important to you."

Kate redialed. Calla answered. Floundering through her questions, Kate soldiered on. The increasing tension in Calla's voice made Kate uneasy. "Yes," Calla responded flatly, "Hal wears contact lenses. Why? Yes, Phillip wears glasses. Yes, we're in debt," Calla said, adding stiffly, "but, really, Kate, is any of this your business?"

Carefully Kate explained what had been going on. The murders, the attempts on her life. The fire at The Last Resort. Hal's connection to the computer bugging. Everything. When she finished, the line hummed between them, Calla's breathing raspy.

"I have to go," she finished with a gasp. "I can't handle this, Kate. None of this makes sense."

Back at the house, Jed was jittery, fidgety, pacing from room to room as he waited for the Gainesville ophthalmologist to return his call. When the phone rang, he listened, his gaze holding Kate's as he wrote the information down on a pad beside the phone.

*Hal.*

Kate's stomach tightened with misery. More lives were about to be destroyed. And no matter what Jed insisted, she couldn't believe that Calla was involved, not even when the phone rang again, and Jed handed it to her, saying, "Calla."

Listening to her friend's frantic plea, Kate turned her head so that she wouldn't have to see Jed's taut face. She knew what Jed thought. But she had to make this decision based on her own instinct, her own knowledge of her friend.

"I'm going to meet Calla. She's crying, Jed, and falling apart. I have to let her explain. She asked me to come alone because she doesn't want to talk over the phone."

"I won't let you do this, Kate. I'm going with you."

"I know you want to," Kate said gently. "But I have to do this by myself. She's my friend, and she needs me now. I trust her with my life."

"That's exactly what you're doing if you go alone." Anger heated Jed's eyes. "Too much has happened, Kate. Too much is out of control. You *need* me, no matter what you think. You need protection."

"Not from Calla."

At Kate's words, Jed picked up a vase, his narrow fingers gripping it so tightly that she feared it would snap in two. *"Kate,"* he snarled, "listen—"

"Calla would never hurt me." Kate rested her hand over Jed's. "I know you want to protect me, take care of me. But this is my problem. You have to tell D'Amico and Roberts what we've discovered. If Hal's behind all this, it will break

Calla's heart. And apparently Phillip's debts are so bad that he's facing prison. He made some terrible financial decisions at his brokerage firm. Calla only recently learned how bad the situation is. That's why she's been pushing for bigger accounts. It's a mess. And she needs me.'' Kate slung her purse over her shoulder and fished out the keys to her car. ''I wish I could make you understand, Jed, but I can't. You have to trust me on this.''

''I can't, I won't.'' He seized her wrist. ''Don't do this to me, Kate.''

''Oh, Jed,'' she whispered, the stark terror and fury in his eyes giving her pause, ''I have to.''

On the way to the island and the meeting place Calla had picked, Kate chewed the edge of her thumb, wishing she had given in and brought Jed with her. Everything had seemed so clear when Calla had called, but now as the sun moved toward the horizon, red rays bleeding into the gulf, she thought of Hal's painting, of the viciousness of the attacks. If she'd brought Jed along, she could have made Calla understand, surely?

The bottom line was that Kate missed him. He'd been at her side for every minute of these horrible days, and she wanted him with her now. Digging out her phone, she tapped in her number first, hoping he was still at the house. When he didn't answer, she left him a message, saying only to call her, and then pushed the button that dialed up the Blazer phone, a number she'd programmed the day they'd gone to Coco's on the Pier. That number, too, rang until the voice mail came on. Reluctantly, she left him a message, this time wanting him with her so badly that she told him exactly that, told him that she'd been wrong. She needed him with her.

The sun was a blaze of red and gold when she pulled in to the cove not far from the ruins of The Last Resort. She, Calla and Hal had picnicked here once, and the memory of that lost innocence left her melancholy as she slid her phone into the pocket of her lightweight suit jacket and got out of her car.

Looking down and lost in memory as she walked to the wooden picnic table near the pines, she looked up in shock as Hal's chortle broke the stillness.

"Hal?" She stopped, her shoes skidding on the crushed shells.

Hal held a gun to his mother's head. "Surprised, Auntie Kate?" The affectionate name sounded obscene. "I fooled you, didn't I?"

"For a while." Kate's gaze met Calla's. Weeping silently, Calla shook her head, a slight movement that brought Hal's attention back to her.

"I overheard Ma call you. I knew she was going to tell you everything she suspected. She knew I'd broken my sunglasses, and when you told her y'all had found that broken piece, I knew I had a problem on my hands. You made me mad, Auntie Kate, because I thought I'd picked up all the pieces." He pouted, a reminder of the boy he'd been, the child she'd loved because he was the son of her friend.

"Mistakes happen, Hal. You made a bunch."

"I suppose I did. But I'm not going to make any more." He glared at her. "You've run out of luck this time, Auntie Kate."

"Oh? Why's that, Hal?" With one hand in her pocket, forcing herself to remain casual, to show none of the fear leaching all her strength and courage, Kate felt along the face of her phone, judging by familiar touch when she'd reached the numeral *1,* the number that dialed Jed's phone in his Blazer. She pressed, praying with every ounce of faith she had that Jed would pick up the phone, that he would hear Hal and understand what was happening.

"Because this plan is perfect. It's going to look like you killed Ma. See, you raced away from here with Ma in the trunk of your car. Everybody knows you drive too fast, Auntie," he said seriously. "You're going to speed off the bridge with Ma. You'll both drown."

"But why would you want to kill me or your mom?" In spite of the fear paralyzing her, Kate moved closer so that the phone would have a better chance to pick up what they were saying. "I've never harmed you, Hal."

"You saw me."

"What?"

"At the Port of Tampa. When I was making arrangements with the captain of one of your ships." At her expression of incomprehension, he made a face. "Don't be stupid. You saw me setting up the next delivery of the workers from Haiti, you know you did."

Buying time, trying to reach the little boy she remembered behind this stranger's eyes, Kate faked a calm she didn't feel. And in her mind she called to Jed over and over, willing him to hear, willing him to come to her. "I didn't see you that day, Hal. But that was you who ran me off Gillette Road?"

"Of course it was. And me who killed that detective. She was too close to figuring everything out, so I had to solve that problem, you see. I like solving problems, Auntie Kate. I'm good at it. I didn't expect to see Frank there that night, though. That was a surprise. You were supposed to be there with her. Not him."

"Because you'd been keeping track of me through the computer?"

With Calla clasped tightly to his side, Hal beamed at Kate. "Wasn't that clever? I knew everything that was happening. Almost everything," he added. "You must have talked with Frank after you left the office."

"You're right." She inched closer. "But why do you need to kill me, Hal?"

"Money, money, money," he chanted in a mad singsong. "Ma and my step-papa cut me off. Said I needed to be more responsible. Tough love," he sneered. "So I solved that problem, too. That's why I made the agreement with your captain to short you on deliveries and use the space to bring in laborers. He gave me a cut from each delivery. I was afraid you'd found out and I'd go to jail. 'Cause he was smuggling drugs, too. That was his own deal, but I didn't want to get caught.'' Hal's sense of pride was malevolent, with an evil she couldn't begin to comprehend.

''And now I've set it up so that it will look like you killed Ma. Everybody will think it's because of the business insurance. Oh, I know, I don't get that money, it's only for buying Ma's share of the business, but I'll eventually get it. See,'' he said earnestly, jabbing his mother with the pistol that Kate knew would be deadly at the range she and Calla were, ''Phillip would sell the business, and with Ma's personal insurance eventually coming to me from her estate and the proceeds from the sale of the import company, I'll be rich. Isn't that a good solution?'' He pushed Calla ahead of him and approached Kate.

''No, Hal,'' Kate said, and let amusement touch her face, ''you haven't thought this through. What's supposed to be *my* motive for killing my partner, my friend? You've made a big mistake.''

''Think so?'' he said so cheerfully that her blood turned to ice. ''Money again, Auntie Kate. *You* needed the insurance money from the business policy. It only pays to you if Ma dies unexpectedly. Everybody needs money. Me. Phillip. Ma. Why should you be any different?''

''This won't work, Hal. Too many loose ends.'' Kate could start with a list of about ten, but all the loose ends wouldn't do her and Calla a damned bit of good. She wasn't going to spell out to Hal that Jed knew, that the police had the information about the sunglasses, that if Ben survived, he would be able to tell the police about the shipping invoices and what they meant.

''Enough. It's getting late, and I'm tired of talking,'' Hal said petulantly. ''What's done is done. You and Ma know what I've done. You're my problem right now. It'll all be a terrible tragedy, you killing Ma, but I'll survive. Unlike you. Now open the trunk. Don't be scared, Ma,'' he said sweetly, and smacked her across the head, letting her tumble into the trunk as Kate opened it.

She'd thought she had a chance to kick the gun away from him, but he surprised her with the swiftness of his attack on Calla, and then the gun was tight against Kate's side.

"Now get in the car, Auntie Kate. I think a sharp blow against your head will do. The car will go off the bridge, I'll jump out in time, and this problem will be solved, too."

Only a few miles away, Jed heard the voices and smashed his foot onto the accelerator, dust spurting behind the Blazer. Muffled, the voices came to him with chilling clarity. His phone had rung and he'd picked it up, startled to hear Hal's voice and then Kate's. Realizing immediately what had happened, he clutched the phone to his ear, listening in horror as he raced down the island road.

He had one chance to stop Hal's plan, Jed realized as he arrived at the narrow, one-lane bridge that was the only bridge off the island. Although he'd contacted the detectives and brought them up-to-date, they would never arrive in time, not even if he hung up on Kate and called them.

He was her only chance.

They would play one more game of chicken. Again and again she'd thrown up to him that he never backed down, never surrendered, never backed away. The night they'd made love, he'd tried to show her he'd changed, that he could let her into his life, that he trusted her judgment. And then, damn it to hell, he'd gone all heavy-handed and told her she couldn't meet Calla alone.

He hoped Kate would remember the night and understand the day. If she did, they had a chance. If she would surrender her pride, too, and have a little faith in him. If they were lucky.

This time, Kate couldn't stop her car. She would have to have faith that he could handle the situation, because she would need to hit him broadside, letting him and the Blazer take the force of the impact.

If she didn't, if she tried to stop or turn in the narrow space, her car would spin out of control and off the bridge. She would have to trust him this time to take care of her.

They would both have to surrender. Kate, her pride. Him? His need to be the last one standing. In that moment it seemed an easy surrender. Kate's would be the hard one. She would not surrender easily her pride and her utter confidence in her ability to handle her car and the situation. Clever Kate, to think of using her phone as a microphone.

His heart shuddered as he saw her red car barreling toward the bridge. Staying inside his car so that Hal wouldn't become suspicious, Jed waited, his engine purring. At the last second he would have to angle his car and block her smaller one. If there's time, he thought distantly, he might have a chance to roll out, but to give Kate, sweet, sweet Kate a chance to survive, he would probably have to remain in the car, guiding it and maintaining as much control over its direction as possible. He would have to use every skill he had to keep both cars from ratcheting out of control and into the water below with its furious tides and sharks.

No one, not even him, would be able to fish her car out of that maelstrom of currents under the water.

Preparing himself, he took a deep breath and let his mind go empty. He would give her the only chance he could. And if it worked, it would be his chance to have her in his life again, to hold her in his arms, to have her sweetness filling him and giving meaning to his world.

Kate's mind raced as she ran through one possibility after another. Hal's gun dug cruelly into her side, and in a blur of slowed-down time, everything around her seemed sharpened to her hyperalert senses. Could she unclip her seat belt and roll out of the car before Hal pulled the trigger? Before the car spun off the bridge? Hal's first, automatic reaction, no matter what she did, would be to pull the trigger.

The bridge was around the next corner. She had to decide. But how could she? She couldn't abandon Calla in the trunk. Perspiration slid down her back. Her hands gripping the wheel with all her strength, she rounded the corner and saw Jed's Blazer at the opposite end of the bridge, blocking it.

Something in her expression caused Hal to turn and look at the bridge. Screaming, he whipped back to her, reaching for the steering wheel with one hand, raising the gun with his other.

The gun was away from her side. That was all she knew. She had a moment to act. It was the only opportunity she might have.

As she prepared to move, Jed's car roared straight at her down the wood-railed, frighteningly narrow bridge. Through her terror, a laugh bubbled up. Damn him. He'd never given her room to maneuver.

She remembered their last game of chicken at The Last Resort and tried frantically to figure out what game they were playing now, what the life-and-death rules were.

In the last split second, before Hal could react and while the gun was away from her side, she pressed her foot hard on the accelerator and turned sideways toward him, swooping her right arm up and blocking the downward smack of the gun, aiming her shiny red car straight for Jed. She saw Hal's head hit the dashboard, the gun tumble to the floor.

As the car rocked toward Jed, she hoped that she understood his message. She blinked, Jed turned, stopping his car, and the two cars slammed together with a scream of metal on metal, the angle of his car absorbing the forward momentum of hers.

Her head whipping back and forth, Kate held on to the wheel with every ounce of her strength, desperately trying to control her car as it plowed broadside into Jed's.

Jed saw Kate's white face, her uplifted arm as the gun came toward her. Muscling his steering wheel so that his car would stay on the bridge as Kate's car pushed, pushed, pushed them ever closer to the wood railing, he kept the two vehicles locked together. With a dreadful squealing of brakes, the cars finally stopped.

He lifted his shaking hands off the wheel.

The front tires of his car rested just over the edge of the bridge, and he slapped his door open, leapt out and ran to Kate.

Dust swirled in the twilight, metal groaned, and he saw her car door open as he ran toward her, saw her roll onto the bridge and scramble to her feet, running toward him, her hair streaming behind her, her arms open wide to him.

As she jumped into his arms, her legs wrapping tightly around his waist, he buried his face in her hair. "Oh, you're a tough cookie, you are, sweetheart. And I'm shaking like a spit-scared recruit. If you think I'm ever going to let you walk away from me again, you're crazy."

Her small hands gripped him tightly to her. "I'm not crazy, you fool."

Kate let him carry her back to his car, then they phoned for the police and he pulled Calla from Kate's trunk. Trembling and lacking his bravado, Hal was a pitiful, loathsome specimen tied with Jed's lovely tie to the steering wheel of Kate's car. She didn't regret for a second the ruin of the tie.

Over the next days as Booger and Jed moved into her place, Booger happily lounging under the tree in her backyard, she teased Jed. The silly man couldn't keep his hands off her. He needed to have her within arm's reach every second. And she felt the same way. One morning she laughed as she, Jed and Booger moved in sync in the backyard, all of them touching.

Jed took her with him to supervise the rebuilding of The Last Resort and let her choose the material for the restaurant, although he insisted, along with Sparks, that she was "tarting the place up and ruining a respectable dive with her notions of fancy chairs and stuff."

All of them, even Tuba Tony, who'd missed all the excitement, visited Ben every day. Kate insisted on paying for the hospital bills. Every time she left the hospital she wept, Ben's poor, burned self reducing her to tears even as he tried to joke through the tubes down his throat.

"Hormones," she explained, since that explanation seemed to silence the men quite nicely.

Calla let Kate buy out her share of the business. "I can't stay here, Kate. I love you, and you're the best friend I ever had, but I'm carrying too much guilt. I need a fresh start. Somewhere else where I won't think of the horrors my son's committed. I won't leave you in the lurch, though. I'll stay until after the trial."

Jed missed Calla's sass, but neither he nor Kate could change Calla's mind.

She hadn't posted bail for Hal.

Three weeks later Kate returned with Jed to the construction at the restaurant. A full moon shone down on the gleaming new wood, turned the beach golden.

She had a plan. Jed had been treating her with kid gloves ever since she'd almost lost the baby, and she was tired of it. Like her, her baby was a survivor. It was time for a woman to assert herself, she decided, grabbing his hand and towing him toward the beach behind The Last Resort.

"Hey!" He resisted her pull on the new tie she'd bought him and which he wore every other day, delighted that she'd picked it out. "What's up?"

She tilted her head. The corners of her mouth pulled up with amusement. The poor lug hadn't a clue. "Uh, you want *me* to answer that question, big guy?"

"Sure, but you'll have to come closer than you are now." He grinned at her.

"Everything in its time." She tugged him behind the sand dune where she'd left a thick blanket and a bottle of wine in a cooler.

"Ah. I see."

"Do you, Jed? Do you really see how much I love you? Because I do, you know. And I came so close to losing you, to never realizing how much I needed you in my life. I thought I was fine. I was. But I had no idea how empty my life was without you until you came back into it."

"Pretty good bodyguard, aren't I?" he asked smugly,

skimming his hands down her hips and unbuttoning her skirt with his clever, fast fingers.

"You are," she said seriously. "You saved my life."

"You're letting me have your fine body as payment, then?" He shot her a sharklike grin as he unbuttoned her silvery silk blouse and took her long string of pearls between his teeth, nibbling closer to her bare breasts. "Works for me, but I'm thinking of a long-term payout, cookie."

"I could see that." Her knees buckled as he slid the damp pearls over her nipples, blowing lightly against them until they puckered into hard nubbins. "Oh, Jed, I love the way you think."

She collapsed under him as he took them to the ground, her back against the soft cashmere of the blanket. Her hand rested on the steady beat of his heart, a heart she knew she could count on for the rest of her life. "You know the nicest games, Jed," she whispered into his ear as he lowered himself to her.

"Nice?" he muttered, tightening his arms around her and rolling to reverse their positions. "Come and kiss me, Kate," he murmured into the curve of her breast as he looped pearls around one nipple, dragging them against her skin and down to her belly button.

"Well, perhaps *nice* isn't exactly the right word." She sighed blissfully as he proceeded to show her a new twist on an old, old game. "But I do adore a man with literary aspirations and the good sense to know when to surrender to a woman."

"Maybe I was born a fool," he said, reaching into his pocket and slipping out a tiny package, "but I'm teachable."

"That you are." She sighed with satisfaction, sliding her palms over the long muscles of his buttocks. Then, as he waited, she took the square from him and pitched it unopened into the cooler.

He ran his fingers down the bare length of her spine, sketching drawings on her spine in the moonlight. "Oh, excellent Kate," he said. "A woman after my own heart."

She raised her head and looked deeply into his eyes. "Do I have your heart, Jedidiah Stone?"

His chest moved under her as he linked their hands, the matching rings glinting in the moonlight. "My heart, my soul. All of me, Kate. You and your baby—*our* baby, forever."

"Forever's a start," she said, sinking down onto him.

Above them, the moon pulled the tide outward, an endless, irresistible force.

\* \* \* \* \*

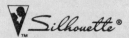

If you enjoyed what you just read,
then we've got an offer you can't resist!

# Take 2 bestselling love stories FREE!

# Plus get a FREE surprise gift!

**Clip this page and mail it to Silhouette Reader Service™**

| **IN U.S.A.** | **IN CANADA** |
|---|---|
| 3010 Walden Ave. | P.O. Box 609 |
| P.O. Box 1867 | Fort Erie, Ontario |
| Buffalo, N.Y. 14240-1867 | L2A 5X3 |

**YES!** Please send me 2 free Silhouette Intimate Moments® novels and my free surprise gift. Then send me 6 brand-new novels every month, which I will receive months before they're available in stores. In the U.S.A., bill me at the bargain price of $3.57 plus 25¢ delivery per book and applicable sales tax, if any*. In Canada, bill me at the bargain price of $3.96 plus 25¢ delivery per book and applicable taxes**. That's the complete price and a savings of over 10% off the cover prices—what a great deal! I understand that accepting the 2 free books and gift places me under no obligation ever to buy any books. I can always return a shipment and cancel at any time. Even if I never buy another book from Silhouette, the 2 free books and gift are mine to keep forever. So why not take us up on our invitation. You'll be glad you did!

245 SEN CNFF
345 SEN CNFG

| Name | (PLEASE PRINT) | |
|---|---|---|
| Address | Apt.# | |
| City | State/Prov. | Zip/Postal Code |

\* Terms and prices subject to change without notice. Sales tax applicable in N.Y.
\*\* Canadian residents will be charged applicable provincial taxes and GST.
  All orders subject to approval. Offer limited to one per household.
  ® are registered trademarks of Harlequin Enterprises Limited.

INMOM99                                        ©1998 Harlequin Enterprises Limited

"Fascinating—you'll want to take
this home!"
—Marie Ferrarella

"Each page is filled with a brand-new
surprise."
—Suzanne Brockmann

"Makes reading a new and joyous
experience all over again."
—Tara Taylor Quinn

See what all your favorite authors
are talking about.

*Coming October 1999 to a retail store near you.*

HARLEQUIN®
*Makes any time special ™*

Silhouette®

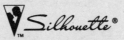

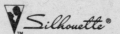